Book 4 of *The Order of the White Boar*

'Brilliant ... heart-breaking ... brings the uncertain and dangerous times after the Battle of Bosworth to life.'

Wendy Johnson, member of the Looking for Richard Project

'A wonderful work of historical fiction . . . altogether a very enjoyable book for both children and adults.'

Isabel Green, *Ricardian Bulletin* of the Richard III Society

Also by Alex Marchant

The Order of the White Boar
The King's Man
King in Waiting

Time out of Time

As editor

Grant Me the Carving of My Name
Right Trusty and Well Beloved…
(both sold in support of Scoliosis Association UK)

SONS of YORK

Book 4 of *The Order of the White Boar*

Alex Marchant

Marchant Ventures

First published 2022

Copyright © 2022 Alex Marchant

The right of Alex Marchant to be identified as the author of this work has been asserted in accordance with the Copyright, Design and Patents Act, 1988.

All rights reserved. No part of this publications may be reproduced, stored in or introduced to a retrieval system, or transmitted, in any form or by any means, electronic, mechanical, photocopying, recording or otherwise, without the prior permission of the copyright holder.

ISBN-13: 9798811480777

Cover illustration: Oliver Bennett, morevisual.me

To

Maya and Grace

my daughters of York(shire), for living alongside King Richard, Matthew and his friends all these years!

Contents

1	June 1487	11
2	The Invasion Begins	13
3	'England, My England'	24
4	The Messenger	30
5	Within the Shadows	37
6	Games	42
7	Crossing the Sands	52
8	Nothing to Fear	66
9	'The More You Fight …	72
10	'Fit to Wield a Sword'	85
11	Return to Middleham	92
12	Jervaulx Abbey	98
13	Words of Love	107
14	Pursuit	112
15	'Perfidious York'	122
16	Homecoming	129
17	The Distant Cousin	138
18	Farewell to York	145
19	'The Bloodiest Battle'	153
20	Storm Clouds Gather	161
21	The Advance	171
22	'Arise Sir Matthew Wansford'	176
23	Playing Dead?	188
24	Aftermath	200
25	A Matter of Life or Death	211
	Post Script	220

Cast of characters

The Order of the White Boar
Matthew Wansford, a merchant's son of York
Alys Langdown, ward of Henry Tudor
Roger de Kynton, squire to John, Earl of Lincoln
Elen, companion to Alys

On the march
Edward Plantagenet, King of England, son of Edward IV*
John de la Pole, Earl of Lincoln, nephew to Richard III*
Francis, Viscount Lovell, Richard III's friend and chancellor*
Sir Thomas FitzGerald, brother to the Earl of Kildare*
Sir Henry Bodrugan, a knight of Cornwall*
Sir Thomas Broughton, a knight of Cumberland*
Captain Martin Schwartz, a mercenary*
Robert Mallary, a gentleman of Northamptonshire*
Giles Mallary, his brother*
Hugh Soulsby, a squire, nephew to Lord Walter Soulsby
Harry, a local boy

Across the spine of England
Abbot Laurentius of Furness*
Abbot Haslington of Jervaulx*
John, Lord Scrope, of Castle Bolton*
Thomas, Baron Scrope of Masham*

In York
John Wansford, a merchant
Mistress Wansford, his wife
Frederick Wansford, his son*
John, Agnes, Peter, Sarah, Richard and Anne Wansford, his sons
    and daughters
William Mallary, a gentleman of Northamptonshire*
John Mallary, his brother*

Known to history ...
Henry Tudor, King of England (usurper)*
Elizabeth of York, Queen of England, his wife, sister to Edward
    V*

Arthur Tudor, Prince of Wales, their son*
Elizabeth Woodville, mother of Edward V and Elizabeth of
	York, later Dame Grey*
Richard, Duke of York, her youngest son*
Thomas Grey, Marquess of Dorset, eldest son of Elizabeth
	Woodville, elder half-brother to Edward V*
Edward, Earl of Warwick, son of George, Duke of Clarence*
Margaret Plantagenet, dowager Duchess of Burgundy, sister to
	Richard III and Edward IV*
Henry Percy, Earl of Northumberland*
John de Vere, Earl of Oxford, Lord Great Chamberlain*
Edward Woodville, Lord Scales, brother of Elizabeth
	Woodville*
Thomas, Lord Stanley, Earl of Derby*
Lord Strange, his son*
Sir William Stanley, brother to Lord Thomas*
Lady Anne FitzHugh, wife to Francis Lovell*
Gerald FitzGerald, Eighth Earl of Kildare*
Lady Anne Tyrell, wife to Sir James, governor of Guînes*
Walter, Lord Soulsby, a knight
Ralph Soulsby, his son
Master Ashley, a merchant of London
George, natural son of George, Duke of Clarence

In the past ...
Richard III, King of England*
Anne Neville, his wife*
Edward of Middleham, his son*
Edward IV, King of England, his brother*
George, Duke of Clarence, his brother*
Richard, Duke of York, his father*
Richard Neville, Earl of Warwick, his cousin, known as the
	Kingmaker*

* Historical figures

The Code of the Order of the White Boar

a b c d e f g h i j k l m n o p q r s t u v w x y z
u v w x y z a b c d e f g h i j k l m n o p q r s t Monday
r s t u v w x y z a b c d e f g h i j k l m n o p q Tuesday
o p q r s t u v w x y z a b c d e f g h i j k l m n Wednesday
l m n o p q r s t u v w x y z a b c d e f g h i j k Thursday
i j k l m n o p q r s t u v w x y z a b c d e f g h Friday
f g h i j k l m n o p q r s t u v w x y z a b c d e Saturday
c d e f g h i j k l m n o p q r s t u v w x y z a b Sunday

1

June 1487

No more than a bowshot away across the water, thousands of heavily armed men waited – still, silent, ready.

For more than an hour they had been assembling, swarming in ranks like worker ants. The air above them had been thick with bellowed orders and the clashing of arms, though the stamping of their boots had been muffled by the sand beneath. But now all was quiet as a strange silence settled. The gentle whisper of the waves sucking at the shingle and the distant cry of a swooping gull were the only sounds that crept into my ears. The narrow shoreline was dark with these armoured bodies, stretching in rows from one end of the beach to the other.

Never before had I seen so many soldiers. Save once. On another summer morning almost two long years before. When the forces of the usurper Henry Tudor had gathered to challenge my master King Richard and his royal army. Then I had been far away – perched atop a church tower, shielded from the thunder and screams and treachery of the battle. Now I felt I could almost reach out my hand to touch these men where they stood to attention, waiting, across the shallow waters. Jewel-coloured standards fluttered in the early breeze and the razor-sharp points of halberds and pikes bristled high above the myriad steel and leather helmets.

I swallowed. It was a daunting view to one unused to it. Despite all I had seen on that August morning two years before, I was awed at this spectacle. And surely the usurper would be too – when he came face to face with this army that now mustered to challenge him.

For this was the army brought to England by my new master, Edward Plantagenet – nephew of my late master, King Richard – who sought to reclaim his crown. These warriors had travelled with him from his safe haven in Ireland to restore the throne to the rightful king. A Yorkist king, not a Lancastrian upstart who had only won his crown through treachery on the field of battle. And these soldiers and their masters – whether English gentlemen or Irish lords or German captains – would follow him and fight for him until death, as I too had sworn to do.

Barely an hour before, the scene had been very different. Barely an hour before, when our ships had just rounded the immense sandspit that sheltered this shore and dropped their anchors so our invasion could begin …

2

The Invasion Begins

Barely an hour before, I was gripping the ship's rail with both my hands and watching in wonder. The swell of the sea was gentler now we were at anchor in the lee of the great sand bar. Our crossing of the Celtic Sea had been less blustery than our previous one across to Dublin, almost six months ago, just before Yuletide, but still my world rocked more than I found comfortable. Focusing on the work of those around me helped me to forget the queasy lurching of my insides.

At this moment, I was craning over the ship's side to watch as my old master's warhorse, Storm, was lowered down from the ship's high deck – down, down, towards the white-crested waves far below. The sailors did their job well, hauling with care at the winch and pulley system by which the pale-grey horse was being inched downwards, as they might when unloading wine casks or bales of wool in more normal times. So too did the groom who sat astride him, bending over to mutter calming words into his ear the whole time. The stallion kicked out once, twice, with a high-pitched whinny, as his hooves first struck the water, but the groom adeptly unbuckled and slipped off the wide canvas sling beneath his chest and belly, whipped the blindfold from his eyes so the horse could see no danger lurked about him, then urged him forward to swim across the final deep stretch of sea.

Storm forged through the last waves, his head held high, his regal neck slicing through the spray. Then, hooves crunching on shingle, he bunched his well-muscled hindquarters and, scrabbling with his sturdy forelegs, heaved himself up on to the sloping beach. The groom swung down from his back as the stallion shivered and shrugged droplets of seawater from his pearly coat, before leading him out of the shallows to join the other horses, my own new mount among them, amidst the forest of sea holly and swaying yellow poppies above the tide line.

Once my old master's horse was safe ashore, my gaze scanned elsewhere on the beach and back aboard the ships. Everywhere people were at work – sailors, soldiers, gentlemen, campfollowers. I had not seen such frenzied activity since our neighbour back in York's Stonegate had lifted the straw-plaited lid from the bee skep nestled in a niche in his backyard wall to offer me a glimpse inside. The busyness of those honeybees going about their usual tasks – building the buttery-gold comb, feeding their grubs, dancing in their neat, age-old figures of eight – was echoed here this morning, everywhere I looked, upon every ship in the water and on the pebble beach fringed by its wildflower meadow. I breathed now the salt tang of the ocean not the warm scent of spring honey, and men's shouts and commands took the place of the sleepy drone of insects. Yet, all about me, the same industry prevailed.

Below me now, pitching upon the choppy water, yet another rowing boat bumped up against the oak timbers of our ship's hull. Its oarsman held the rope ladder steady while a dozen or so soldiers, with bundles, armour and weapons, lowered themselves into the swaying innards of the boat. More bundles, barrels, packs, stacks of harness, followed, tied on ropes snaking down from above. As the boat settled further down in the water, the oarsman hollered and held up his hands to halt the loading. Then he sat again and pulled on his oars to ferry his cargo – human and other – to the beach.

These actions were being repeated all around me, on the landward side of the fleet of ships now riding the waves just offshore. On the shingle itself, the opposite was happening – the unloading of rowboat after rowboat, with the splashing of soldiers wading ashore, bundles and weapons held high above their heads, and the slinging of packages from hand to hand by chains of men linking shallows to foreshore. Piles of gear littered the pebbles in all directions, like mole hills in a spring meadow, while above the beach wagon after wagon patiently awaited their loads.

Dominating everything was the towering castle, its patchwork stone walls stained pink in the early morning sunlight. The glassless windows of its massive keep yawned black as they kept watch over our disembarking army. Beyond the parapet far above, I could just make out the flash of gold – a flapping banner catching and throwing back the rays of the midsummer sun now rising above the horizon. In the first pre-dawn light, as we had sailed past the sandspit towards our anchorage, Edward, standing ready and eager on the ship's forecastle, had pointed to it.

'Look! The abbot is flying the sun in splendour,' he had cried at the sight of his late father's symbol shining proud above the castle, stitched upon this huge flag of murrey and blue, the Plantagenet colours. 'Lord Francis said he would prove his loyalty to me. So did Alys.'

This ancient castle of Piel had finally been chosen for our landfall after much discussion. Both before and after Edward's triumphant coronation in Dublin, his lords and gentlemen – among them Lord Francis Lovell, King Richard's most loyal friend – had argued over where to start the invasion we hoped would restore our young king to his throne. Built by a long-ago abbot of Furness Abbey, to control the trade in wool across and along the sea lanes between England and Ireland, this castle crouched, stout and strong, on the tip of a wild hilly land jutting into the Celtic Sea. There it commanded the southern approaches to the far north-west of England where many men still loyal to the family of York had their lairs, among them Sir Thomas Broughton, who had recently joined us in Dublin, and also it seemed this present abbot of Furness.

Once the decision had been made, my friends Alys Langdown and Roger de Kynton had reminisced about a visit they had made to the beautiful abbey many years before when they lived in the household of our late master,

King Richard, when he was still Duke of Gloucester. As at every great house in which they had stayed on their journey around these distant parts, the duke, his lady, Duchess Anne, and their entourage had been royally entertained by feasting, music and mumming. Yet what had remained strongest in Alys's mind was the memory of the majestic landscape, with its high wooded crags and mirror-like lakes reflecting the blues or cloudy greys of endless skies.

I saw little sign of such grandeur here, where the beach rose gently to a low mound on which the castle stood. But as I thought of Alys now, I cast about for a sight of her. We had not met, of course, since before our departure from Dublin. But surely she was somewhere there upon the wide, shallow slope of sand and grass leading up to the castle's walls.

She was not easy to spot in the teeming crowds, dressed as she was once more as a boy, her slender form swathed in drab-coloured clothes like so many upon the shore and her light-red hair caught up and concealed in an old soldier's cap. But before long I spied her.

She was one of a party of both men and women clustered at the crest of the beach, hefting bundles and sacks from the heaps on to the waiting carts. There, I guessed, she could choose what to lift, making sure nothing was too heavy. She was too far away for me to see her face, but from her sturdy movements I could imagine the determination in her eyes and the set of her jaw. She would not give herself away if she could help it. I knew I must not risk drawing attention to her either, by staring too long at some peasant lad working one among many. Yet I could not drag my eyes away just yet. She paused a moment to straighten up, drawing the back of one hand across her forehead as though weary. As she bent again to grasp another bundle, I wished I could be there beside her to help her with her task.

'Have you spotted her?'

Roger broke into my thoughts, his voice quiet for

once. He leant forward over the rail beside me. I noticed my knuckles shining white as they grasped the polished wood and loosened my grip. At my feet, Shadow stretched, her shaggy, narrow hindquarters pointing skywards and her clawed forepaws scraping against the planking of the deck. Her mouth lolled open in a pink, sharp-toothed yawn before she rose to touch noses with Belle, Roger's hound, who was sidling towards her past his smart leather boots.

'She's up by the wagons,' I said, in a similar tone to Roger's.

He grunted, taking care to look everywhere at the busyness about us, everywhere, that is, except in Alys's direction.

'Lord Francis sent me to fetch you.' His voice was now at its normal pitch. 'He wants you to attend Edward as he's rowed to the beach. And I'll be with Earl John, of course. We'll all be in the last boat. The abbot has sent word that he'll be here to greet Edward shortly.'

I nodded, watching the two hounds as they settled down on the deck between our feet, flank to flank, larger Shadow alongside more delicate Belle, both pure white muzzles resting on outstretched forelegs. Roger followed my gaze and stroked the instantly snoozing Belle with one toe.

'Do you think we'll get away with it?' Barely above a whisper again.

I shrugged. The sideways glance Lord Francis had shot us on the morning we sailed arrowed back into my mind.

I had been leaning on the rail like this, staring astern at the Pool of Dublin as its stone quay and merchants' warehouses glided away from the frothing wake of our ships. The farewell party had already turned their horses' heads to return to the city and Edward had retired into the depths of his cabin, muttering about shedding his heavy armour. He had worn it to impress the crowds who gathered on our route to the harbour, cheering and wishing him well. With his body servants fussing around him, I could tell he had no need of me. But Lord Francis and John, Earl of Lincoln, Edward's older cousin, had lingered on deck, alongside Sir Thomas FitzGerald, who was accompanying us on our venture on behalf of his brother, Lord Kildare. Our host had made his own farewells on the harbourside, at the very spot where he had greeted Edward when he had first stepped ashore in this country all those months before.

My mind was misty like the far-off hills as Ireland faded into the distance, our time passed there soon to be no more than ghostly memories. But Earl John's voice broke into my musings and banished them in a second.

'My lady Alys did not come to see us off then, Matthew?'

I started at being addressed so, though in recent weeks the earl had become used to seeing me as his cousin Edward's close companion. But my mouth uttered without hesitation the words that my friends and I had agreed.

'No, my lord. We all made our farewells privately last evening after supper. Alys did not want to cause Edward any distress – or indeed herself.'

Something flickered in Earl John's blue eyes, and I cursed myself inside. Had I made a misstep with those last words? He had come to know Alys also since his arrival in Dublin. Did he know her well enough to distrust the idea that she was so easily upset?

Yet perhaps he understood her better than I realized. The flicker became a half-laugh, and a nudge of Lord Francis's arm.

'From all I've heard of her previous exploits, I can well imagine my lady Alys was disturbed at our leaving without her. But no doubt she will find plenty to occupy her, now Lady Kildare's son has been born.'

My breath trickled out in relief. But then his gaze dropped down towards my feet.

'Yet is this not her hound? It is almost the twin of my little cousin's hound – the one I gave to young Roger.

Though this one is a more fitting size for a hunting dog.'

Right on cue, young Roger had appeared, coming to my rescue. As ever at his heels was Shadow's 'twin', Belle, once the pet of our late, lamented friend little Ed. As the two ghostly hounds brushed noses in greeting, Roger bowed his head to Earl John.

'Your baggage is safely below decks, my lord.'

The earl responded with a nod before returning to his question.

'Is not this my lady Alys's hound? I'm surprised to see it here with us.'

Roger's reply was glib, as was his habit.

'Alys was worried that Belle would pine if separated again from Shadow. They have become so close since we came to Ireland. And she knows Matt is still grieving for the hound he lost at Lowestoft.' I was glad he did not turn his eyes to me as he said this. 'So she gave Shadow to Matt for now.'

'That is very kind of Alys,' remarked Lord Francis, a doubtful expression upon his face.

'Aye, my lord,' agreed Roger, unfazed by the lies he was telling. 'She said she'd reclaim her when Edward has reclaimed his throne – and then we can all enter London together in triumph.'

Earl John laughed again.

'That is a fine plan. And one that we must make sure is soon fulfilled. If only to satisfy Lady Alys's desire for victory.'

A broad grin unfurled across Sir Thomas's face. 'And we must be doing all in our power to keep my lady happy, to be sure.'

'Indeed, yes, Sir Thomas,' said the earl. 'That is something I have learnt the importance of over recent weeks. She has often made it clear exactly what her wishes are, especially on matters relating to our young king and his prospects. You know, I truly believe I shall miss Alys's lively, impertinent ways.'

He nudged Lord Francis again and Sir Thomas

had winked and tipped his cap to his companions as they moved on to other topics of conversation. But Lord Francis's glance …

'Perhaps we should have left the hounds behind in Dublin as Giles suggested,' I said to Roger now, recalling that look. It was his turn to shrug.

'It's too late now. The deed is done. Come on, we'd best be going. I think I spy the abbot's welcome party arriving.'

Back on shore, beyond the carts, a solemn procession was making its way towards the main gateway of the castle's outer bailey. At the head of a company of armoured horsemen strode a man in dark robes, holding aloft a colossal gilt crucifix. Sunlight flashed from the many gems encrusting it. In the midst of the party rumbled a closed carriage, gaily painted, curtains drawn back a little to reveal several richly clad gentlemen within. All around, soldiers, sailors and campfollowers fell to their knees. Each made a sign of the cross beneath their bowed head, before rising and continuing their tasks as the procession disappeared into the depths of the castle.

I yielded to Roger's tug on my sleeve and, with the hounds, followed him back below deck to collect my bundle. Or rather, bundles. When we had left Dublin, my musician friends in Lord Kildare's household had presented me with a gift of a harp, now protected from salt spray and all weathers by a leather bag all its own. I slung it on my back, settling its strap across my chest, then we returned to daylight to await our next orders.

Lord Francis had emerged on deck in the meantime and was now directing matters, as he did so often these days. He clapped a hand on my shoulder.

'At last, Matthew. I thought Roger had got lost trying to find you.' His tone was light-hearted for once as he pointed over the side of the ship. 'Hop down into the boat, both of you. Your bundles will be lowered to you. Edward and John will be here soon.'

I swung myself over the rail, Shadow clamped

under one arm. To my relief, she did not squirm, as though she sensed how precarious our descent would be if she did. My foot searched for, then found the first rung of the rope ladder, but before I climbed down, I cast my gaze back to the beach. The chaos was mostly cleared away now. The carts were trundling one by one up the slope towards the castle's outer walls, the campfollowers straggling after. I couldn't spot Alys among them. But assembled on the lower part of the foreshore were the companies of soldiers, now fully disembarked.

This was my first sight of them gathered all together, not hurrying off to their various billets in Dublin or scattered upon the many ships. And they were now not busy clusters of worker bees. Rather they resembled columns of ants, rank upon black rank of them. Waiting, still, silent, ready for their orders.

After a moment's hesitation, struck by the impressive display, I clambered down into the rowing boat, followed by Roger, and we both squeezed past the oarsman. As we settled ourselves on to the narrow plank seat – bundles and hounds stowed beneath – a single shout arose, then a sudden, strident clanging of steel and stomping of feet. I craned my head round just as the dark phalanx of men upon the shore parted, like the Red Sea in the Bible story. Revealed, at the top of the beach, was the shining crucifix, still lifted high above the head of the black-clad monk. Behind him paced slowly, on to the dark pebbles, a score of fine-robed gentlemen, at their head a man who I guessed was an important church official. A gigantic jewelled cross rested upon his chest and one hand clasped a staff sprouting what looked like an unfurling frond of golden bracken.

Roger elbowed me and whispered, 'The abbot of Furness. I remember him from our visit with Duke … with King Richard.'

In His Grace's wake marched armour-clad soldiers from the earlier procession. They lined up beside the other men and soon all the actors were in place, the abbot and his companions standing just out of reach of the lapping waves.

Silence again upon the shore. All around was motionless, save the boat rocking beneath us, and the waves beneath that, gentler now the frenzied activity on the water had ceased. Above us sounded the dull slap, slap of wet rigging against the mast and spars – above that, the flap, flap of Edward's royal standard in the fresh morning breeze. Beyond all, from the far side of the sand bar, out towards the open sea, came the distant screaming of wheeling gulls, diving, hunting, oblivious to the tension that gripped me.

Boots scraped on the deck high above, then a blare of trumpets split the air. Rousing cheers soared from the assembled companies of men, alongside a huge clamour and clash of weapons and armour. I could not see him, but I knew from the hurrahs that Edward had at last emerged from his cabin. And with a 'peek, peek, peek' I could hardly hear above the racket, a pair of startled oystercatchers that had been skimming the waves near the shoreline dashed about in alarm, scudding past our boat and sweeping on out to sea in a flurry of black, white and orange.

My eye was drawn from them upwards, to where Edward loomed now above the ship's rail, his steel-gauntleted arms flashing aloft to acknowledge the acclaim. Then, preceded by a liveried gentleman and aided by Earl John and Lord Francis – one to either side – he eased his leather-clad leg over the side and lowered himself down the ladder.

The rowboat tipped a little to one side as first the gentleman, then Edward, stepped into its belly. For ease of climbing, Edward wore only leather armour upon his lower body, but his upper was again clad in plate armour intended to impress. His shining breastplate and arm grieves were topped by a helmet of exquisite workmanship, open to the front so his face could be seen by everyone. And upon the helm was perched a gold coronet that dazzled with gems.

The roar from the shore continued as Edward steadied himself in the swaying boat. The gentleman with him I recognized as Giles Mallary, Lord Francis's man, who had travelled with his lordship to Burgundy in the early spring and then to Dublin. He winked at us now, holding fast to the rope ladder as first Earl John, then Lord Francis, followed Edward hand over hand down its rungs. They both edged along to take their places upon plank seats towards the stern, but Edward shook his head as they urged him to sit too. His face was pallid as though his insides still quailed, as I knew they had when he first awoke on this challenging morning, but he spoke with a new firmness I had come to expect in recent days.

'No – I shall stand. They shall see their king as I come to shore.'

And stand he did, his feet planted wide, balancing against the roll of the sea, as the rowing boat pushed away from the ship's side and the oarsman pulled for the beach.

3

'England, My England'

We pitched camp that night some miles north of our landing site, at a place our local guides called Swarth Moor. It was unlike any moor I had ever known, being rather rough heathland at no great height above the sea, a gentle slope away from the nearest village. No bilberry or heather sprang underfoot to soften the ground beneath our blankets, and no curlews or lapwings soared above. The salt scent of the sea still lingered, and stonechats and warblers hopped about the bushes and the long meadow grasses.

It felt good to make a start on our journey at last, after all the weeks of waiting, and to see Edward so happy at setting foot in England after almost two years away. My stomach had lurched with trepidation during our crossing of those last yards of sea – with Edward upright in the bows, his armour blazing, his legs braced against the rocking of the boat. But all tension shattered as soon as the prow scraped upon the gravel and he had leapt out on to the beach ahead of the rest of us, spurning the helping hand offered by Giles Mallary. As his boots crunched the shingle, he had bent down to grasp it in handfuls, raising them towards the sky. Then, slowly opening his fists, he let it trickle back to earth through his fingers, as all about him sank to their knees.

'England.' His voice, slightly raised, slightly husky, reached my ears. 'My England.'

More trumpets had blared, and Lord Kildare's herald – sent with us just for this purpose – had thundered, 'Edward Plantagenet, by the Grace of God, King of England and France, and Lord of Ireland.'

The voices of all the men there gathered – lords, soldiers, sailors, monks – had risen once more in thunderous cheering. As Roger and I had followed Lords Lincoln and Lovell on to the beach to stand with our king, Edward had glowed in pleasure as if lit from within.

I was reminded of that other time he had gloried in being seen in all his kingly splendour – on the morning of his coronation in Dublin only days before. As he emerged from the great west door of Christ Church Cathedral, his step was lighter, his smile broad, his eyes sparkling, reflecting the azure sky above. Upon his head then – perched on his wavy fair hair, not a steel helm as now – had been a different crown, an ancient, simple circlet borrowed for the holy ritual from a venerable statue of the blessed Mary, mother of Christ. But soon he had swapped it for this coronet of golden fleur-de-lys and bright cabochon jewels, specially made and sent to him by his aunt, Margaret, Dowager Duchess of Burgundy – the better to display his magnificence and his powerful allies.

Here, though, newly arrived in his English realm, he knelt, crowned head bowed, to receive the abbot's blessing and welcome, before embracing him and the lords who had come to greet him. He then led the triumphant way between the ranks of troops up the beach towards the castle.

Roger and I, with Giles, had followed Edward and all the lords, the soldiers closing in behind us as we scrambled over the wave-tumbled pebbles and midnight rocks clad in sunshine-yellow lichen further up the slope. Crossing the seaweed-strewn highest tideline, bladder-wrack popped and shiny blue mussel shells cracked beneath my boots, while all about us black and red moths flittered skywards. A few more steps and we were passing over the bridge across the outer moat, under the red-stone arch of the castle's western gateway and across the outer bailey – crammed with riding and packhorses – before entering the relative calm of the inner courtyard overshadowed by the lofty keep. There, in its draughty great hall, Edward – and we – had finally broken our fast and rested a while. Then, accompanied by the gentlemen and soldiers of the welcome party and many others who had gathered earlier at the castle, we set off on the first leg of the journey, with more blessings by the abbot and his brothers ringing in our ears and speeding us on our way.

That way had at first been across the salt marsh beyond the castle, picked along a narrow pebbly causeway. The wagons and packhorses had passed along it earlier while we were at breakfast, so as not to delay the main party on this cramped track. Soon the road began to rise and the shallow pools and clumps of marram grass to drop away to either side, and our wider surroundings became more visible to me.

By this time the tide was at its lowest ebb, as it had been at its highest at our dawn arrival. To our right now stretched out an immense sweep of flat sand, the like of which I had never before seen, or even imagined. Mile upon mile of dull yellow sand, reaching back the way we had come, ever onwards into the distance northwards, and across to the east, where the greyish mounds of faraway hills looked like nothing more than a bank of low cloud on the horizon. Here and there the late morning sunshine glanced off tidal pools stranded by the sea's retreat, and was that far-off silver ribbon the course of a slow-moving river winding across the sands? All else was flat and still, save the odd dark speck of a wading bird. It was the strangest, bleakest, most desolate landscape – yet, in its way, also one of the most beautiful.

My horse, a quiet, sturdy old bay from the Kildares' stable named Caesar, ambled to a halt as I stared in awe at what lay before me. The oncoming riders grumbled as they twitched their mounts to avoid a collision. But a local lad walking nearby, with whom I had shared bread during our meal in the castle, paused beside me. He gazed the way I did, his hand, flat, shielding his eyes from the bright sun.

'It's a sight, isn't it?' he said in his broad accent.

I nodded, made dumb by what I saw.

He brought his hand down in a slap upon Caesar's

neck, a swift smile upon his sun-beaten face.

'You'll get to know the Sands well enough these next few days. Always treat them with respect – and they may let you go on your way.'

With these cryptic words, he grinned again before striding off.

I urged Caesar into movement once more, not wanting to fall too far behind the foremost riders – among them, of course, Edward and their lordships, protected by their own close companions as well as knights who had greeted us at the castle. Marching in our wake was the greater mass of troops – the Irish, English soldiers who had arrived in Dublin with various Yorkist gentlemen, a large company of German pikemen and handgunners sent by Duchess Margaret just before the coronation, together with the newly mustered local men. Glancing over my shoulder, I could see them snaking still along the narrow causeway, dark against the grey-green marsh. Had they all even left the grassy hillock upon which we had landed yet? If I squinted against the sunlight, I could just spy the lumpy pinkish-grey shape of the castle, now so far behind us.

The land continued to rise, though our road still ran close to the coast and its sweeping views across the Sands. But before long, I glimpsed an edge of jagged hills far to the north. Then, as the sea began creeping stealthily back across the wide sands, we turned our backs upon it, taking a track that led inland. I was by now again within the cluster around Edward. Alongside me rode Roger, from whom I had become separated as the party jostled across the causeway. He did not share my amazement at the immensity of the Sands, and only looked forward to when we would finally halt for the evening.

'It's been a long day,' he complained, stretching his back as best he could while in the saddle. 'And I'm not so used to lengthy rides as you.'

'I suppose not,' I said, thinking back across recent weeks. 'But if you'd ridden out more with Alys and me in

Dublin, you'd hardly notice it now.'

'I would have liked to, believe me.' He grimaced, not meeting my eye. Had he detected a touch of resentment in my tone? 'But you know how Earl John always kept me so busy with my duties.'

'Never mind.' I tried to soothe away any discomfort between us. 'You'll soon get used to it again. And you'll have plenty of chance, by the looks of it. It's going to take some time to pick our way through that country.' I pointed towards the hills rising ahead of us.

'Maybe or maybe not,' he returned, his gaze following the direction of my finger. 'I heard Lord Francis tell the abbot at breakfast that he means to be at York within a week.'

'A week! To York? Is that even possible? That must be … well … I don't know how far.'

At just the mention of my home town, my heart thrummed in my chest with excitement. It had been so very long since I had been there or met any of my family.

But Roger only frowned, wrinkling his freckled nose.

'From the way he said it – and the abbot's reaction – it must be a very long way indeed. But I'm sure we'll cope. We'll have to.'

He didn't appear very convinced, as he shifted again in his saddle, rubbing his seat. And then a thought struck me.

'We may. But will Alys? Don't forget, while we may be riding, she'll be walking all that way.'

'Have you seen her since we left?'

I shook my head. I had not caught sight of her again, though my eyes sought her constantly.

'I think she must have left Piel Castle before us, with the wagons.'

'We'll have to find her when we halt – check that she's OK. If we can do it without drawing attention to her.'

Knowing her as we did, we might have guessed it

would instead be Alys who found us. Yet before that, I had to endure another, less welcome meeting.

4

The Messenger

The tents had all been put up, the campfires lit, pans of food set to cook upon them. A warm evening it might be, but hot food in our bellies would be a comfort to us all after our day's exertions. The water was already springing in my mouth at the enticing aromas rising from the cooking pots all around when, to my disappointment, Giles Mallary came to summon me to Edward's tent. He plonked himself down on the ground in my place next to Roger as I rose to do his bidding and sniffed the air appreciatively.

'Don't worry, I'll eat your stew if it's served before you get back. It won't go to waste.' He nudged Roger and stroked the heads of both hounds, flopped exhausted on the grass at his feet. 'I'll keep Roger here company too and look after Shadow for you.'

I had first met Giles and his brother Robert on my brief visit to England the previous autumn. At that time they had remained behind in Lowestoft to arrange a diversion, allowing our party to sail safely over to the Low Countries with Lord Francis. Both Mallarys had later travelled with his lordship back to Mechelen in February when Earl John took flight to Duchess Margaret's court, and Roger had been thrown much into Giles's company before their lordships had joined us in Dublin. They differed in age by several years, but they had struck up a firm friendship, finding they enjoyed similar pursuits, such as hunting and hawking. Despite Giles's long family loyalty to Lord Francis, Roger was adamant that we could trust him in our little deception over Alys. They both now waved me on my way, falling straightaway into a lively debate about how good the hunting might be in the countryside we'd ridden through this day

My stomach was surely rumbling loud enough for those around me to hear as I crossed the short distance to Edward's royal tent. Stitched together from wide panels of Plantagenet murrey and blue, it had been pitched at the very centre of our camp. There it towered like a sentinel over the hundreds of smaller tents radiating in neat lines out across the flat heathland to the wagons and horse lines at the edges.

The guards at the tent's entrance stamped to attention as I approached and one pulled aside the flimsy curtain that served as a door. Before I ducked within, a strong memory grasped at me, and I hesitated.

Above, on the pinnacle of the tent, the royal standard rippled, its lions, lilies and roses lambent in the deepening blue of the summer evening sky. The buzz and bustle of the camp all around, the harsh feel of the canvas as I clutched it for support, the scents of cooking, horses, men's sweat, the now-familiar throat-catching reek of gunpowder – all whisked me back to that night before the battle when I had entered King Richard's tent in just this fashion. Then I was not expected, was stricken with guilt at my subterfuge, terror at what should happen. Now I was summoned, awaited. Yet still I felt … what? Apprehension? Fear that I should not be there? That I was an imposter?

I gulped – the noise deafening within my head.

'Go in, lad.' The guard's rough voice hammered through my remembrances. 'Lord Lovell is waiting.'

I stooped beneath the flap he held up for me, emerging into the warm, torch-lit cavern within. Half a dozen or more gentlemen were mustered beneath its lofty canopied ceiling – Lord Francis, Earl John, Sir Thomas and Captain Schwartz, the leader of the Germans, among others.

Edward himself sat behind a table strewn with papers, jugs and goblets, his face pale in the lamps' glimmer. He no longer wore his armour, and his coronet lay discarded upon the tabletop. The flickering of the brands drew forth blood-red glints from the ruby-studded gold.

Again the memory was sharp – of when I had before crossed the threshold of a royal tent. Yet then my master had leapt to his feet at the sight of me, strangely as I had thought at first – before I knew the mission that would soon be mine. Now his nephew only glanced in my direction as the guard announced me, before turning back to the discussion, swirling his goblet in an absent manner.

Lord Francis, though, broke away from the group of gentlemen. He took my arm and guided me to a poorly lit corner, where bundles and boxes were piled alongside a skeleton-like wooden campbed, not yet swathed in the fine bedlinen set ready.

'Matthew,' he began in a quiet voice, 'I thank you for coming. Edward and I have decided you should attend him at night while we are on the march.'

I bowed my head, in part to hide some disappointment. Roger and I had hoped we could be together, among the other squires.

'Of course, my lord. But would not one of his squires …?'

'Edward himself asked for you. And I agreed it will be useful to have you on hand to write any letters or notes that may be necessary. It is not just because you and he are friends.'

'Yes, Lord Francis. I have all my writing things here ready.'

I patted my pouch where, these days, quills and ink bottle always resided alongside my pen-knife and several, more precious things. The shadows gathered about us did not allow me to read his lordship's expression as he continued.

'He has also begged Roger de Kynton from Earl John for the next few nights.'

So Roger and I would be together, despite our different masters and duties. And maybe … but no, I did not let myself think of whether Alys was part of Edward's plan too. And perhaps that was just as well, as Lord Francis was watching me closely, through the gloom.

'I believe I can rely on you, Matthew.' His tone was quiet still. 'As King Richard did. We are in a difficult time now – delicate even. I trust you will let me know if anything is amiss. Or if Edward – well, if Edward …'

But before he could finish his hesitant request – or I could learn what might be worrying him – muffled voices outside the tent caught our ears. Then the flap was thrust aside by one of the guards. Stepping inside, he removed his helmet and bowed towards Edward and Earl John. Edward still sat in the carved oak chair, with the earl on his feet beside him.

'Your Grace. A messenger from Lord Soulsby.'

A hiss.

Only as Lord Francis glanced back at me did I realize I had made the noise.

His lordship gripped my arm and murmured, 'Stay here', before striding across to join the other gentlemen.

I did as he bid. My unthinking reaction to the name had startled even me, and my chest was heaving as I gulped in my breath again. It was best to stay away from the others' notice until I could compose myself.

'Lord Soulsby?' Edward was saying. 'But wasn't he Lord Stanley's man?'

'Aye,' Earl John agreed. 'And still is.'

'He rode with William Stanley against good King Richard in his final battle,' said Sir Thomas, his face full of anger. 'I hear he now consorts with that traitor at Tudor's court too. Why would he be sending messengers to us here?'

'We cannot trust him,' Lord Francis said, his words terse.

Earl John shot him a look over Edward's head, before bending down towards his king.

'Yet, Edward, both the Stanley brothers and Lord Soulsby were loyal to the old king, your father.'

'But not to the old king's brother – also king

himself,' retorted Lord Francis. 'Nor yet to his son. They have served Tudor these past two years, though likely they all knew Edward was alive.'

'As did I serve him.' Earl John's reply was calm. 'After a fashion – and to others' eyes. It did not prevent me then joining my cousin and swearing my oath of loyalty to him. The Soulsbys and the Stanleys have ever watched to see which way the wind blows.'

With a start, I recalled the self-same words uttered by King Richard two years before.

'Now perhaps Soulsby sees the wind blows strong from Ireland.' Earl John raised his cup in salute to Sir Thomas, who returned the courtesy and drank deeply. The earl did not touch his wine as he continued.

'He has sent me tokens of his interest in this venture. I did not speak of it before as I confess I have little faith in him myself. I gave him no details of our plans, save what all knew – that perhaps we would invade to reclaim Edward's crown. Clearly he has a man in these parts who has watched for our coming.'

'As, no doubt, has Tudor,' put in Lord Francis.

'No doubt,' said Earl John, 'but he is not here to meet us. Soulsby's messenger is. We should perhaps hear him out.'

'Lord Soulsby was loyal to my father and rode against my uncle Richard, you say.' Edward's voice rose into the strained air between the two men.

'Aye,' said Lord Francis, turning his attention to Edward again. 'And that means he rode and fought for Tudor. He did not seek to restore you to your throne.'

Earl John also looked down. Edward was gazing ahead, his features impassive, yet his fingers now gripped the arms of the chair.

'Aye, Edward. At that time none knew where you were, or even whether you still lived. Our uncle Richard – for good or ill – had allowed people to believe what they would about you and your brother – or not think of you at all. I think that was his aim. That you should fade from people's minds until none thought to cause trouble on your behalf.' He paused, before continuing, 'I do not counsel that we should trust Soulsby. Just that we should listen to what he has to say.'

Edward glanced from one man to the other, then to Sir Thomas and the dark-featured captain who stood next to him. Each inclined his head in turn, Lord Francis after the briefest hesitation, and Edward gestured to the still-waiting guard.

'Send him to us.'

The man bowed and retreated back through the tent flap.

Edward thrust himself upright in his seat, placing his hands flat upon the tabletop as though for support. His gentlemen arranged themselves about him. I pressed myself further into the shadows, curious as to what would unfold, loath to remind anyone of my presence.

A few moments of silence passed, then the scuff of feet on the turf outside and some murmured words heralded the arrival of the messenger. The cloth flap was thrust roughly aside and a tall figure shoved his way into the tent. The wings of the great black bird upon his surcoat appeared to flutter in the flicker of torchlight as he slipped off his helmet and bowed a fair head to Edward.

'Your Grace.'

The messenger's voice was gruff, deeper than when I had last heard it. For I found now I had good reason to be grateful for the shadows all about me, hiding me from his view.

As he straightened up, I saw once more that hateful, handsome face I had seen so often in nightmares, seen again only months before as I fled across the harbourside in Lowestoft. The broad cheeks, ruddy in the glow of the torches. The crooked nose, legacy of when my fist had crunched into it several years ago. Beneath it, the well-shaped mouth, so ready to stretch into smirk or leer as the situation required. Now, as he stepped forward at a signal from Edward, those lips parted to say,

'Hugh Soulsby, Your Grace. Sent by my uncle Lord Soulsby to bring you his most loyal greetings.'

5

Within the Shadows

A torrent of fear, anger, hatred washed through me, a freezing, then a scorching tumult of emotion. Waves pounding in my head, a whirlpool in my stomach, my limbs numb, refusing to move. Yet if I could have stepped forward, it must have been to strike him. But no, not in front of my king and his lords. And if I did, what would happen? In the past, I had always come off worse – except once, when I had the help of my faithful hound, Murrey ...

I shrank back, though still motionless – shrank back within myself, within the darkness, within the horrors replaying within my mind's eye. The taunts and bullying at Middleham, the treasonous words in London, the vicious stab at Leicester, the murder done at Lowestoft. The surge of my hatred rushed again. Yet I had to master it – now was not the place or the time to free it.

Still, silent, I remained within the shadows as Edward spoke.

'Welcome, Master Soulsby. My lord of Lincoln here tells me he has received messages from your uncle.'

'Aye, sire. My uncle sent word before of his intentions. Now he has sent me with news of men who will join you tomorrow from our Westmoreland estates. Lord Soulsby himself stands ready to meet you later on your way south.'

Edward settled back in his chair. 'But your uncle has not come himself?'

His voice was quiet, but clear. Lord Francis's eyes flicked down to him, then back to Hugh.

Hugh bowed his head again in assent.

'He felt it best to wait. To gather more men from his southern manors, and join your army on its march to London.'

'But he sent you.'

Lord Francis's words were not a question – and were voiced as calmly as Edward's had been. But Hugh flashed him a glance as though uncertain of his meaning. And that look catapulted back to me all the doubt that Lord Francis had shown just moments before – and also on the eve of the battle. When he had entered a tent such as this to tell King Richard of Hugh's request to depart to his uncle's camp, and thus that of Lord Stanley. Lord Francis – who had been fighting alongside his friend, striking towards Tudor, when the Stanley brothers' cavalry had thundered into the king's rear the next morning. Who had survived, when his friend had been cut down by the traitors.

What was going through Hugh's mind? He faltered, then recovered himself.

'He … I – I'm here as a token of good faith, my lord. My uncle – he says he has no son to send you. He trusts you will accept me in his stead.'

Though the light was not good, a mixture of uncertainty, pride, smugness, flitted across Hugh's features.

'No son.' I recalled Elen's words months ago at Gipping about Hugh's cousin, Lord Soulsby's own son. Ralph. The young man who had been betrothed to Alys when she was only twelve. Elen had spoken about his being unable to meet with visitors, acting more like a child than a grown man – since he had struck his head so badly during his fight with my friends and me at Lowestoft. What did that mean for Hugh?

Edward's face was a mask. He gave no sign of remembering that night and that fight when he also had sustained serious injury – at the hands of Ralph himself. He glanced up at each of his advisers in turn before coming to his decision.

'Send a message to your men to meet us at Cartmel Abbey tomorrow forenoon, Master Soulsby. Meanwhile, take your rest here tonight. You may eat with us while Captain Schwartz's men find you a billet and make sure your mount is attended to.'

'Tomorrow forenoon, Your Grace?' Hugh asked. 'You mean you aim to make camp there tomorrow night?'

'Nay,' said Lord Francis. 'We've sent ahead to tell the abbot to expect us soon after midday. He is ready to attend his king at dinner.'

'But, my lord,' Hugh protested. 'It's a good day's journey around the top of the estuary and on to Cartmel.' Puzzlement now chased all else from his face. 'The roads are poor and the hills steep. I have often travelled them myself. With an army of this size, and wagons too, you might still not arrive even by nightfall.'

A smile touched Lord Francis's lips. 'That is why tomorrow at low tide we will make our way across the Sands.'

My stomach hollowed out with fear at his words. We were to travel across the vast, flat expanse of sand I had seen that morning? No rumour had reached us that it should be our route. And the warning words from the local lad on our ride came back to me. How safe would such a crossing be?

The notion shook Hugh too. His cheeks paled and his eyes narrowed, darting from Lord Francis to Edward to Earl John and back.

'Across the Sands? But that is perilous!'

'Indeed,' agreed Lord Francis. 'But we shall have the best local guides. And, as you say, it will save us two, perhaps three days on our journey. Time that may prove all too vital for our plans.'

Hugh ran the tip of his tongue along his lower lip to moisten it, but he pulled himself together and bowed.

'Then I must send word to our men as soon as I can. They will have to move fast if they are to meet us at Cartmel.'

Edward motioned to him to go, and he slipped back out through the tent flap without another glance around. But even once he'd left, the strain of those last moments hung in the air.

Earl John was the first to break the silence.

'Perhaps Soulsby is acting in good faith. Or he would not have sent his nephew as a messenger. The word is that Soulsby will soon make the boy his heir – now his son is incapable. Ralph Soulsby still shows no signs of recovering fully from his mysterious accident.'

His accident? I almost snorted at the word. I felt again the sticky blood on my hands, heard once more the thud of Ralph's skull against the wall as Roger, young Richard and I cannoned into him. Saw his face white as he lay senseless upon the ground. It had been no accident, not truly. Nor was it mysterious to me and my friends, whatever Hugh had or had not told his uncle and others.

Yet was Hugh now to profit by our actions? Had hunger been mingled in his eyes with those other emotions as he had waited for their lordships to consider? The hunger of ambition perhaps. Did Hugh see himself taking Ralph's place? As heir to the Soulsby estates, to their fortune? His own father had been only a knight, executed for treason against old King Edward years before. But his uncle was a baron – and one whose only son was not now fit to meet with visitors, let alone to take his place at court and parliament, if what Elen said was true.

'It does not make me happy to trust Lord Soulsby,' Lord Francis was saying.

'I like it no more than you,' replied Earl John. 'But we need all the men we can gather. No matter what our speed on the march, if Tudor is now at Kenilworth as we are told – and once he gets word of our landing, he will move then towards us – it may be difficult for men from the south to join us. They will have to pass him.'

'Your uncle Richard learnt to his cost not to trust Soulsby – as also the Stanleys.'

'Then we must keep young Soulsby close and make sure his uncle knows that we do. He may not play so fast and loose with his life as Lord Stanley did with his son.' Earl John's face was sombre as he spoke. 'I do not understand why my uncle let Lord Strange live when Stanley did not join him on the battlefield. Yet he ever had too forgiving a nature.'

My mind flashed back to the eve of battle when the king had spoken lightly of his 'hostage' – and to the sullen, yellow-haired young lord in the royal tent the next morning. Then my glimpse of him alongside Hugh later that day on the streets of Leicester forced its way into my mind, and I shivered at recollection of the vicious stab, the clapping, the laughter.

Lord Francis's quick eyes must have caught that tiny movement, although I hid still in the shadows.

'Matthew, go after young Soulsby. Make sure he sends a local messenger to his troop – doesn't think to go himself rather than return here to supper.'

Edward raised an eyebrow at the words. Was he surprised that Lord Francis should order me about in this way? But as I moved to do his lordship's bidding without question, all he said was, 'Be sure to return yourself after supper, Matt. And bring Roger and the hounds too.'

Did the light of conspiracy shine in those blue eyes despite his tight smile? As I bowed my way out of his presence, I had little time to think on his meaning before my own emotions took over.

The flare of anger and terror within me at the sight of Hugh had not yet died away. Yet Lord Francis had commanded me to follow him, and I must not let him down. So I forced the fear and hate deep down within me, like gunpowder tamped into a cannon's barrel, and emerged into the near-darkness of the busy camp.

Cooking fires and scattered braziers threw only a dim, flickering light on the tents clustered about the royal pavilion. Squinting, I did my best to spy Hugh among the many soldiers and campfollowers bustling this way and that. After just a few moments, I was ready to give up and admit I had failed in my task. But then, from the deep shadows behind me, a voice called out.

6

Games

'Do you seek Lord Soulsby's messenger, lad?'

I spun round, alarmed. Full of dread at the thought of Hugh, my breath caught in my throat. Yet it was only the guard who had earlier hustled me into Edward's tent.

Feeling a fool, I nodded, sure my panic was splashed across my face. But the guard appeared not to notice.

'He's just left, heading towards the horse lines. That way. If you're quick, you'll soon catch him.'

I mumbled my thanks and hurried the way he pointed. Only a score or so yards ahead, the red glow from a brazier lit up a bulky form in grey and green surcoat and iron sallet, hastening away.

Hugh.

He hadn't gone far, not as far as I would have expected. Had he been lurking after his dismissal, maybe listening outside the tent?

Whatever the case, I had no desire to gain on him. So I hung back a little myself, hoping he would not look round, then followed. I did not consider my actions if he did not do as Edward had instructed.

He wended his way between huddles of soldiers, sitting and standing about tents and campfires. The clinks of cups and scraping of spoons on bowls amid their raucous laughter rose to my ears through the still evening air and reminded me of my empty belly. But still I trailed Hugh on his determined path.

A stand of wagons, fully laden, mounded up before us, and then beyond were ranged another band of men. Their accents, rather than the limp, night-shrouded pennon hoisted above, told me they were local troops. One or two called out to Hugh, jesting, as he passed, but he returned no response.

Just ahead now, silhouetted against the last orange embers of the long-gone sunset, loomed the horse lines, shadows from the locals' campfires playing across myriad legs and sleek flanks. Beyond, I knew, were only guards – a good number of them, but placed there to stop assault from without, not prevent a single man leaving from within. A lone horse was tethered at the end of one line. The harness still upon its head and the wide-winged raven stitched upon its saddle cloth gleamed in the glow from the closest fires.

Without thinking, I cried out, 'Master Soulsby!'

My voice was thin and reedy to my ears, hardly able to carry through the night air. But the broad figure in front of me halted, turned slowly. One hand rested on the pommel of his sheathed dagger.

Again, with little thought except to the task I had been given, I called, 'Master Soulsby, Viscount Lovell bids you send a local messenger to your troops – and then to join the king at supper.'

A curse, swiftly stifled. Then he stepped towards me.

He surely could not see my face, veiled in the darkness. Could not know who I was from my voice alone. But I saw in the fireglow his fingers start to draw his knife, and heard the faint hiss of steel against sheath.

Unnerved, and aware now of my foolish mistake, I took a pace back – and trod on something behind me. I staggered as my ankle cricked on the unexpected softness underfoot.

A second curse, then a laugh. Hands gripped my shoulders, holding me upright.

'Take care, lad.' A gruff local accent. 'I'll be needing both my feet in the fight against Tudor.'

Twisting my head, I found myself gazing up into glittering eyes in a friendly weather-beaten face. Another face loomed beyond. As I turned back, Hugh was resheathing his dagger, his face set in a scowl.

'Needing a messenger sent, are you, sir?' The second soldier stepped forward, past his mate. 'Just let me know the details and you can return to His Grace in two shakes.'

'And is this your horse, master?' My saviour also advanced on Hugh, shielding me from his view. 'I'll unsaddle him for you and get him his feed.'

How close I had come to disaster – averted only because my calls had attracted the soldiers' attention! Now, while Hugh was cornered by them, I swiftly made my retreat, stumbling back towards the wagon line.

I passed the locals' camp, beckoned onwards by the bright fires of the main encampment. The mouthwatering scents of roasting meat and stews drifted on the air towards me, along with chat and laughter. The bulks of the carts rose dark alongside me and I was still some way from the sanctuary of the next throng of men and tents, when the thumping of boots assailed my ears and strong hands seized me from behind. They shoved me roughly to the side, forcing my face into the side of the nearest wagon. Sharp splinters scratched my skin and a voice rasped in my ear.

'You miserable little tick! Order your betters around, would you?'

It was Hugh, of course. He must have concluded his business with the local soldiers with unwelcome speed.

He swung me round to face him and cuffed me across my cheek, slamming my head to the side so hard my ears sang. I righted myself, hazily focusing on his face – higher, but only inches from mine. Yet the glimmer from the faraway fires showed the snarl on his features dropping away and his eyes widening.

'You!'

To my amazement, his fist unclenched, releasing me, and he drew back. I tensed to flee, but then was stunned by what was scrawled across his face, just visible in the dim light. The shock of recognition was driven away, not by fury as I expected, but by something else.

Another raw emotion, vivid within his eyes.

Was it – fear?

Surely that was not possible.

Whatever I had glimpsed was wrestled from his face as we stared at each other across the darkness. His chest was heaving from his run, mine from my own terror, and my cheekbone throbbed from his blow. But I could not now be the first to move.

I thrust my chin up in what I hoped was a defiant gesture. From behind him, beyond the wagons, came the noise of hoofbeats rising to a trot, then fading into the distance. He glanced over his shoulder towards the sounds, then glared back at me. He had conquered his earlier emotion.

'I suppose I should have expected to find you here,' he spat.

I did not reply, simply held his gaze, while casting about for what to do next. I was too far from the main camp to hope for help from that direction – and I could not expect my earlier saviours to hear us again.

As though riled by my silence, Hugh spoke again. His voice was still harsh, but quieter.

'You always turn up where you're not wanted. I should never have let you go at Lowestoft.'

His words jolted me out of my fear, into anger of my own.

'What? *You* let *me* go?' My hands balled into fists by my sides. 'I left you bound and trussed like a chicken. And I should have killed you.'

The all-too-familiar smirk unfurled across his broad face and in his tone. The shadows were not dense enough to disguise that.

'But you didn't, did you? You couldn't. You were too weak.' He hesitated. 'Anyway, I didn't mean then. I meant last time. When you were at the harbour with your friends.'

His disdain at that last word rang out despite his hushed tone.

My mind snapped back to that early morning the previous autumn. Catching sight of Hugh emerging from the tavern in Lowestoft. The dash across the quayside to the Flemish ship. The thumping of my heart as I stood on deck and watched him mount and ride calmly away up the score without a backward glance. My astonishment that I had escaped from him – after all that had gone before. My mystification at why …

'I thought it was just because you were alone,' I said. 'You didn't fare so well on your own before – even without my friends around.'

'I had my orders,' he shot back, rattled too, perhaps, by the memory of our last fight.

'Which were?'

'I don't have to tell you.'

'But we're on the same side now, aren't we?'

He was silent. The darkness had closed in further among the wagons, concealing what might now be in his eyes or his thoughts. Then,

'I suppose so. But only because my uncle says.' Another pause. 'We were told just to watch for Yorkists. See what they did, not engage with anyone. Just to report back to him.'

'Because you messed up so badly before?'

Anger flashed in his retort.

'No. They were just our orders, that's all.'

'But why would Tudor not want you to stop us? He knows we're his enemies. He must have known we were on our way to Edward.'

'Did I say our orders were from the king?'

It was my turn to be silenced.

After a moment, I stammered, 'But … but why would Lord Soulsby …? He's Lord Stanley's man and … and Stanley is Tudor's stepfather.'

A chill ran through me at Hugh's quiet laugh, eerie in the still night.

'It may not suit him always to be Stanley's man – or Stanley to be Tudor's. They have their own plans, play their own games. They always have. I don't ask. I just do what I'm told.'

My mind was racing now, and I felt as though I stood on shifting sands. Who could be trusted in all of this? My thoughts flew back two years to the night before the battle, to what King Richard had said about changing loyalties and the difficulties of balancing them. And then to their lordships' discussion earlier. Now I stood facing he who had been my bitterest enemy – only to find I might have to accept him as an ally.

Perhaps Hugh was coming to the same realization. His tone had changed, become less vicious, less cutting. The anger, the fear – if such it had been – had softened as we spoke, though a sneer remained in his voice.

Yet my acceptance would not come so easily.

'And you always follow orders, do you?'

'Of course. Don't you?'

'Even if it means being here, with me? Doing what King Richard would have wanted?'

'I served King Richard well,' he insisted, 'despite all he did. Now I serve my uncle. He serves Lord Stanley. We're loyal. It's what we do.'

My turn now to laugh.

'Loyal? Lord Stanley doesn't know the meaning of the word. Nor his brother. I was at the battle, don't forget. I saw what happened. Earl John, Edward – they're mad if they trust any of you now.'

'Well, that's up to them, not you. You have no say or influence here. You'll simply serve them too. Blindly, like an old faithful dog.'

Words of protest sprang to my lips, but he swept on.

'Is it really because it's what old Dick would have wanted? He stole the boy's crown after all. And now he's dead. Would it really matter to him who rules now? Why does it matter to you?'

'But Edward – his family – I—'

Yet now I could speak, I found I had no ready

answer – despite all my many months attending Edward, in Burgundy, in Dublin, on our various journeys.

Hugh didn't let me flounder long before he pushed me on to other unsteady ground.

'Or is it just to impress Alys? I know she was with you in Dublin.'

The heat rose in my cheeks. Had there been light enough to see, the flush would no doubt have vied with the bruise that must be purpling there.

'Don't you dare speak her name! We're just friends.'

But the tumbling out of my words told him his dig had struck home, like a small boy poking an ants' nest and seeing the insects erupting from their burrow. I could have cursed. His voice was tinged with triumph as he said,

'Do you forget she was promised in marriage to my cousin Ralph? Who you cowardly left for dead at Lowestoft. The injury to his head was so bad he is like a small child now. And if he doesn't recover – and if my uncle makes me his heir as he's promised – she'll—'

'Masters?'

The single word broke through the darkness behind Hugh. He broke off. His head moved a fraction as though he glanced towards the sound, but then back to me, perhaps not daring to risk shifting his attention.

'Yes?'

'Supper is ready, masters,' came the light voice again. 'You do not want to miss it.'

A hesitation. Then Hugh's shadowed face bent towards mine.

'We'll continue this another time,' he muttered, then stalked back towards the main camp.

The person who had spoken from the dark came towards me. I had supposed it was just some lad, perhaps sent by Roger or Lord Francis to find me. But now, to my astonishment, it was revealed as Alys. Her face, beneath her dark boy's cap, was a pale glimmer caught by the distant firelight.

'Matt – what on earth?' she whispered as she grasped at my arm. Under her cool fingers, I felt my sinews tense, my fist clenched. 'I was searching for you and Roger. I heard raised voices, and realized one was yours. Then I saw ... Matt, what is Hugh doing here?'

'Turning up like a bad penny – as always.' I did my best to joke but couldn't. Though Hugh was gone, my breathing was still shallow, my chest tight.

She fired more questions at me, so I filled her in on what had happened since I was called to Edward's tent, up to my encounter with Hugh. I stopped at the point before her name was mentioned, but what had she overheard at the end? Had she understood Hugh's insinuation? Relief crept through me when she said,

'We must warn Lord Francis about him. Or, rather, you must. We cannot let him jeopardize everything.'

It was evident her concern was for our venture, for Edward, rather than for herself.

'Lord Francis doesn't trust him,' I assured her. 'Nor does Earl John. Neither I think does Edward – for all he made mention of Lord Soulsby's loyalty to his father ... and his betrayal of King Richard.' My discomfort at Edward's tone when speaking of his uncle wormed into me once more, but I pushed it aside. These were different times. 'It was he who insisted Hugh stay here with us so he can be watched. Perhaps he has learnt from other people's past mistakes.'

'Perhaps.'

She fell quiet for a moment as though thinking. And into that silence, to my shame, burst an enormous gurgling rumble. My face flamed again, but though the darkness might hide that, there was no concealing where the noise came from. My stomach was complaining of its long neglect.

Alys laughed.

'Oh, Matt! Supper truly is ready – past ready, I'm sure. We must get you some before you suffer any more hardship this evening. Come on. Where did you leave Roger and Shadow?'

Together we made our way as quickly and quietly as possible back through the main camp to where Roger sat with Giles Mallary and the two hounds. Despite our stealth, we caused mayhem as first Shadow, then Belle, leapt about in excitement at Alys's arrival. Both dogs managed to land a lick or two on her face before she could calm them down. Her eyes darted about the nearby groups of soldiers and squires in case any showed interest in the reason for the hounds' enthusiasm. But at most they glanced across to the commotion and smiled before returning to their chat or games of dice.

Rather than following through on his threat to eat all the supper, Giles had made sure some stew was saved for me. When he hauled the cooking pot over from where it was keeping warm in the embers of the nearest fire, we found just enough left for Alys too. We each used a hunk of wheaten bread to scoop it straight out of the pot, before all four of us shifted further away from the other soldiers so we could talk in private.

For Roger and Giles's benefit, I related again all I had witnessed in Edward's tent: my shock at Hugh's arrival, their lordships' concern at Lord Soulsby's intentions, the plan to march across the Sands on the morrow. When I spoke of Edward's last order to me – to make sure I brought Roger and the hounds to join him after supper – followed by my suspicion of his real intent, Alys's response was full of disquiet.

'Edward said, before we left Dublin, that he'd try to smuggle me into the royal tent with you both if he could. But I told him it's a very bad idea and I'd have to find somewhere else to sleep.'

The far-off fireglow revealed her eyes lowered as though in modesty at the very notion of sharing a tent with three boys. But her next words showed what her real worry was.

'What if word should reach Lord Francis or Earl

John that a strange lad had joined you? And with Shadow here too? He'd no doubt put two and two together and know it was me. And then I should be lost.'

With that, Hugh's final words came back to me. The idea that if he took Ralph's place as his uncle's heir, he would also inherit his cousin's marriage plan. And I knew we had to do everything we could to protect Alys from that fate.

7

Crossing the Sands

'Don't step away from the path we show you for any reason.'

The voice of the guide was raised as he addressed the scores of soldiers and campfollowers gathered about him. Roger and I, both hounds sitting neatly at our feet, were standing at the edge of the group, our horses' reins loose in our gloved hands.

'Don't do it,' the guide continued. 'But if you're stupid enough to, beware the tide and the quicksands. The incoming tide is fast, faster than a man can run, and it can cut you off in minutes. If you fall into quicksand, whatever you do, don't struggle – you'll just sink all the more quickly.'

He ended his speech with a broad grin, as though he was looking forward to us making all these mistakes. I wanted to ask what we should do if we were cut off by the tide or did fall into quicksand. But there was no time. Before I opened my mouth, the man strode off to join the other guides.

They had all now finished their warnings to various groups scattered around the packed-away campsite and were making their way towards the front of the army, which had already begun to move off. As the people around us collected together their belongings ready to follow, only Roger remained to see my grimace.

He just laughed at it.

'Stop worrying, Matt. All will be well. We must just do as the guides tell us. Lord Francis and Earl John wouldn't be taking us across the Sands if they didn't believe it was safe.' But then a frown edged on to his face. 'Although … do you know what "quicksand" is?'

I had not a clue. But before I could tell him, a man

walking past said darkly in a local accent, 'You don't want to know.'

Other soldiers around him pealed with laughter as they marched on, but one, an older man, halted. A wry smile wrinkled his tanned face as he turned to us.

'You're not from these parts, are you, lads?'

We shook our heads.

'Well, make sure you pay heed and do what the guides tell you. Quicksand is the work of the devil on this coast. It looks like normal sand. Feels like it too, until you put your foot full down on it. Then it a-quivers and a-quavers like a cow's fat belly, and it sucks you right down into it till you can hardly move.' He gestured with both hands to demonstrate this predicament. 'The more you fear and the more you fight, the more it will suck you down. Out on those sands there are places that could mire a cat, for all a cat's lightness of step and fleetness of foot. And there'll be more of them after all that rain we had last night.'

He went to walk on, then swivelled back again, as though he'd sensed my unspoken thought.

'If you start to feel you're sinking, don't stop walking – just keep going. But if you should get caught, it's best to stay calm and call out. And pray your friends can get you out before the tide comes racing back in and drowns you.'

With this, he tipped his sallet to us and continued on his way after his fellows.

Roger's earlier mirth had long since fled as he listened, and his expression now surely mirrored my own. Even before mention had been made of tides and sinking, my first sight this morning of the immense sweep of the Sands had reawakened my dread of the crossing. Even Hugh had called the attempt perilous.

But now I clasped my friend by his shoulders.

'You're right, Roger. All will be well. You and I will not be so foolish as to disregard the guides, or step beyond where they step. It will be no great difficulty to keep on the tracks of an army four thousand or more strong!'

So saying, and sounding braver, I hoped, than I felt inside, I grasped my reins and hauled myself into Caesar's saddle. In a moment, and as always far more elegantly, Roger had also swung himself upon his mount. Together we urged our horses forward and were soon riding alongside the column of men marching across the heathland towards the shore.

We had not broken camp early. The guides had said we should not start our journey until the tide was on its way out. That had been welcome, as it allowed time for gear – and people – to dry out after the rainstorm overnight. Had Alys been among those without suitable shelter when the downpour burst upon us? Not all campfollowers had secured a place within a tent, many having to make do with bedding down beneath a wagon.

Roger and I had not seen Alys since she left us the evening before, accompanied by Giles. He promised he would find her a comfortable place to sleep among the campfollowers. When he returned to us, settled by then in Edward's tent, he assured us she would be safe, whatever the night should bring. I hoped now he had been right.

Edward's face clouded when we told him she would not join us. Later, when the first raindrops pattered, then pounded, on the outer skin of the tent as we lay awake talking in the dark, he urged us to find Giles, to tell him to fetch her. We refused, insisting it would be, not only immodest, but also risky if we wanted to keep Alys secret. Edward rose and prowled the tent in darkness for some time, before throwing himself back on his campbed and turning away without a word more. It had been an uncomfortable night for Roger and me – for all that we were in the warm and dry.

As on the day before, we kept watch for Alys as we rode. But it was no surprise we didn't spy her before we descended the final slopes towards the Sands. More local troops had arrived to swell the army while we were camped at Swarth Moor. Sometimes we struggled to spot even Edward's banners among the many that now bristled above the heads of men and horses.

Roger and I had become separated from the royal party earlier in the morning when we sought Giles for news of Alys and how she had fared overnight. Before we found him, the guides had begun to issue their cheerful warnings to the assembling columns of troops. But it had, anyway, been good to escape for a time from their lordships and their companions, who now, of course, included Hugh. He had sneered at us without speaking as we emerged with Edward to join the rest of the company, breakfasting in the open air on this sunny morning.

Now, up ahead of us, Edward's party broke away from the main body of the army and halted, allowing us the chance to catch up. To the right, towering oaks and elms on a low, wooded hill half-concealed a grey stone gateway and a cluster of buildings. A procession of black-clad monks were advancing to meet the small company arrayed under the huge royal standard, flying proud in the stiff breeze from the sea. As Roger and I rode up, the monks' richly attired leader finished greeting Edward and ushered forward a brother bearing a small iron-bound chest.

After more bows and blessings, Edward and their lordships made their farewells and continued on their way, with Roger, me and the hounds once more in tow. The chest was stowed safely within the closed carriage Lord Kildare had supplied to carry Edward's treasure. I had snatched a glimpse inside before we embarked from Ireland. As well as his crown, sceptre, robes and other precious items, the carriage held caskets of coins to pay the army. Overheard discussions among their lordships and Captain Schwartz told me soldiers did not come cheap, whether they fought for pay, as the Germans did, or simply needed to be fed and armed. Abbots and priors might not supply fighting men-at-arms, but they could show their loyalty to their new king in other ways.

Before us now the flower-starred heathland sloped down to the Sands and, as the foremost companies of the army set foot upon them, their stark flatness struck me again. Here, though, they were not so featureless, with orange sunlight glinting off two river channels and a distant craggy rock that cut through the mud, and the far shore appeared closer than the morning before. Green, tree-covered hills mounded up only three or four miles away across the beige expanse.

My spirits lifted a little at the sight. Perhaps the crossing would prove less dangerous than I had feared.

'Well, here goes.'

Roger's cheerfulness rang false to my ears, but I smiled at him in return. I clicked my tongue at my horse to encourage it – and me – and together we stepped off the last of the grassy land on to the sand.

There was no jolt, no faltering, no misstep, no sinking feeling. The sand beneath Caesar's hooves was as firm as the turf had been. Before us the sandy ripples left behind by the retreating tide were sliced through by myriad tracks of foot-, hoof- and wheel-prints, but none was more than a fingernail deep. If the hollow drumming of marching troops on the grassland had given way to a softer, denser, sandier sound, it was scarce noticeable. The tumult of creaking wheels, jingling harness, rowdy laughter and cheering song that had accompanied the troops the previous day masked any change underfoot.

Had I expected muddy chasms to open up as soon as we set foot upon the Sands? Perhaps. My dreams overnight had been full of such terrifying holes and hollows, and since the guide's warning, my fears had only worsened. But now I breathed again, and drew the fresh salt air, slow and deep and calming, into my lungs.

The crossing passed quickly enough after those first, long-drawn-out moments. And my earlier worries were soon forgotten as I took in the sights and sounds all around us.

Beneath me, tangled patterns of prints – of man,

beast and the delicate toes of wading birds. Trails of weed and tiny translucent skeletons of crabs, giving way to spiral casts thrown up by burrowing worms and the glossy blue of mussel shells. Above, black darting dots of swallows swooping for insects, the shrieking of gulls disturbed by the army from their scavenging on the sand flats.

To the north, my eye was drawn to the ancient black stumps of a ruined jetty or breakwater, jutting up from small mounds of sand. Then beyond – to distant jagged hills piercing the clouds, past where the Sands narrowed and the shores seemed to close together. Were those the steep hills with poor roads at the head of the estuary that Hugh had warned of? I glanced back to where he rode among their lordships' gentlemen, his face expressionless. Despite all his misgivings last night, this flat crossing now appeared preferable to such a climb.

Before the dark skeleton timbers were long past, we came to the first of the rivers carving its way across the Sands. The brown, slow-moving water barely rose above my horse's fetlocks and the footsoldiers splashed through it without a care. The next was a different matter. Before we arrived at its edge, guides came back to give us all warning. Those of us who were riding were advised to dismount and guide our horses down the bank, and if we valued our boots, to take them off and sling them around our necks or across the saddle. Even Edward, riding Storm as he had the day before, joined us on foot, walking tall at the head of the royal party. Despite his disappointment last night, his mood was merry enough this morning. Laughter drifted back to us as he and Earl John plunged into the river alongside one another.

The water reached above their knees and Edward laughed again as, knocked off balance, he staggered sideways and clutched at his cousin for support. Storm snorted and tossed his head at the noise and the jerk of the rein in Edward's hand, but he followed his new master, picking his way with care down the side into the stream.

I glanced at Roger, who returned my look with a grin.

'One, two, three,' he counted, and pinched his nostrils with his fingers as though about to jump into water well above his head. I punched his arm, then together we stepped into the muddy flow.

The water lapped high up on my thigh and I gasped at its cold clutch. For an instant, my thought sped to those high, craggy hills to the north. Might snow still be melting from their peaks into this river, although it was now early June? Tales of such things had been spun by foreign merchants visiting Master Ashley's house and I had stood amazed. Was it perhaps true, even here in England?

But as that first freezing shock wore off, a tugging at my legs replaced it. The flow of this river was much faster, stronger – enough almost to drag me along with it. But as Caesar and then Roger's horse followed us, stepping down gingerly into the water, their bulk diverted the worst of the current to either side of us.

A whine came from behind.

It barely reached my ears above the trampings and trundlings and splashings of the men, horses, and carts arriving at and jumping or sliding into the river upstream of us, or hauling themselves or being hauled up its far bank, some score or more yards ahead. Turning, I was in time to catch sight of Shadow leaping headlong into the water, paddling sturdily towards me. But behind her, stranded, was little Belle. She trotted one way, then another along the bank and whimpered as she gazed at us and at her hound cousin, so confident in the water. Her soft brown eyes held a pitiful expression as she whined once more.

Roger too had stopped and glanced round. Now he threw me his rein, saying, 'Lead my horse for me, will you, Matt?' before wading back and gathering up the small dog in his arms.

'She's worse than a child sometimes,' he

complained, but his tone was tender. Together – me leading both horses, he carrying his precious cargo, Shadow swimming ahead – we forded the churned-up watercourse before scrambling up the further bank.

The only other landmark of note on our crossing was the rocky outcrop I had spied from the shore. As we drew near, a low, craggy hill revealed itself. Fringed by pebbles and topped by scrubby trees and bushes, it no doubt transformed into a tiny islet at high tide. Upon it perched the smallest church I had ever seen. Its single bell tolled in greeting as we passed, and from its doors spilled half a dozen black-clad monks. Their cheers and cry of 'God bless King Edward and God speed your venture' prompted the soldiers closest to echo their hurrahs. Those shouts rippled outwards, forwards, backwards along and across the columns of men-at-arms, and in a moment the cheers and huzzahs and clashings of weapons of the entire army were deafening.

Edward, once more aboard Storm, slipped off his shining helmet and bowed his thanks to the brothers. Then he raised the helm high in the air, the army roared once more, and he spurred Storm into a canter, drawing his small company of lords and gentlemen (and Roger and I) along in his wake as he swept to the head of the procession.

In this fashion – the royal standard resplendent above the foremost riders, the parade of loyal troops marching behind – we approached the far shore just as the sun tipped past its warm noonday height. Gradually the soft, muddy sand under foot and hoof changed once more to tidelines of murky brown seaweed and wracks, then to clumps of marram grass and sea pinks clinging to sandy mounds. Sculpted banks and narrow channels carved deep through reed beds followed, before salt marsh at last gave way to the grass-clad soil of the shore proper and our horses scrambled on to dry land. As I urged Caesar up the slope towards the trees edging this shore, I sent up a prayer of thanks to the Virgin and Saint Christopher for carrying us safely across the perilous Sands.

The guides still leading the way, we soon came to an opening between the massed trunks where a hollowed-out trackway began. In a moment we were swallowed up by the cool shade of the forest, a welcome contrast after the growing heat out on the Sands. All about us song tumbled down from birds hidden in the swaying tree tops high above. The track itself was wide enough for several horses to travel abreast or two carts to pass one another with ease, but a few paces off the roadway to either side, the trees and bushy undergrowth closed in. Everything beyond was invisible to our eyes.

From where Roger and I were riding close behind Edward and their lordships, I saw Sir Thomas exchange a glance with Earl John.

''Tis a fine place for an ambush, I'm thinking. For his safety, His Grace the king should not perhaps now be at the head of the army.'

Though clearly Sir Thomas had meant to speak quietly, as always his powerful voice carried to the ears of those further away. Riding the other side of the earl, Edward glanced at his cousin. In the semi-twilight of the woodland, his face was pallid.

Lord Francis, next to him, reached across to grasp his arm.

'Nay, have no fear, Edward, Sir Thomas,' he said, with a smile. 'This is good Yorkist country. The people hereabouts are loyal to our cause. And the greatest of them is the Abbot of Cartmel, who is even now overseeing preparations for our dinner. Besides, I sent outriders ahead at low tide last night to scout the way.'

'And some of them now approach, I suspect, my lord,' said Captain Schwartz, who rode on the far side of Lord Francis.

His ears must have been sharp to hear them above the racket made by the army at our back, but sure enough, a moment later four riders cantered round a bend in the track some hundred paces ahead. Their leader was revealed as Robert Mallary. With his companions, he reined his horse to a halt before us and bowed low in the saddle.

'Your Grace, your lordships.' His familiar gruff voice. 'I bring my lord the abbot's greetings, and news that all is ready for your arrival at the abbey. The way is clear and should take us no more than an hour or so.'

Robert did not lie, on either count. And I, for one, was grateful when the end of our long morning's journey came and the royal party rode through the buff stone gateway of Cartmel Abbey.

The abbot and his foremost monks were waiting on the steps up to his venerable church and their welcome was warm. And so, thanks be, was the dinner. Fresh sea trout and oysters, fished early in the morning before the tide receded from the very sands we had crossed; vast venison and mutton pies; spiced fig and honey pastries; a pudding made with early strawberries and hindberries from the abbot's sheltered kitchen garden served with a jug of rich new cream. Fare fit for a king – of course.

After the final course of crumbly cheese made from milk from the abbey's own flock of sheep, Roger and I were happy to be dismissed the royal presence, as Edward and their lordships were ushered into the abbot's private chamber behind his magnificent dining hall. Only the king's closest companions had been entertained in the abbot's residence and as we made our way back out to the abbey courtyards, Hugh was just leaving the guesthouse refectory in the company of Giles and Robert Mallary and a number of other gentlemen. He scowled at us before sauntering with them towards the gatehouse and the rest of the army, gathered for their meal in the extensive pastures outside the abbey precinct. Giles, however, must have made his excuses as, with a few words to those around him, he peeled away from the others and came over to us.

'Charming company, your friend Master Soulsby,' he said as he came up. But he chose not to add to his comment, turning instead to the matter of Alys. 'I spotted her when I was tethering our horses before dinner. She was with those helping the abbey servants to serve food and drink to the men. I did not see her so very close, as I dared not go too near. But she appeared none the worse for her first night on the march.'

I was somewhat reassured by his words, though still worried that she would be finding not only the march difficult, but also keeping her secret all this time among strangers. A shadow hovered around Roger's eyes too, but Giles carried on before either of us could reply.

'The monks say there are beds aplenty for us in the guesthouse dormitory if we wish to rest. It might be well to do so. I'm told we will set off again an hour or so before sunset.'

'Not till then?' Roger asked. 'That's strange. Why so late?'

'I've no idea. Perhaps to allow time for more troops to join us? I've not heard that Lord Soulsby's company have arrived yet. Maybe I should catch up with young Hugh and check. Lord Francis asked me to keep an eye on him anyway.'

With a flash of smile, Giles bid us farewell and hurried off through the gateway.

After the worry and trials of the morning, I had no objection to resting before our journey began again, so Roger and I climbed the stairway to the large chamber that served as sleeping quarters for the abbey's guests. A number of their lordships' companions were already snoring on the wooden-framed beds.

I had no intention of sleeping. But we each settled down on a straw mattress and, after a few whispered words, Roger turned his face away from me, dragged a blanket over his head and was almost immediately asleep, with Belle curled up in the crook of his knees. I pulled from my pouch the book of tales of King Arthur given to me all those years ago by little Ed, but after reading a few lines only, I too was ambushed by sleep.

The sun had crept down the length of the

dormitory's tall arched windows before a trumpet blare in the courtyard outside roused me. A few minutes later, the royal party was assembling in front of the church. A weighty wooden chest was lifted into the treasure carriage, and with a final salute to the abbot and his brethren, we rode out through the gateway, following Edward's banner to the head of the gathered army once again. We passed Hugh at the head of a large party of horsemen and men-at-arms clad in the Soulsby green and grey livery. At a shouted command, the troop fell in behind our company.

The road leading from the abbey gateway was narrow and edged on one side by a wall the height of a man. In the pasture beyond a score or more deer were grazing peacefully, several spindly legged fawns sticking close to their mothers. Only one or two raised their heads from the grass to view the cavalcade passing so close.

Roger pointed. 'That must be where the pies at dinner came from.'

'But they're taking no more notice of us than sheep would,' I said in my surprise. 'Usually they flee at the merest sign of humans.'

'The brothers must husband them like sheep,' he said. 'I doubt monks are allowed to hunt, after all, and my lord abbot must have his venison from somewhere. Especially if he is to entertain kings.'

Little Belle was slung once more across his saddle bole to keep her safe. As we rode past the deer, her nose quivered and her head lifted, her dark eyes staring at the quiet herd. Upon the ground, Shadow was not so placid. She darted towards the wall, raising her muzzle to quest the air, then dashed backwards and forwards pawing at the stones. Finding a sturdy wooden door a few yards on, she scrabbled at it with her forepaws, yapping.

I whistled to her, then called her name, but she heeded me not. She did not even turn her head when I shouted.

'Masterful control, lad,' one soldier heckled as he marched past, and the whole column erupted in guffaws.

My cheeks blazed and I slid down from Caesar, grabbing at Shadow to haul her away. She struggled, trying to dig in her heels, but for once I was stronger. As I dragged her after me, she still sniffed the air and gazed back with her sad hound eyes.

Stifling his own laughter, Roger threw me down a length of rope to slip through her leather collar and he held this makeshift leash while I remounted. Meanwhile, he had kept one hand on Belle to pin her to his saddle.

'And Shadow is usually so obedient,' he said, then added with a badly concealed smirk, 'For Alys at least.'

'It just shows what a strong scent can do to a hound,' I shot back. 'Even one not trained for the hunt. I remember our dogs reacting the same way when out in the woods around York.'

'I suppose any smell is far stronger for them than us,' he admitted, as he handed the end of the rope to me. 'You had best keep an eye on her for the time being.'

Shadow became her normal calm self again as we left the abbey precincts and rode once more through light-mottled woodlands. Before long the shadows were lengthening and, where they could be seen through the interlaced branches, the few fluffy clouds above us were stained a delicate pink. Hardly a breath of wind drove them, but the air was cooling as the evening wore on.

The track we were following sloped now downhill and twisted and turned to make the way less steep. Roger lowered Belle to the ground so he could manage his reins more easily and, deeming it safe once more, I released Shadow from her tether. The two hounds loped along between our mounts, side by side, touching noses and glancing up at us from time to time, as though to check we were still there.

Far behind and high above, a ruddy glow was creeping across the sky, and all about us twilight stole among the tree trunks. The woods thinned and then disappeared altogether. As the royal party rode out from the shelter of the trees, a wide vista was revealed before us in the half-light. A wide and – to me – terrifying vista. For ahead of us stretched, not only a gentle slope of scrub and rough grassland, but, once again, a vast, flat expanse of sand, darkening now to grey in the last of the evening light.

8

Nothing to Fear

This next crossing of the Sands – of this second huge, shallow estuary from which the tide had retreated beyond our sight – was very different from the first. This time no sun shone to cheer us. Soon it had set fully behind the hills to our rear, the last rosy glow in the sky fading and the dusk deepening into night.

The distance to cross was also far longer. Perhaps twice as long. Certainly it seemed so. As I rode with a heavy heart down the final yards to the salt marsh, the far shore appeared very far indeed. A band of darkest grey on the horizon, between the light grey of the dusky sky and the dull grey of the almost endless sands. Was that band distant hills? Here and there it was starred with a twinkle of light. A village? Fishermen's cottages? Perhaps we would meet with a welcome there before too long. But they looked so very far away.

At the head of the army, the guides kindled lights. Soon brands were held aloft all along the column of men and beasts and carts as it emerged from the woodland on to the shore. Giles and Robert Mallary, riding one to each side of Edward and his companions, had the honour of lighting their lordships' way. And with no priory this time to delay our progress, the great procession wound its way without hesitation on to the muddy flats.

The words of the guides and local men that morning – and my own empty bravado – circled in my head.

All will be well, stick with the guides, step where they step, easy to follow a huge army …

But tides, quicksands, sink …

Yet the sea was clearly far out from here. That must be why we lingered so long at Cartmel – to start the crossing at the right time. It was all in the plan. There was nothing to fear.

Alongside me, Roger's face was pale in the torchlight as he leant down to grasp Belle by her scruff and haul her up to drape across the saddle in front of him.

'Just in case she tires and begins to fret. I might not hear her whine.' He stroked her head, then glanced back at me with a strained smile. 'It'll be fine, Matt – just like this morning. Nothing to worry about.'

I glanced down. Shadow, a ghostly shape sticking close to Caesar's heels, was gazing up at me with a whine of her own. I clicked my tongue at her and the horse, and urged us all forward, dutifully following our king.

An eerie start we had to the journey. From the early passage through the reeds – where the booming calls of bitterns I remembered from childhood rambles in the countryside resounded through the dusk and a lone raven stalked across the mud before spreading its wings to flap slowly away – to the darkening strangeness out on the Sands themselves. The clamour of the army was deadened by the heavy hushed dark all around and above us. From time to time, song would break out somewhere in the column and be taken up by companies of men in front and to the rear. But always, after two or three verses, it faltered into silence. The grim tramp, tramp, tramp of marching feet was often the only sound.

The thinnest sliver of moon barely helped light our path. Few stars pierced through the ragged shreds of cloud, and only the scatter of torches guided us on the weary march. By the time we forded the river channel in the middle of the Sands – another shallow, gentle flow, thank the Lord – even the handful of faint lights on the distant shore had vanished.

By then it must have been close to midnight. And, yes, that shore could not be so distant now, after the miles we had marched across the mud. We were getting closer to this journey's end with every weary step. Of course we were … though nothing could be seen beyond the feeble halos of the torches, and the black bulk of the train of soldiers and horses, or heard above the incessant tramp, tramp of feet and hooves and creaking of wheels – and the odd defiant snatches of song.

Sometimes I would catch myself drifting off to sleep, swaying as if drunk atop my horse, having to grasp the saddle to keep myself upright while I shook dreams away once more. Through the dark I could just make out Roger's indistinct shape. From time to time, he too would sway and lurch and grab in the same way. A stray glint from a Mallary torch sometimes caught the shine of his eye or pale teeth bared in a strained grin. Mostly, though, I felt alone in the near total blackness, relying on Caesar to carry me forwards, with only the unceasing beat of the army's march for company.

The tramp, tramp, tramp of boots on the sand – mesmerizing in the heavy darkness.

Then, for a bleary second, I was back in Middleham. A warm summer's day. The touch of breeze off the moor. The mewl of a buzzard high above. The rolling gait of old Bess beneath me. My friends laughing. Murrey dashing off after a rabbit, vanishing among the roots of an ancient, wind-twisted tree. A whimper, a whine. Where was she? Had I lost her?

Then – a sway, a lurch, a clutch. And far below me, as I gripped my saddle to cling on, I spied black trails of sea-twisted weed scarring the grey of the sand. The tideline? We must be close to the other shore. But against the dark patterns – a ghostly glimmer.

Shadow. Tense, alert. Point of nose, point of tail – sharp, a faint quiver. A whimper.

And then she was off – sprinting into the darkness.

Without thinking – dopey still from my doze – I wrenched Caesar's head around and kicked the beast to follow her.

I mustn't lose her, not Alys's hound. I mustn't lose another hound.

The horse didn't resist, but cantered into the pitch

black after her – a spectral shape dashing ahead. And from the surface of the sand a hundred – more – small dark shapes rose – spread wings – flew into the night. A flock of birds disturbed from their nocturnal feeding.

'Matt!'

My name called from behind – Roger?

Far behind.

Here was just the dull thumping of hooves, the air cool against my cheek, a streak of white across the dark sand ahead, chasing the birds, black fluttering shapes, wheeling now above and around us.

My head clearing – but, oh so slowly.

What had I done?

Dragging Caesar to a halt, I whistled to Shadow.

She stopped – a pale shape against the darkness. Half-turned, then turned back. Trotted on. Slower, but still following her nose and the exciting flurry of the birds in flight.

I cursed and pushed the horse again into a stumbling run.

Further and further from the army …

Its noise was fading behind me. Or was it now to the side? Had we turned back across the Sands in pursuit of the fluttering birds?

The sound and swirl of wings and the darkness confused my senses. I glanced back over my shoulder as I clung to my jogging horse, loath to lose sight of Shadow still surging ahead into the maelstrom of feathers.

Back there and to my right, the flicker of lights. Brands held high, but receding from me.

Then, as I looked ahead again, the swirling fluster of wings soared up, away from us, up into the star-studded, raggedy-clouded sky.

A moment of still, dark silence. Then –

Another light. Out there. Beyond the disappearing birds, beyond the leaping hound.

Out upon the Sands. Where it shouldn't be.

Shaded now, dimly pink. Part hidden.

Shielded behind a hand?

I hauled Caesar to a stop. Shadow, cheated of her prey, also halted, nosing the mud for any trace of scent.

But that light …

It was motionless, far away from the troops.

Someone else who had become separated from the main column? How? And why were they not rejoining the army?

Hardly knowing what I did, I slipped down from Caesar on to the sand. Called Shadow softly to heel. This time she came, now no birds remained.

Together, boy, horse, hound, we crept towards the light. Why – what prompted my suspicions – and how I supposed we would not be seen, I did not stop to consider.

The light bobbed and ducked as we drew nearer – still scores of paces off. Dim figures milled about it, concealing it, then revealing it, as the shadowy bulks of horses, then men, came between it and me. Hushed voices drifted through the cool night air. No words, only sounds, whispers.

A dark shape broke away, horse and man together, heading back towards the army. Another lingered with the light, shielded again.

As the muffled hoofbeats died away across the mud, another voice – not hushed now – was flung in my direction.

'Who goes there?'

I froze.

A man's voice. A familiar voice.

But why out here on the sands?

Yet was it my place to challenge him – as he had me? Or just to report back on what I had found?

Darkness was on my side. I had no glimmer of a lantern to light me, or to give me away – though clearly he had seen or heard something as we approached.

He took a step towards us, moved his hand away from the lantern. Lifted it.

'Hie there? Who are you?'

The light shone full upon his face. And my nerve broke.

It was Hugh.

9

'The More You Fight …'

I tugged on Caesar's reins to drag the horse away, to flee. Pulled on Shadow's collar too, thrust her back the way we had come.

She whined once, gazing up at me. I hissed at her, and she ran off, stepping lightly across the sand.

A wordless shout behind us, the clump of running feet upon the mud.

I yanked again at the horse to hurry him. He reared a little, tossing his head, then shied away to the side, pulling the rein from my grasp. I lunged towards him to grab it, and as I did, it was as though I had stepped clean off a cliff. One moment my feet were on firm ground, the next the ground gave way beneath them and I was floundering ankle deep in cold wet sand.

The horse neighed in alarm. As my arms flailed to regain my balance, one struck the dangling rein and spooked him again. He wheeled away in panic before I could seize the rein and galloped off into the darkness.

Fighting against my own panic, I tried to pull first one foot, then the other out of the clinging sand. Only as I felt first one, then the other sink further into the quaking mud did the words of the local man and the guide that morning nudge into my mind.

'Don't struggle – you'll just sink all the more quickly.'

'The more you fight, the more it will suck you down.'

The memory came too late. The clutch of the cold sand now reached almost to my knees. It was creeping higher and higher, seeping over my boot tops, as I struggled to keep myself upright. Each time my body swayed, trying to right itself, my feet settled just a little deeper down and were snared a little firmer in the sand's grip.

The blood was pounding in my ears. I closed my eyes, drawing in a deep breath in an attempt to calm myself. As I opened them again, my shadow lengthened on the sand before me, cast by a light at my back.

A harsh laugh rang out.

'You again!'

I made to twist towards the light and the words, but at this merest movement the sand sucked once more at my booted feet and they inched even lower. Now my knees too were clamped firm, my thin hose offering no defence against the freezing dampness.

'Spying on me, were you?'

I turned my head cautiously as far as I could. Out of the corner of my eye, I could see Hugh looming several paces behind me, the lantern lowered now towards the ground. He patted the sand just in front of him with the toe of his boot, then pulled it away as the surface quivered.

'Quicksand,' he said, his tone less certain. 'You should have watched where you put your feet when you ran off to report on me.'

'I wasn't spying,' I protested, taking care not to move. 'Shadow chased some birds. I came after her to catch her. I saw your light, then you and – well, whoever you were with. I – I didn't want to intrude.

My words were lame, even to my ears.

'Intrude?' Hugh laughed again. 'What was there to intrude upon? I was sending a messenger to my uncle, that's all. To say his troops had arrived safely. I forgot to at Cartmel.' He checked himself. 'Not that I have to explain myself to you.'

Had his explanation sounded too pat? As though rehearsed? And he didn't say why he had needed to move away from the army to send his message.

But at this moment, I cared little why he was there.

'Get me out, Hugh.'

A moment of silence.

I craned round at him.

He had not moved since he tested the sand. Now he raised the lantern to illumine both our faces.

'Why should I? We're all alone out here.'

He was right, of course. Though I could still hear the tramp, tramp of the army, the column was a long way away. I doubted my voice would carry so far, even if I shouted for help with all the breath I possessed. And if it did, who would hear it above the noise of the soldiers all around them?

He bent towards me, staring into my face. His own was impassive as he said,

'And the tide will be coming in soon. With you stuck here, I could just leave you to die. And no one would ever know.'

I fought to keep the fear from my face, even as I longed to turn it away. If he saw my terror, would he carry through his threat?

Perhaps my struggle succeeded. Still with no expression on his face, he put down the lamp and straightened up.

'Let's see what I can do. Catch hold of my hand.'

Relief washed through me, first at his words, then as he leaned forward.

I stretched back my hand as best I could, careful still to keep my movement small. Hugh swung his own hand towards me as though to grasp it. But at the last instant, he teetered and, in trying not to overbalance, his swing became a flail. That flail became a clout that caught the side of my head as he fought to regain his balance.

The shock of the blow rattled my teeth together and sank me further into the sand. Before I could still the movement, the top of the mud was halfway up my thigh.

'Oops,' Hugh said behind me. 'My mistake. You're too far away for that to work. I'll have to find something else.'

The words were innocent enough. But did I detect

a smirk beneath them?

He disappeared out of the ring of lantern light and returned a moment later leading his horse. He halted it near the edge of the quicksand, then, slipping its reins over its ears, threw them towards me.

Once, twice, three times he threw them. Each time they fell short of my grasping fingers, then slithered further out of my reach as the horse backed away in alarm. And each time, of course, my lunge towards the leather straps had only one outcome – another slippage into the shifting sands beneath me.

Was he doing his best to help? Or was this failure deliberate, along with his apparent attempt to grab my hand?

Whatever the case, he was my only hope.

And his next words chilled me – or at least the part of me that was not already chilled beneath the freezing sand.

'I'll have to go for help. I'll be as quick as I can.'

Before I could object, he picked up the lantern and, gathering his reins upon his mount's neck, swung himself into the saddle. Turning the horse's head, he gazed down at me.

'Stay there till I get back. Oh, of course, you won't be going anywhere, I suppose.'

His features were demonic in the light cast upwards by the lamp.

Any pride I might once have had deserted me.

'Leave me the lantern, at least,' I begged.

'How shall I find my way back to the army without it?' he asked in response. And with a snigger, he dragged his horse about and, raking his heels against its sides, urged it into a swift canter.

Craning round, I watched as his light dwindled into the distance. He was heading in the right direction, at least. Beyond that single bobbing glow, a sparse scatter of glimmers like distant glow-worms showed where the army still marched. Faint snatches of song drifted back towards me above the muted tramping of feet.

Straining to project my voice back over my shoulder, I shouted as loud as I could. Once, twice.

My voice was lost in the eerie deadness of the Sands, as I had expected.

I now had to place all my trust in Hugh. It was not a happy notion.

And then another thought struck me. How would he find his way back to me with rescuers if I had no light to guide them?

The darkness was pressing on me from every side, and with it the beginnings of despair.

I tried to bat such fears away and tell myself at least I wasn't sinking any lower into the sand. Struggling had caused that, I knew, and with care I could avoid moving too much. But I was stuck fast almost up to my waist now, and the cold and the pressure of the sand were becoming painful. Something was digging into my hip too. Yet in a moment, my irritation at it fled. Of course! It was my pouch. And in that pouch was my tinderbox.

I had been about to sink at least as deep into despair as I had into the sand, but this offered a chink of hope. Yet would the tinder be dry? And could I even reach it?

With utmost caution, I edged my fingers into the cold grainy sand at my waist and worked them down until their tips met the leather of my pouch. The movements were small and appeared not to disturb the sand – no jolt or slow creep plunged me further into its depths. Slipping my fingers towards the drawstring, I grasped it and slowly eased the whole pouch up out of the clutching mud. It emerged with a loud sucking noise, but no buffet against my body from the surrounding sand. A quick rummage and the contents were revealed to be mercifully dry. Within a few seconds, I had struck light from the tinderbox on to a stump of candle.

The glow was feeble in the intense darkness, like a firefly dancing in the depths of a moonless summer night.

But at least it was light, and as I held it up, it fanned the flame of my hope a little.

In truth, though, deep within me scant hope remained. I could still see and hear signs of the army, but it was too far away for my miniscule light to attract attention, any more than my shouts had. Hugh alone knew I was trapped out here, and I had little faith he would truly seek any help for me.

Roger must have seen my foolish chase after Shadow. He had cried out, hadn't he? But what could he do? Alert their lordships or the guides? The guides surely would know how to get me out. But would they or their lordships think one boy worth searching for on the dark and dangerous Sands? After all, what value was I to the venture? Not enough to permit any delay to the march. Before long the tail end of the army would arrive at the far shore. And it would be too late then for anyone to think of returning to seek me.

My spirit dipped even as the tiny candle flame guttered in the breath of breeze.

My legs were numb with the cold and squeezing of the sand, and shivers ran through my whole body. Nearing midsummer we might be, but the nights here were cool, especially now it must be long after midnight.

And with that idea of passing time came another thought.

One that chilled me even more than the night air.

The tide.

In the morning – it now seemed so very long ago – the guide had warned us the tide came in faster than a man could run. And Hugh said it would be coming in again soon. Had it already turned? When would the sea flood back in to this wide estuary? How long … how long did I have before the inrushing water overtook me and … and I drowned?

I shouted again. Shouted for all I was worth. Feeling the wave of terror washing through me, swamping me. Even the fear of sinking further into the sand was thrust to one side as I filled my lungs with air and bellowed for help as loud as I could. But the exertion only made my body rock again in the mud and – yes, to sink a little further into it.

What a choice lay before me!

To carry on shouting in the vain hope someone would hear, and take the risk of sinking more – perhaps under the sand completely. Or to stay quiet and still – and simply wait for the tide to reach and then overwhelm me.

Either way – death or death …

But to do something, anything, was better than doing nothing.

My screams tore into the darkness around me. Soon the sand was pressing against the lower part of my chest, making it harder for me to suck air into my lungs to yell again. The effort was wearing me out. Before long my hollering tailed off, dying away into uncontrollable sobs.

The glow of the candle stump no longer offered me any comfort. I lowered it until the back of my hand rested on the quivering surface of the sand and stared into the flickering heart of the tiny flame.

How long I stared at the flame, mesmerized, I couldn't say.

Seconds?

Minutes?

Hours?

Before a new sound wormed its way into my consciousness, a new glimmer at the edge of my vision.

The urgent yap, yap of a dog.

A dim light moving closer, growing bigger.

A pale streak advancing low across the sand. Two shadows following.

I twisted round a little to see better. The streak formed into a shape, a familiar shape. A moment later Shadow bounded into the halo of candlelight, shuddering to a halt several paces short of me. She stretched out one forepaw on to the quavering surface of the sand, then withdrew it sharply, turning and yapping again.

Behind her, two figures hove into the circle of candlelight.

I shrieked at them. 'Stop there! Don't come closer.'

The hands of the foremost flew up to smother a gasp. A boy clad in workers' clothing, rough cap jammed firmly on their head. Eyes wide as they stared in horror at my plight.

'Matt! What on earth—?'

I almost laughed in relief. Not just at seeing someone who could help, but at seeing –

'Alys! Thank the Lord. Help me!'

The second figure came up alongside her, carrying a lantern and stick. A boy, similarly dressed, perhaps a little younger than us. He shot a glance at her.

'Alys?' The burr of his voice marked him as local. 'But I thought you were called Dick? What –?'

'I … we … I can …' Alys began, then hurriedly, 'Look, it doesn't matter now. We need to get him out. How—?'

She took a step forward.

'No!' the boy and I cried together, he thrusting out his stick to bar her way.

'He's stuck in quicksand,' said the boy. 'You mustn't go near. We'll need help to get him out. And the tide must be on the turn by now.'

'The tide?' Alys's face, always alabaster, was whiter than ever in the light cast by the lantern. 'Then we must hurry. I'll stay with him, keep him company. You go back and get people to help. Go quickly.'

The boy nodded. 'I'll go as fast as I can. But if there are quicksands hereabouts, I'll need to test my way with this.'

He raised his sturdy stick again.

Alys grabbed him, twisted him about and pushed him back the way they had come.

'Then get going. You hold his life in your hands.'

He hurried off, taking the precious lantern with

him, leaving us with only the candle stump, much to my unease.

Alys turned back to me and knelt gingerly on the sand next to Shadow.

'Oh, Matt! What happened? When Shadow came and found me, and tugged at my sleeve and wouldn't let go until I followed her, I knew it was something urgent. But this—'

She broke off. The candlelight glinted off tears springing in her eyes.

'Everything will be fine now you're here,' I said to reassure her – with a confidence I didn't in truth feel.

At her prompting, I gave a brief account of all that had happened. Shadow's mad dash after the wading birds, coming across Hugh, my misstep into the quicksand, how any movement made things worse. Hugh's promise to return with aid. I didn't tell her of my terror and despair.

Alys scolded Shadow for her part in my misfortune, then hugged her close and buried her face in the fur on her neck. When she re-emerged, she had blinked away her tears.

'She was at fault at first,' she said. 'But we must be grateful Shadow is an intelligent hound, and knew how to bring help. Let us hope Harry is as clever, and can as quickly find someone who knows what to do.'

Neither of us mentioned the tide again, though it was forever in my thoughts.

To distract me from my plight, Alys told me about her day and the night before. About how she had befriended the boy called Harry when Giles had found her a place to sleep among the supply wagons. They had journeyed together on the march from Swarth Moor to Cartmel, then across the second stretch of the Sands. He had shown her how, as a young lad, he was taught always to carry a long stick if he ventured out on to their expanse. With it he could probe the sand before each step in case there should be the tell-tale quiver and sucking of quicksand.

How much time passed, I could not tell, but the cold brought a shiver to Alys's voice as she chattered, and my neck and shoulders ached with the strain of turning to listen. But at last, from out of the darkness floated the sounds of calling voices and many feet, and the dipping lights of torches.

Alys shouted in return and held aloft our shrinking candle stump. Soon a rescue party was assembling along the edge of the quicksand, those few scant paces from where I was marooned. At their head were Harry and, to my surprise, Roger. Two of the local guides I recognized from the morning accompanied them, together with Giles Mallary, a number of local soldiers and, to my dismay, Lord Francis.

At sight of him, Alys shrank away to the far side of the little group, dragging Shadow with her.

The guides busied themselves delving into the packs they carried, while Roger filled me in.

'You quite scared me when I saw you dashing off into the darkness. It happened so quickly. I must have been asleep. But I knew I mustn't follow you, so I went to ask a guide for help.' He gestured towards one of the men laying out his gear upon the muddy ground. 'Then someone found your horse wandering loose on the sands. By that time, there was such a hubbub that Lord Francis got to hear – and he insisted on joining the search. We were so relieved when we came across this lad – and he was able to lead us back to you.'

Not so relieved as I was, I wanted to say, though no doubt my voice would crack with the emotion welling up within me. But before I could speak, Roger was elbowed out of the way by the guides.

'Now, lad,' said one, staring down at me. 'You've got yourself into a fine mess and no mistake. You must have thrashed about a good deal to have sunk so far.'

'Did we not warn you all not to do that?' asked his mate.

'Gentlemen.' The men both bowed as Lord

Francis himself stepped forward. 'Now is not the time for chiding him. Please make haste before he sinks quite beneath the sand.'

'I've never heard tell, my lord,' said the first guide, 'of anyone going completely under the sand. Though the tide would probably get them before that, I reckon.'

'Then you'd better move fast before that happens here,' retorted his lordship, earning my eternal gratitude. 'We don't have too long, I believe.'

Yet, for all that, it would be a long and laborious time before I was freed.

'Lean back your head and shoulders as far as you can,' said the second man, as the first used two sticks to manoeuvre a thick cloak across the surface of the sand behind me.

It was a strange command. I had no wish to lower the top of my body into the sand to join the rest of it.

But his lordship said, 'Quickly, Matthew – do exactly what they say. They know best.'

So I did as I was bid.

It was hard to force my head back like that, and to feel my shoulders settle into the soft mud. But to my relief, the sticks and cloak stopped them sinking.

Then the first guide's voice came down to me.

'Do you feel your feet lift a bit?'

And I did. Just a fraction. But it was the first upward motion since I stepped into the wretched stuff.

More odd instructions followed. I had to move my legs in small circles as slowly and gently as I could, and definitely not try to pull them up as that would suck me down once more.

As I wiggled my feet, I felt another tiny shift upwards and the odd sensation of sand slipping down past my ankles to fill the space beneath. I wiggled again, and once more my legs floated upwards. Just an inch or so, but more sand slid downwards.

And slowly, but slowly, the guides conjured their

magic. Slowly, but slowly, my feet and legs worked their way towards the top of the sands. They had warmed up, but were aching mightily, when after an age of these tiny deliberate movements, the lower parts of my body at last broke through the final layer of mud and rested upon the surface.

A quiet cheer rose from those watching.

My chest was heaving with the effort. I closed my eyes and lay in a daze for some moments.

'Now, lad.' The guide's voice broke through my exhaustion. 'Don't linger. You must wriggle backwards across the sand towards us. The cloak and sticks will help hold you up. Spread out your arms and legs too, and take it slowly.'

'But not too slowly,' said his mate.

His tone was tense, not jesting now, and as I spread my arms wide, I understood why. Cool water trickled against my fingers, water that had not been there moments before.

Was it – was the tide coming back in?

My heart leapt into my throat at the idea, but I fought to keep myself calm. I must focus first on getting across these final few feet.

I inched towards my rescuers – not an easy thing to do in such a position. As I slithered on my way, squirming first one shoulder then the other backwards across the surface, a guide said quietly, 'Those without horses should leave now, my lord. One of us can lead them safely to the shore and drive stakes in the sand to guide the way for the rest.'

'Aye,' agreed Lord Francis. 'Once we are finished here, you shall ride with me, and Giles can take Matthew behind him. And Roger.' He raised his voice as though Roger was at some distance. 'Roger – you shall take my lady Alys with the first group. And I shall speak to you first thing in the morning, my lady.'

In my shock at his words, my creeping motion ceased, and I was rewarded with a hiss from the guide.

'Keep moving,' he urged.

I had indeed felt myself subside a little, despite the buoyancy lent by the cloak. A sudden weight as though of lead in my stomach made it difficult to start again, but I knew I had to. My worry about what would happen to Alys now Lord Francis had recognized her would have to wait. After all, my immediate terror was of the water flowing fast now over my outstretched fingers.

I heard no objections from Alys or Roger before the bustle of the leaving group faded away into the distance. And mercifully it was not long – and the water had become hardly deeper around my limbs – before my head and shoulders edged within arms' reach of my remaining rescuers. Giles and the guide grasped my upper arms and dragged me towards them. My heels scored a groove in the sand's surface before they heaved me upright and stood me on my own two feet at last.

My legs, quivering from the cold, the exertion and the fear, gave way at once. Lord Francis, ever vigilant, caught me before I quite fell back to the ground. And then, within a few moments, a warm cloak was flung around my shoulders and I was clinging to Giles's waist as his horse cantered, splashing, through the dark rising waters, following the lanterns held by the guide and the stakes planted in the sand by his mate – across the last few hundred yards to the welcome safety of the shore.

10

'Fit to Wield a Sword'

'He says he will leave me at the next safe house we come to. He thinks that will be Jervaulx Abbey.'

Alys was telling Roger and me of her interview with Lord Francis the next morning. At first she had been aggrieved, but her tone soon softened into weary resignation.

'Edward tried to stick up for me. He said it was his idea that I travel with him and the army, and that he wanted me to stay. But Lord Francis overruled him. He said there is a battle coming and he wants me nowhere near it. Earl John agreed. He said he couldn't lead an army made up of women.'

'He said what?' I asked, also indignant on her behalf. And ours.

'At least he said it with a smile. Not like Lord Francis. And he offered me his tent to use and a servant while I'm with the army.'

'That's something,' soothed Roger. 'You'll be comfortable again, even if it's not for much longer.'

'Well, yes,' she admitted. 'It wasn't easy, living among the campfollowers. Or pretending to be a boy all the time. But I would do it all again to be able to stay longer with you and Edward.'

The army had made camp not far from where we came ashore in the early hours of the morning, and we all snatched a little sleep before setting off again. A horse and women's clothing – neither very suitable for a lady – had been found for Alys, and now she, Roger and I were riding together near the rear of the royal party, as the column of troops and wagons wound up into low hills at the start of our journey.

Giles Mallary was riding just behind. Lord Francis

had ordered him to keep an eye on us after what had happened.

'Which is pretty funny,' he joked, 'when you consider I was part of your little conspiracy too.'

What trouble his lordship thought we could get into now, I knew not. But maybe his concern was more to keep an eye on – or us apart from – Hugh Soulsby. Hugh rode once more with the royal party rather than at the head of his uncle's troops.

I had told Lord Francis of all that had happened out on the Sands, from Hugh's claim to be simply sending his uncle a message, to his promise to fetch help for me. I did not mention his taunts.

Hugh's failure to return with aid was, of course, no surprise. Perhaps I should be grateful he had not contrived some way to cut my throat while I was stuck in the sand. As it was, I was none the worse for my experience, though I would think twice – or three times – before setting foot on any beach in the future. Giles later told me that Hugh, when challenged, insisted he had gone for help, only to find my rescue party was already on its way.

'Lord Francis does not plan to take the matter further at the moment,' he had said. Then added, for once with no suggestion of a smile, 'But don't worry, Matt. We have people watching him.'

I forced my attention back to the present and to Alys's predicament.

'What does Lord Francis expect you to do once he has left you at Jervaulx?'

'He made me promise to stay there until after the battle.' Alys was glum. 'He says he has word that Tudor has left Coventry to march north, though he doesn't believe he can yet have heard of our landing. But he expects to meet him and his allies in battle within the month.'

'So soon?'

'It will seem an age to me if I'm stuck at

Jervaulx,' she replied. 'But when the victory's won, I suppose he will send for me to join you all in London.'

'And if we lose?' Roger gave voice to what had stolen into my mind too.

'Hush, Roger,' Alys snapped back. 'You cannot think like that. Edward is rightful king. Right is on our side, and therefore God will be too.'

We had believed the same about King Richard two years before, but still the usurper had won. But I stayed silent.

'Whatever happens,' she continued to Roger, 'you and I will find out together. Earl John offered you as my companion when I am left behind.'

A grin unfolded across Roger's face. He bowed as best he could from atop his horse and made an elaborate show of kissing his hand to her. For an instant I was transported back to our days at Middleham, when the two of them would play at knights and ladies.

'A task I will accept with good will, my lady. Glad am I that he has such faith in me to protect you from harm.'

Unusually she did not return his smile or his pleasantry.

'Don't get too full of yourself. Earl John may not have said it, but what he means is he won't miss you in any battle that may come. In fact, no doubt he thinks it's better all round if you're safely out of the way.'

But as ever, her words failed to deflate Roger or spoil his good humour at the news that his time on the march was now limited. He struck up a cheerful song about hunting and feasting, which was taken up first by Giles, then others of the gentlemen about us. Soon even Alys shrugged off her sombre mood and joined in.

I alone did not. Once more I was about to lose my two closest friends – at a time when perhaps the most difficult trial of my life was approaching. For I was expected to remain with Edward until the outcome of the invasion was known.

Giles had delivered me to the royal tent after my rescue from the Sands. The sight of my mattress unrolled and the warmth of Edward's fire had been welcome, as had the hot food saved for me.

Edward eyed me as I sat huddled within Giles's thick cloak, spooning the aromatic stew into my mouth.

'I hope you will soon be recovered from your ordeal, Matthew,' he had said without emotion after listening to my tale.

'I'm sure I will,' I reassured him. 'I am but a little bruised and sore.'

'Good. I expect you to be fit to wield a sword and fight by my side when the battle comes. I will need all my loyal companions around me at that time.'

Cold flooded over me again, worse than had assailed me out on the Sands, and the food lost its savour. No hint of humour touched his voice. He sounded very like his mother or Aunt Margaret – more serious than either his uncle or father. They, aware of where my talents really lay, might have spoken such words in jest. Edward surely knew training with weapons had not been my highest priority in either Mechelen or Dublin. Not since my time at Middleham had it been expected of me, though from time to time I had tried to practise. But that had been with a child's wooden sword, either alone or with my fellow apprentice in London, Simon. For all that I had once longed to become a knight, and now even had my own steel blade courtesy of a gift from Lord Francis, I had for some time assumed that was not to be my path in life.

Much later on our ride that day, as we gazed from high rolling hills back on sweeping views towards the Sands – so innocent now in the bright sunshine – I screwed up my courage to speak to Roger about it. Once he had been as hopeless with a sword as I, but since becoming a squire had enjoyed – or endured – more years of training with various weapons masters.

To my relief, he did not make light of my worries.

'Of course I'll help you, Matt – as well as I can

anyway.' He gestured back to where Giles still rode in our wake. 'Though you'd probably be better asking Giles. He tells me he's a noted swordsman in his part of Northamptonshire. Though how much we can rely on his own claim, I know not.'

'What's that?' Giles spurred his horse alongside ours. 'Did I hear my name?'

'Matt is a little rusty with his swordplay,' Roger said airily. 'I thought you might help him polish up his skills.'

'I'd be glad to,' Giles replied. 'Once we make camp and our duties are over, come and find me. I'll see if I can beg some training swords from one of the armourers.'

I thanked him, though less than happy at the prospect of my inept swordsmanship being revealed to Giles. Alys was watching, silent, but with one eyebrow raised, no doubt aware that such skills as I possessed would need more than just polish.

In the late afternoon, we marched through the sleepy town of Sedbergh, clinging to the skirts of a looming hillside. Battalions of swallows and swifts swooped and screamed just above our heads as we passed the ancient church and market cross. They cared less about the thousands of troops than did the town's residents, who shuttered themselves within their grey stone houses, strung out along the narrow main street.

We pushed on another few miles before halting to pitch camp. Among the patchy trees and scrub littering the valley floor, Roger, Giles and I found a small, secluded clearing to practise swordsmanship before the light failed.

I discovered I had not forgotten everything I ever learned about wielding a sword – just that what I had learned had been very little. In truth, I had probably found that out when I faced Hugh on that fateful night in the score at Lowestoft. Giles was a patient teacher, though, and applauded me for my efforts to continue learning in the years since I left King Richard's service.

'I cannot teach you much in the little time we have, Matt,' he said, serious once more. 'But perhaps you need not worry. You will likely be on horseback and at the rear of any battle if you are with Edward. Kings and their generals rarely plunge into the front line of the fighting, from all I've ever heard. You perhaps know enough already for any fighting you may do on horseback.'

My thoughts flew back to King Richard in his final battle – to how his standard had flown in the thick of the fiercest fighting on foot so many times on that dread day. I was hardly reassured.

'But King Richard was a seasoned warrior,' protested Roger, when I mentioned it. 'Edward … well, I have no doubt Edward is brave, as his father was before him. But he has never fought in a battle – or even seen one. Do you think Earl John would let him risk himself at his first?'

'He will most likely stay aboard Storm, towards the rear, where he can be seen and rally the troops as need be.' Giles was thoughtful. 'Maybe not so far back as Tudor was, of course. I hear he remained far to the rear, protected by pikemen, while my lord of Oxford fought his battle for him. And he was a dozen years older than Edward too. I doubt our young king would prove such a coward, even at his first taste of action.'

He spoke the truth, as I could bear witness. Tudor's red dragon standard had never been close to the fighting. Not until the tide of battle had turned and King Richard had seized his chance to take the fight to his challenger. Even then, the man who wished to be king cowered behind his bodyguard while others fought and won his crown for him.

The memory of the treachery on that day prodded me to anger, and in our next bout, I surprised Giles with my fierceness and at first managed to beat him back. But, before long, he knocked my blunt training sword out of my grip and had me on the ground at his mercy.

He extended his hand to haul me back to my feet.

'Well done, Matt. You could do worse than take that anger with you into battle. Now, let us try again. And don't forget, pay attention to your footwork this time.'

11

Return to Middleham

Later that evening I wished we had spent less time at swordplay and more in Alys's company while we still could.

When we returned to the royal tent, I was tired and aching, from both my mishap on the Sands and the unaccustomed exercise, not to mention the number of times Giles had walloped me with the flat of his blunted blade. My mood was not improved as Edward greeted us with unwelcome news.

'John and Francis held council this evening and have decided to push on quickly tomorrow. Just a small party of us on horseback. The army will follow at its own pace, commanded by Captain Schwartz and Sir Thomas.'

Roger wrinkled his brow at his words.

'Why? What's their plan?'

'They aim for us to reach Jervaulx Abbey by nightfall. They expect more troops to join us there, and will hold important discussions with the abbot and other gentlemen.'

'Us?'

Edward's face was inscrutable. 'You are John's squire, Matt is my … well, my companion, I suppose. And Alys …'

'Alys will be coming too?' I tried to keep my voice steady, to hide my disappointment. But Edward grimaced too as he responded.

'Aye. Francis insisted. He knows she's a good horsewoman and will have no trouble keeping up the pace. It looks as though we shall lose her company sooner than we expected.'

Alys herself was philosophical when we met her early next morning. She was breaking her fast outside Earl

John's tent, waited on by his servant.

'What choice do I have in the matter? We must just make the best of the time we have left together, Matt.'

That time proved to be little enough, and barely suited to companionable conversation, given the pace at which we rode that day. Scouts had been sent ahead before sun-up, though they were hardly needed, except perhaps to warn of the approach of the army. Local folk had long been fiercely loyal to their Yorkist kings, and everywhere they emerged from houses and barns and cheered as we passed. When I praised their zeal, Alys pointed out that Lords Francis and John would not otherwise have taken the risk of riding so far ahead of the main army, with the protection of only a few dozen Germans and local troops – Hugh's company among them.

By mid-morning we were already riding through a more familiar landscape. Fields edged by thorn hedges had given way to rough pasture cut through with drystone walls that almost grew out of the earth, and to the north rose huge moor-clad fells, their summits wreathed in cloud. Rivulets trickled down towards the valley floor through a carpeting of sedge and bracken. Green it all was at this time of year, but in a few weeks it would be blazing gold and purple with heather as summer drew on. Where would we be then?

A persistent drizzle set in towards noon. Soon we were soaked through as we made our way hour by weary hour along this deep dale, sculpted now between towering hills to either side. Lines of ancient walls ran down from the tops, broken only by the occasional barn and channelling us towards our destination. We saw hardly a soul now save the odd shepherd, tiny with their scattered flocks upon the heights.

Gradually, though, after the briefest of halts for a hurried meal of bread, dried meat and cheese, the vale widened, and I recognized the unfolding shape of the countryside around us. Then, well on into the afternoon, a cry went up from Roger.

'Pen Hill!'

Edward, riding with us, shot him a quizzical glance and Roger had to explain his excitement. That familiar brooding bulk, resembling a sleeping hound rising above the dale, had been the site of many of our pleasures while we had all lived in Duke Richard's household at Middleham Castle.

'It was where we captured Lady.' Roger's face was wistful. 'She was my first hawk. I had to leave her behind at Sheriff Hutton when … well, when Alys and I rode down to London.'

I knew why he hesitated. Lady, the focus of countless happy hours, had been lost to him after King Richard's death. Roger was always careful not to mention our old master in front of Edward if he could help it – unlike myself.

He soon rallied, pointing again.

'Over there is Bolton Castle.'

On the far side of the dale a stout square keep reared up among a scattering of trees, a sky-blue and yellow standard flying proudly from its turrets.

'Bolton? Isn't that the seat of Lord Scrope?' asked Edward.

Lord Francis, his horse pacing just a little ahead, caught his words.

'Aye, Edward. A loyal ally of King Richard. He and his brother Lord Thomas have promised to meet us this day at Jervaulx. They will bring a strong force of men to serve you too.'

An image sprang into my mind of the hearty gentleman I had encountered from time to time at Middleham. The last occasion was the snowy boar hunt more than four years before that almost proved fatal for both him and our little friend, Ed. He must have recovered well from his bloody goring that day if he now proposed to ride to battle with King Richard's nephews.

Our fast pace soon brought us within sight of more recognizable landmarks. But far from boosting Roger's chatter, the well-known landscape seemed to suppress it. Alys too was quiet. Our first sight of Middleham itself, the castle crouched against the side of the sheltering hill, sparked no exclamation from either. Rather it was Lord Francis, turning again in his saddle, who drew Edward's attention to it. As he spoke, he appeared to be choosing his words carefully, but did a shadow pass across his hazel eyes?

'There is the castle of Middleham, Edward. You may remember it from your stay. It is no more than a league now to Jervaulx. We shall not pause here.'

I had expected my spirits to rise as we approached the place that held so many happy memories for me. Of that long summer when first I had met Alys, Roger and Ed, and we had formed the Order. Those cosy autumn evenings in the company of Duke Richard and his family. The innocent days of that final spring before the duke's life was turned upside down – and with it, my own. Yet, to my surprise, Lord Francis's words caused me no regret. Not only my friends' mood, but my own, was subdued as we trotted along the road into the outskirts of the village.

Our despondency was echoed throughout the company. Song had often broken out from one group of riders or another to speed our way that day. Not now. We drew near the market square with its well-remembered stone cross in silence, bar the clatter of horses' hooves. To either side, cottage doors opened as we passed, and townsfolk peered out or emerged to stand and watch us without a sound. Men and boys returning from the fields also lingered along our way, gazing up at us, expressionless. Above all, the immense outer wall of the castle loomed.

The main gateway was barricaded by the massive wooden drawbridge, hauled up from its usual place lying flat across the deep moat. The entrance no longer offered us its old welcome. This once-loved home turned a blank, unseeing face towards us. A breeze swept down from the hills beyond, chilling me.

Yet upon the castle's high battlements men kept watch. Shouts arose as we came closer. More cries and muffled sounds came from within the outer courtyard. Lord Francis's hand and those of his gentlemen stole towards their sword hilts.

Beside me, Alys glanced across, uncertainty written in her eyes. And deep within my gut, a hollow fear gaped, nudging my own fingers to grasp the pommel of the barely familiar weapon now bumping against my side.

Our party halted. The leading riders swung their mounts' heads towards the castle gate. Lord Francis, and Giles and Robert either side of him, spurred their horses ahead of Edward and Earl John. Tension was scrawled across all their faces.

The chains of the drawbridge rattled and creaked as it was lowered slowly to rest upon the side of the moat. Beyond, the steel teeth of the portcullis were disappearing into the upper reaches of the gateway and the heavy wooden doors being dragged wide by armoured men. Through the yawning opening poured a large body of mounted men-at-arms, bristling with pikes, spears and axes. They rode, hooves drumming, across the drawbridge and down the cobbles towards us, then clattered to a halt, just yards away from Edward and their lordships.

Lord Francis and the Mallary brothers stood steady in the middle of the roadway, their horses' hooves planted firmly on the cobbles. For the briefest moment, the two parties stared at each other in silence.

Then the fully armoured leader of the men-at-arms removed his helm and bowed, flashing at Edward a balding head fringed by wisps of reddish hair.

'Your Grace, the garrison of Middleham is at your service. The usurper cannot command our loyalty. We will ride with you to reclaim your throne.'

From all sides shouts and cheers rose, and with them my spirits, and as the enlarged company turned and trotted down past the market cross, scores of townsfolk came to applaud and wave us on our way.

It was only later we learned from Giles that, although Lord Francis had sent word of our approach to the castle's commander, no response had been received. Until the moment the commander had doffed his helm, none had known what the garrison's decision would be – whether to confront our small party or to join us.

12

Jervaulx Abbey

Lighter of heart and lighter of mood, the royal party soon travelled the final few miles to Jervaulx Abbey.

The ancient buildings of this abbey I remembered well from the day of the boar hunt, when my friends and I had accompanied both little Ed and Lord Scope to its infirmary and then ourselves had recovered in the warmth of its guesthouse. The abbot greeted Lord Francis as an old friend, as he had Duke Richard on that occasion, and he accorded Edward and Earl John all the honour of their royal rank as he bowed them into his own lodging. That evening the whole company of gentlemen – and Alys – were entertained with a sumptuous feast that more than rivalled the one provided by my lord the abbot of Cartmel, if with less of a flavour of the sea. That was no hardship for me. In recent months I had had plenty of dealings with that element – enough to last me a lifetime.

As their lordships rose from table after the meal, the abbot drew Edward aside for a few words in private. Alys, Roger and I waited for him by the door of the dining hall. When he joined us, his eyes were clouded.

'What's wrong, Edward?' asked Alys in concern.

'Nothing,' he said straightaway. Then, after a moment's reflection, 'Well, Abbot Haslington said perhaps I would like to attend evening service and – as he put it – pay respects at the resting place of my royal cousin.'

Alys gasped.

'Oh! Poor little Ed.' A look full of guilt passed between her and Roger. 'I quite forgot this is where he is buried.'

'That was the last time we were here, wasn't it?' said Roger. 'It must be more than three years ago now.'

'The late Prince of Wales, the abbot called him.' Still distracted, Edward hadn't observed their distress. 'But he never really was that. It was my title before ... before my father died.'

'Yes, he was,' Alys said stoutly. 'I was at his investiture myself, in York.'

'And so was I,' chimed in Roger. 'It was so magnificent, people thought it was a second coronation.'

'It doesn't matter how magnificent it was if he had no right to it,' Edward retorted.

'Parliament gave him that right – just as it took away your right to be king,' Alys flashed back, her pang of remorse thrust aside. 'It wasn't his choice or his fault, any more than it was yours. He was just an innocent little boy. And he was your cousin.'

Edward stared at her, a mix of emotions chasing across his face. Roger's glance flicked from one to the other, then to me. The deep discomfort within his eyes mirrored my own.

At last, Edward said, 'I suppose you're right. I'm sorry. He was not responsible for what his father did any more than I ... It will do no harm for me to visit his tomb. Come, the service will be starting soon.'

He headed out the door, followed by Roger.

Alys lingered, gazing after them. I took her arm and gave it a gentle squeeze. She turned to me, her forehead creased as though she didn't recognize me at first. Then her frown slipped into a wan smile and, returning the pressure, she led me after the others.

All the gentlemen who had dined together were already packed into the exquisite abbey church as we entered. The stout form of Lord Scrope, fresh from enjoyment of his supper, was squeezed on to the seat next to Lord Francis. On his other side sat Earl John. He beckoned to Edward to join them there, close to the ornate rood screen that hid this public part of the church from the choir where the holy brothers sang and worshipped.

Alys, Roger and I found seats where we could. I

was grateful to be towards the back of the nave, far from where I now spotted Hugh. He stared stolidly ahead throughout the service, save when required to kneel, turning to neither left nor right to speak to the men around him. Perhaps he was mindful of being watched still. Giles and Robert Mallary were settled a row or two behind him. Giles, who I now knew saw and heard everything, bobbed his head to us as we came in, before seemingly focusing his own attention solely on the service.

Hearing the familiar songs and prayers in the voices of my fellow countrymen was a pleasure, as had been the accents of the abbot and local gentlemen at supper. I had spent so long out of not just England, but my own native country of Yorkshire, that my eyes pricked with tears at the sound. And the heavy scent of incense beguiled me back to my early days as a choir boy at our great Minster in York – before all my adventures began. Yet when I joined in the 'amens', my voice sounded alien to my ears.

Once the service ended, the unseen monks bustled out of the church through their private door. The gentlemen and other worshippers, talking amongst themselves, were mostly on their feet and leaving too.

Lord Francis ushered Edward and the earl to the central aisle of the nave. As the crowds parted around them and dispersed, a small casket of stone was revealed, set on a low plinth upon the floor. The two older men knelt before it, crossing themselves and muttering brief prayers. But Edward hung back, his stance awkward.

Standing once more, Lord Francis grasped his shoulder, spoke a few words, then released him and led the earl from the church. As they passed us, loitering, uncertain, he glanced our way and signalled back towards Edward.

'Come on,' said Alys, her words barely above a whisper.

As the three of us walked along the nave to where Edward stood, from the corner of my eye I glimpsed

Hugh. He was still there, lurking in the shadows by a column. I did my best to ignore him.

'Edward,' Alys was saying as we came up to him, 'do you wish us to pray with you?'

Misery was etched on Edward's face as he gazed down at the stone slab in front of him. It was not the tomb I would have imagined for a prince of the realm. Smaller than any I had ever seen in a great church – of course, Ed had been only a boy – it was also plain, with no effigy or symbols carved upon it. Only his name was scribed there, in square-cut letters, each a handspan across.

E – D – W – A – R – D.

The click of a door catch, the tap, tap of feet on stone. Across the aisle from us, a figure came into view behind the veil of pungent incense hanging still between the columns. It hesitated, then, parting the mist-like tendrils, moved forward into the flickering light shed by the candles in their tall iron holders.

It was a boy, no more than ten or eleven, clad in the livery of an abbey servant. He spotted me, standing towards one end of the plinth, and bowed his head.

'Forgive me, master,' he said softly, in the broad local accent I had missed so much. 'I come here after my work of an evening to pray for the little lord. I saw him lowered into his grave with gentlemen and ladies weeping all around. But now no one comes or prays for him, save the holy brothers in the choir. I don't like the idea that he's all alone.'

He knelt at his side of the simple slab, lowering his head. I spied gentle blue eyes and a strong chin, before his curtain of fair hair flopped down to shield them.

The others didn't notice the interruption. Alys was still talking to Edward in muted tones, with Roger putting in word or two of his own. Before long, Edward gave way to their cajoling. He slipped to his knees beside the tomb, hands clasped at his chest, head up but eyes tight shut. Alys knelt likewise, a pace or so behind him, as did Roger, after removing his cap.

In the fluttering candlelight, among the threads of incense drifting up into the dark vaulted space above, I watched the two boys – servant and king – kneeling, facing each other across the cold grey stone. Pale faces both. One shadowed, one hollow-eyed. Dark shadowed eyes. And a snatch of a long-forgotten dream edged into my mind. I tried to grasp it, but it vanished again, like incense into the void.

The scrape of sandalled feet behind us. A rustle of rich fabric, the soft clearing of a throat.

Both boys glanced up, Alys and Roger too.

The abbot had entered, a brother attending at his heel. Seeing the strange boy's face, no longer shrouded by his hair, the abbot halted. His manner was stern and he made a gesture of impatience.

The monk stepped forward, flourishing a hand at the boy across the tomb.

'John Broom! Be on your way! This is not your place. You are not fit company for a king.'

His mouth and eyes agape, the boy leapt to his feet and scuttled away into the darkness among the far columns.

The abbot bowed to Edward.

'A word in private, Your Grace, if you please.'

Edward rose without a word, and the two of them strolled away from us back along the aisle.

Beyond, where the rows of columns stretched off into the shadows, did I see a darker shadow move, melting away into the gloom?

Alys and Roger were now also upon their feet. She was gazing to where the unknown boy had scurried away.

'John Broom?' she said, as though to herself. 'I don't remember any families of that name hereabouts.'

'He's just a poor simple boy, my lady,' said the monk, who had remained behind. 'A foundling left at our door as a baby. We took him in, of course. His mother was never discovered. He was found on the feast day of Saint John the Baptist and a sprig of broom was caught up within his swaddling clothes, so we gave him that name. We have several such servants in the abbey – poor forsaken boys. When they are older, they are invited to join our order.'

Alys was barely listening, appearing wrapped up in her thoughts.

'He reminded me of someone,' she murmured. Then she shook her head in dismissal, trying to stifle a yawn. 'Never mind. It's been a long day and a tiring one. Shall we—'

But whatever her suggestion was to be, it was lost to us as Edward and the abbot came strolling back. Edward was nodding and saying, 'Of course, my lord, of course. Just as soon as I can.'

After bestowing a blessing, the abbot and brother took their leave, and the four of us were left alone in the darkening church. The candles spluttered as they burnt down. Not only Alys was tired. Roger too was yawning now, and Edward's eyes were still shadowed, dark rings hollowing them. But he was in no hurry to leave the silent, cavernous building, standing there, staring at the intricate swirls and flourishes of the carvings on the wooden and gilt rood screen overlooking little Ed's tomb.

We all waited for him to speak or make a move.

'The abbot asked me for money,' he said quietly, at last. 'For a proper tomb for my cousin. When I am king.' He paused. 'My uncle Gloucester left instructions, he said, and promised to pay. But then, before the best stone mason could be hired, before decisions could be made ...'

Alys's face was desolate.

'He and Queen Anne spoke of burying Ed at York eventually. That he would have the finest tomb any Plantagenet ever had. They had begun to build a chantry chapel there. But she became ill, and then ... then she died. And he—'

Her voice broke, and she turned her face away. 'It's too late now.'

Edward took both her hands in his.

'I will do it, Alys. When I am truly king, I will build him a fine tomb, I promise you. Or perhaps, if you think it right, I could move him to lie with his mother in Westminster. After all, it's what my father did with his father and brother after they were killed at Wakefield. He told me they were buried first near the place where they fell in battle, but later he had them moved to their home at Fotheringhay.'

I too knew that story, but not from his father. Perhaps Alys had also heard it from King Richard, who acted as chief mourner on that long journey south, for she showed no surprise. She simply held Edward's gaze for a second or two, before saying, 'Thank you.'

He did not release her hands as he spoke on. 'I wish you did not have to leave us. I tried to insist you stayed with the army, but Francis and John would not listen.'

'Even though you're king,' she replied gently, 'I suppose you can't always have everything your own way.'

'I don't see why not,' he said, with a hint of petulance. 'Otherwise what's the point of being king? Although ... well, I do think maybe Lord Francis is right. After all, you will be safer here.'

Alys pulled her hands away.

'So would you be. And Matt. Roger knows it. That's why he's happy to stay.'

A wry smile crept on to Roger's face, but he said nothing as Alys went on.

'And yet you're both choosing to go on. And Lord Francis and John. All of you. Whatever may happen. Well, I would rather have that choice too. Better that than sit here and just wait.'

Edward watched the emotions crisscrossing her face – frustration, anger, unhappiness. In an uncertain tone, he said, 'Francis says he's sent messages to Lady Tyrell and to John's mother to tell them that you're here. They will help you if you need it.'

Alys drew in a deep, deep breath before huffing it out in the most unladylike noise. Exasperation was scrawled across her features too, and she seemed about to hurl a retort. But she bit it back and instead turned to flounce off.

Edward shot out a hand to grasp her arm.

'Alys,' he said, beseeching. 'Don't … please …'

Then, as she glared at him again, his tone altered as though he had come to some decision.

'Alys, don't storm off. May I walk with you? I … I would like to speak with you. Alone.'

Her glare melted into surprise as he folded her arm within his. Too startled to object, she allowed herself to be led meekly along the aisle towards the main west door.

Roger called after them.

'We'll be back at the guesthouse when you've finished.'

Together we watched them leave. As they were swallowed up by the shadows in the long nave, Roger said, almost to himself,

'Well, that quietened her down. So long as he doesn't think he can tame her.'

I was bemused by his words.

'What do you mean?'

'Oh, nothing really. Come on. Let's get back.'

As we turned to go, little Ed's tomb caught my eye, stark in the dying candlelight. Something tugged at my memory.

'That boy,' I said. 'Don't you think he looked a little like Edward?'

Roger's eyes narrowed in bafflement. His mind was already elsewhere.

'What boy?' His gaze followed mine. 'Oh, that servant? Did he? I didn't notice. Mind you, it was rather dark, and with all that incense swirling around … Come on, Matt. Let's go and play dice in the guesthouse. It'll be the last chance we have.'

I let him pull me away from that sad, strange

place. In just a few minutes we were sitting in the cheerful main room of the abbey guesthouse with Giles, Robert and sundry other men. It wasn't long before we were losing our small store of pennies to them.

13

Words of Love

We were still in the guesthouse when Alys came seeking us not long after. I caught sight of her furiously beckoning from the doorway and, relieved to have a chance to escape, I pointed her out to Roger. But he was too enthralled in the game to stop now – while he still had money to lose. So I made my excuses to the company, whistled Shadow to heel, and left the light and warmth of the hall.

Alys was alone in the deserted courtyard, lit only by a scatter of torches propped in wall brackets. She had been pacing up and down, but stopped at the sight of me.

'Roger wouldn't come. He sent his apologies.'

She snorted as she bent down to fondle Shadow's ears. The hound gazed up at her, a tiny whine rising into the evening air.

'It's probably just as well. Roger's no use at times like this.'

'Times like what?'

She swept off again, across the court. As I followed, she stopped abruptly and turned. Her face, lit up by the closest brand, was pale and agitated.

'The daft boy thinks he loves me,' she cried.

'What? Who?'

'Edward, of course.'

'Edward?' The shock of her words was like a slap. 'Why?'

'Good question, Matt,' she flung back. 'I have no idea why he should.'

'No, I mean …'

What did I mean? I didn't want to say the wrong thing. Though that was all too easy for me with Alys. So I tried again.

'I mean – that's wonderful. Isn't it?'

She stared at me as though I had lost my wits.

'No. Of course not. How could it be?'

She set off pacing once more.

I did my best to keep up, trying not to step on Shadow, who was trotting close to her heel.

'I think it must be because there's been no one else around. No other girls our age, or from England, at least. But what should put the notion of marriage in his head, I have no idea.'

She halted, whisking her skirts away from Shadow. As she leant down to caress the hound again, my mind flew back many months to our time together in Mechelen. When Lord Francis had spoken to me of Edward's mood lifting whenever Alys approached.

'You make him happy,' I said. Then thought, I sound like a simpleton. 'I mean, he has always enjoyed your company. Perhaps—'

She was staring at me again.

'Happy? Enjoys my company? Really? Shadow makes me happy – often. I enjoy your company – and Roger's. Mostly. It doesn't make me want to marry you. Or anyone.'

'But one day you must, Alys.' I cringed as soon as I said it, but it was too late to take it back.

'Must? I "must" do nothing. Once I dared not return openly to England, for if I was found, I "must" marry Ralph Soulsby. That has all changed. When Dame Grey entered the convent and Tudor became my—' Her mouth twisted in pain. 'Well, I have no obligation to him – and he has no moral claim on me. He is welcome to my fortune if he seeks it. I can live without it, even if on the charity of friends. But he shall not have me – and nor shall his cronies.'

'But, Alys, if that's so – if you no longer feel you must marry Ralph or … well, or anyone else Tudor says, then you could marry Edward.'

Her stare grew into a glare, reflecting the angry orange glow of the nearby torches.

'But I don't wish to. Don't you understand? I don't wish to give myself to any man.' She drew herself up very straight. 'I cannot marry him, or anyone at all. And nor do I intend to. I'm not fit to be any man's wife.'

'What? Why not?' I tried to make sense of the twists and turns in her speech. 'Not even the rightful king of England? He may well reclaim his throne.'

The glare became a look full of pity. For me, I guessed, for my lack of understanding.

'And be queen? Why would I choose that? What freedom would I have then?'

I scrabbled for an answer.

'The freedom to do what you like – and for the good of the people of England? And the money to do it too?'

'Really, Matthew. Do you believe that? A royal woman free to do any of that? Or would it be the "freedom" to bear child after child for the "good" of the country and my husband? That seems no freedom at all.'

She reduced me to silence. I had no more arguments to send into this particular battle. And the more I considered, the more I asked myself why I had chosen to fight it. My loyalty to Edward? But what of my loyalty to Alys? Or to Lord Francis? His words in Flanders about the best marriage for a king of England came back to me. That a king should wed a foreign princess for political reasons. Was Edward even aware of the importance of that?

'It's probably for the best that I am to stay here,' Alys carried on. 'Maybe it will give him time to forget me. And when he arrives at court in Westminster, there will be so many more beautiful, more suitable ladies for him to meet and fall in love with.'

Her face and her drooping shoulders betrayed her tiredness now the flare of her passion had died away.

'I would still rather have stayed with the army, and ridden with you longer, Matt. That is, if you're sure you intend to ride on with Edward and the others.'

'Of course. Edward expects me to.'

'Does he? Why? Surely he doesn't really expect you to fight in any battle?'

'You didn't hear what he said the other night. Or how he said it. Besides, I promised King Richard.'

'King Richard?' A frown flicked across her face. 'Before the battle? What did you promise him exactly? That you would carry his message promptly to Master Ashley. That's all you told me he said.'

'But I didn't, did I?'

'You must stop telling yourself you failed him, Matt. Just because you didn't take the message straight away. You waited to honour your king and master in Leicester. Had you arrived in London sooner it would have made no difference. Master Ashley could not have moved Edward and his brother more quickly. You more than served King Richard by getting them to safety – at great cost to yourself too. He would have expected no more of you.'

I said nothing in reply. Yet that dread night at Lowestoft was replaying in my memory, along with the oath the Order had sworn.

Alys sighed. 'Well, I'm sure all will turn out for the best, whatever happens. I will say farewell to you properly in the morning, but now I must away to my bed. Warn Roger of what has happened if you wish. I am too weary to tell him tonight. Adieu.'

Clicking her fingers to summon Shadow, she stalked back across the courtyard and climbed the steps to the abbot's lodging where I knew a chamber had been made ready for her. I re-entered the guesthouse. There I discovered Roger had completed his task of losing all his cash to the other gentlemen. He was now watching the gaming and offering the remaining players his valuable advice.

He poured me a cup of wine and joined me on a settle in a corner of the large room. Belle sniffed at my boots, then, disappointed Shadow had not returned with me, she yawned and curled up at his feet.

I told him of all that had passed. At first he did not speak, simply sipping his wine. Then he said, in a more serious tone than usual, 'Perhaps she's right – that it's as well she's staying here. It would be hard for her to ride further with Edward after this. And perhaps with their lordships.'

'But not for you?'

'For me?'

'I thought you might be unhappy.' I chose my words with care. 'I mean, about what Edward said to her.'

Roger's brow furrowed in puzzlement.

'Me? Why?'

'I mean, because you and Alys ... You've known each other so long. I thought perhaps – now you're both older ... now Ralph isn't ...'

Roger's guffaw was so loud Belle raised her head, her ears pricked, and the players paused in their game to cast glances our way. He lifted his cup to them in salute, then turned back to me. His grin was as wide as the goblet's mouth.

'Oh, Matt. Me and Alys? Of course not. She's ... I'm ... Oh, Matt, maybe you'll never understand. We're friends, good friends. That's all we'll ever be.'

Had I read everything wrong all these years? With all their games of knights and ladies and gallantry? Perhaps I didn't know either of them as well as I thought.

'If Alys likes Edward well enough to think of marrying him, then I wish them both happiness. And luck. Believe me, they'll need it.' His smile faded a little. 'But I don't think she will ever marry, if she has the choice. She is – well, she is her own woman, if you like. And she has a mind of her own,' he finished, darkly. Then his good humour reviving, he clinked his cup on mine, clutched forgotten in my hand. 'Let's face it, you and I wouldn't want her any other way.'

And, for all my confusion, as I rolled myself up in my blanket in the guest dormitory minutes later, I knew it was difficult to disagree.

14

Pursuit

I finished the final word with the flourish that had become my hallmark in letters I wrote for Edward and their lordships, then passed my free hand across my eyes as I returned my quill to the ink bottle. In the gloom of the tent I worked by the light of a single candle and its shadows flickered and danced on the canvas walls. I flexed my writing hand as I read back over the letter. From the opening 'Trusty and well beloved we greet you well', to the final 'Given under our signet at Masham the eighth day of June'. Then I was ambushed by a yawn.

The events of the past few days had exhausted me, not just in body but also in spirit. We had not left Jervaulx until late on in the morning, having waited for the main force to catch up and further local reinforcements to arrive. And we had ended our march after only a few miles, making camp just outside the small town of Masham. But for all that, the day had dragged.

The worst of it had been anticipation of the much-dreaded farewells. When they finally came, they had been especially difficult. And Alys, in her inimitable way, made sure they were memorable too.

Edward's gentlemen and closest companions had been assembling in the courtyard in front of the abbot's lodging. Amidst all the bustle, Alys manoeuvred us to ensure she, Roger and I were as far as possible from where Edward and Lord Francis were taking leave of the abbot and his officials. I was just bending to stroke Shadow for the last time before mounting Caesar, when Earl John's voice came from behind me.

'Right glad I am to see you here, my lady Alys. And at last in garb more fitting for a young lady of rank.'

Alys swivelled towards him, twitching aside the

satin skirt of the gown that had somehow been found for her in the abbey. As she curtsied, she blinked away the glisten of tears I had glimpsed a moment before.

'I could not let Matthew go today, my lord, without bidding him God speed.'

'I do realize that now, my lady,' the earl said, politely bowing in his turn. 'Yet after we noticed your absence from the harbourside at Dublin, Lord Francis and I were fooled into thinking otherwise. This time perhaps we can be sure you are staying where you will be safe.'

She flushed at his words. They were lightly spoken, with a jest not far from the earl's voice or his face. But Alys was in no mood for joking.

'Would you wish to see me chained to the church door to be totally sure, my lord?'

'Nay.' The earl's laugh broke the surface. 'To see you here in ladies' clothing is enough. We shall leave the chains to whoever your husband may eventually be – if he has need to stop you wandering.'

Roger shot me a worried look as Alys drew herself up as though to repel the attack, or turn it into an assault of her own. But her response was not the fiery retort I expected. She spoke every word with extreme care, holding herself with all the dignity she could muster.

'Then I trust, my lord, that you will do your work well over these coming days. Or Henry Tudor will have the choosing of that husband for me.'

Her speech, clear and high, carried some distance. Edward and Lord Francis broke off their conversation with the abbot, glancing across at our little group. Even at a score or more paces, I could see Edward's eyes were only for Alys.

Sobered, the earl stepped forward and took her hand. After a moment's resistance, she surrendered it to him, and he bent his fair head to kiss it.

'We shall do everything in our power, I assure you, my lady,' he said, raising his voice as he straightened, still holding her hand. 'For you, for my cousin Edward, and for the kingdom.'

At his words cheers rose from the assembled gentlemen. Before the earl released Alys's hand, he continued more quietly, 'We shall look forward to seeing you installed in your rightful place at court. I hope we part as friends.'

Then, bowing his head to her, he strode off to mount his horse.

Alys's cheeks were pink once more as she drew back with Roger and the two hounds towards the doorway of the abbot's lodging. She raised her hand in a wave as I too clambered on to my horse.

'Farewell, Matt, and stay safe – until we can meet again.'

Edward was by then also astride his mount, Lord Francis and Earl John to either side. He too lifted his hand, in salute to the abbot, but taking in Alys and Roger, before he urged Storm into motion. And so the company had clattered out of the courtyard and made its way across the abbey precinct to join the army on the road towards Masham.

'Are you done, Matt? Is it ready for my seal?'

Edward's voice broke into my thoughts now.

'Aye, it's finished and checked.'

I stood and moved away so he could take my place at the small table littered with my writing things. He read the letter through, then, heating a stick of red wax in the candle flame, dripped a molten drop on to the parchment. It pooled there like fresh blood before he thrust his signet ring into it to complete the seal.

'There. Ready to be sent to the council at York. Francis says we may hear from them as early as the morning. Relays of horses have been arranged along the road to speed the messenger. But he cannot say how long the council will take to make their decision.' The candle flame's reflection leapt in his eyes as he raised them to meet mine. 'I trust your father and his fellows will soon rally to our cause, Matt.'

I bowed my head.

'My father is but one man among many on the council,' I said aloud, but in my head I prayed that all the members would give the right answer.

I folded the letter and ducked outside the royal tent to hand it to the waiting messenger. He mounted and rode off. I watched him weave his way through the surrounding tents towards the roadway. It was strange to think that in a few hours that letter might be seen, or even handled, by my father himself.

As the messenger disappeared, a small band of horsemen passed by. At their head was Lord Francis, both Mallary brothers riding just behind. Giles raised his hand in greeting, then all the riders kicked their horses into a trot, following the path the messenger had taken.

Edward emerged from the pavilion as I gazed after them.

'Was that Francis?'

I nodded without speaking.

'Where are they going?'

'I don't know. But they're making for the York road.'

'York?'

'There are many villages between here and there.' I knew – I had passed through them many times.

'Let's go after them.'

'What?'

'Fetch horses, Matt, and we can follow. Let's see where they go. Francis should have told me anyway – should have asked my permission. I am king after all.'

Was he joking? It was difficult to tell. Shining in his eyes was a light such as I had not seen in many days. Not perhaps since the madcap beginning of our adventure on the headland outside Dublin, or when conspiring with Alys for her to sail with the army.

'But, Edward, it may not be safe.'

'What? Here?' He spread his hands, gesturing at all about him. 'Where all are still loyal to my uncle

Richard and all my family? That's what everyone tells me. What do we have to fear?'

He spoke in a carefree tone, but we both knew I could give him no answer. Mercifully he didn't wait for one.

'Besides, I am tired of all this – all the serious parts of being king, without any of the fun. They wouldn't let Alys stay with us, but why shouldn't you and I go for a pleasant ride? We can send a squire to let John know … once we're well out of the camp, of course.'

There was no arguing with him when he was in this mood. If I didn't go for horses, he might seize any animal tethered nearby and gallop off without even me for company. So I did as he bid and in a few minutes we had passed the lookouts, who snapped to attention at sight of him, and were trotting over the river on the old stone bridge away from Masham. Up ahead, from time to time, we could see the distant figures of Lord Francis and his companions when the bends in the lane allowed.

'We must not get too close,' warned Edward, 'just close enough so we don't lose them.'

It was indeed a pleasant ride through the green meadows dozing in the warmth of the summer's afternoon. As we jogged along in companionable silence, the chirruring of grasshoppers and the bumble bees' drone everywhere overlay the sweet scents rising from carpets of flowers at the field edges. Snowy plates of cow parsley swayed beneath the creamy froth of elder flowers, and more than once the deep pink flash of a bullfinch or a butterfly's azure gleam drew my eyes away from the riders ahead.

Edward was perhaps less caught up in nature's charms than I. Before long he shattered the drowsy quiet.

'Did Alys tell you I declared my love for her?'

His words were unexpected, but matter of fact, undramatic. For all that, I hardly dared look at him. I simply nodded. He carried on in the same tone, though the warmth in his voice grew.

'She has brought me such joy and been a great support all these months. You of all people must have seen that, Matt.'

A pause. Again I didn't reply, uncertain what to say. He seemed unconcerned – maybe, as so often before, bouncing his thoughts off me, happy just to have a listener.

'Perhaps I shouldn't have told her before we parted, but I wanted her to know. Especially if a battle is to come. I have told no one else. I thought perhaps she would be more likely to join us in London after the battle – not run off again. She might run away if she's worried I should hand her over to Soulsby to marry his son.'

Did he expect me to answer? All I could have said at that moment was that he knew Alys less well than he supposed. If anything, his declaration was more likely to make her run away. My heart went out to him. Yet whatever Alys's reply to him had been last night, it had not dented his happiness. Maybe her refusal had been less blunt than her words to me had suggested. Or, perhaps, less clear than she had intended.

To my relief, he did not wait for me to speak.

'You must not tell Francis or John, though. Not yet. I suspect they may have plans for my marriage already – and not ones that involve Alys. But I shall marry who I please.'

Like your father before you, I thought. But I held my tongue rather than speak of it and the trouble it had caused. Nor did I suggest the young lady herself also might wish to marry who she pleased. Or no one. Let him enjoy his happiness a while longer.

We rode further along the road, into the shade of a dense copse of oak and birch. The only sounds were the clopping of our horses' hooves and the distant cluck-clucking of a disturbed blackbird. Until Edward spoke again.

'And particularly don't tell John.'
'The earl?'
'He is my cousin and I shouldn't speak ill of him.

But sometimes I think he is a little too gallant to Alys. For all he has a wife of his own—'

His words broke off as the clucking alarm of the bird flared up again beside us and it shot like a black arrow low across the road in front of our horses. Caesar reared up in surprise and crab-stepped to the side, blundering into Edward's mount.

'What the—?' he cried, as I fought to control Caesar, and he clapped his hand to his sword hilt.

But his choked-off exclamation was not aimed at me. By the time I wrestled Caesar to a standstill, Edward had drawn his sword and levelled it at a horseman emerging from the bushes.

'You! What—?'

'Forgive me, Your Grace. I did not mean to startle you.'

The rider removed his sallet. It was Giles Mallary.

'What are you doing here? I thought you ...' Edward fell silent, his cheeks flushing red.

'You thought I was riding up yonder with Lord Francis?' Giles finished for him. 'I was. Until we realized we were being followed and he sent me back to discover by whom. Please go back, Your Grace. It's not safe for you to be out here alone.'

Alone? I bit back my objection, but Edward had a different one. His colour returned to normal as he lowered his weapon.

'I thought we were among loyal friends hereabout.'

'The families of the dale, yes,' said Giles evenly, not reacting to the barb. 'But there are footpads and vagabonds everywhere. You will be safer back with the army. If you wish, I will escort you.'

'That won't be necessary,' Edward said. 'We have swift horses and our swords if any should attack us.'

I was not sure I could rely on either, and the arch of Giles's brow as his eyes darted my way suggested he felt the same. But I was more taken aback by Edward giving in so easily. He meekly sheathed his sword, hiding its intricate scrollwork inscription.

'But tell me, Giles,' he said as he did so, 'if we cannot go on, where is Francis heading? He left without a word.'

'I'm sure that was an oversight, Your Grace,' soothed Giles. 'His lordship has friends – family, in fact – who own the next manor along this road. He has not seen them for some years, not since he became a fugitive. He wishes to pay them a visit. If they are still in residence. Were he to arrive with a king in tow, I imagine it might cause some disruption.'

'Family? He has family still living?'

'His wife's mother, I believe.'

'I had not realized Francis even had a wife. I have never heard him speak of her.'

Giles bowed his head and pursed his lips to say no more. But Edward persisted.

'Where is she now?'

'Lady Anne? Not here, and safe. That's all that concerns him, and all that I know. And what concerns me at this moment is that you two should be not here and safe too.'

Another time Edward would have bridled at Giles's responses, bordering on insolence as they did. But now he made no complaint, perhaps embarrassed at how easily we had been ambushed. Together we turned our horses' heads to ride back the way we had come.

Giles waited, watching us until we rounded a bend and he was out of sight. I suspected he remained a while longer to make sure we didn't double back, but there was no need. Despite all his earlier bravado, Edward appeared content to return to camp, and once there to sit quietly at supper with Earl John and the remaining gentlemen, before retiring to his tent, where he requested me to play.

I had almost forgotten my harp, though I carried it with me every day. It had survived my misadventure on the Sands, being retrieved with my bundle when Caesar was discovered wandering loose. I released it now from its stout leather bag and ran my fingertips across its many strings. The sweet cascades of notes spilled into every corner of the candlelit tent. As I brought them into line, channelling them into a melody I had learned from the Kildares' musicians, it struck me why, perhaps, Edward wished to hear me. Music ever reminds us of past times. Was he thinking of happier evenings with Alys in Ireland and Flanders?

After a few jaunty tunes, I risked my voice in a song. Too late did I realize the only ones I could accompany on the harp were plaintive love songs. Edward had learned none of the Irish tongue during his stay. Yet though he understood not a word, he soon lapsed into a melancholy mood. He sat nursing his goblet of wine, a faraway look in his eyes. I did not finish all the verses, and switched mid-song to another dance tune, doing my best to lift him and make his foot tap. But it was to no avail. When, after another rousing reel, I took a break to gulp a mouthful from my own cup, he hardly noticed.

I chose again slower melodies when I resumed and left him to his thoughts. My own memory transported me back to other evenings, long before, when his uncle, my old master, had sat and mused in similar fashion. The last time being on the eve of battle …

'Matthew?'

I started at Edward's voice, my hand jerking on the strings and causing a jarring run of notes.

He laughed softly, his face in shadow as the candles around us burned steadily down.

'I'm sorry I startled you. Thank you for your music – until that moment anyway. And thank you for staying with me this far on our journey.'

I lowered my head to him, uncertain what to say, as so often. But he was determined to speak himself.

'I know you're not a fighter, Matt. That you have served me well in other ways. Do you wish to return to Jervaulx, to Alys? I know you would look after her.

Perhaps better than Roger could.'

I was dumbfounded at his words – so different to those he had uttered two nights before. His insistence then had circled in my mind constantly since. That I must stand and fight alongside him, whatever might come. And I had steeled myself for what was on its way.

'I once promised to serve your uncle loyally,' I replied, with barely a thought to what I was saying. 'That I would not fail him in a small service he asked of me. Then I betrayed his trust. I will not do that again. I swore to serve you. Loyalty binds me – always.'

Surprise gleamed in Edward's eyes. He made as if to speak, then closing his mouth, settled back in his chair and sank once more into his own reveries.

I stroked my fingers across the harp's strings again, myself reflecting on the words that had tumbled from my lips. I had reason to think about them often over the coming days … and the following years.

15

'Perfidious York'

The messenger arrived back in the cold light just before dawn. And he had a cold answer for us.

Earl John's face was bleak as he reported the news to Edward.

'The city council will not aid us, nor will it let us enter.'

Edward had received his cousin alone in his tent. Alone, that was, apart from me. A fur-trimmed gown was hastily flung over his nightshirt to repel the morning chill. He appeared pale and vulnerable now as he leaned upon the tabletop, scattered still with my writing gear. But then he raised his head, and his eyes were blazing.

'I should have expected it. After all, they stuck our grandfather's head on a spike on their walls when he was murdered by the Lancastrians. And they were perfidious when my father returned from exile. They would not let him enter either.'

'Not at first, perhaps.' The earl's smile was grim. 'But then he swore that he did not intend to reclaim his throne, and they allowed him in. But remember, that was only days before he marched into London – and then met cousin Warwick and the Lancastrians in battle at Barnet to fight for the throne. Had the battle gone ill for him, no doubt Warwick and old Queen Margaret would have taken vengeance on York for its actions.'

'But I have not lied about my intentions,' protested Edward.

'No. But why should they trust you after what your father did?'

Edward spluttered at this, but the earl lifted a hand to fend off his objections.

'Councils have long memories, Edward. Just like

storytellers, they pass their lore down from one generation to another. And they may have many reasons for their refusal.'

'What reasons? Why should they refuse their true king?'

'You forget that York always favoured the Lancastrians in the past. Before our uncle Richard won it to our family's cause. And Tudor has spent much money to try to win it to his. I saw that for myself when I was there last spring.'

As I listened, my thoughts were swirling. I wanted to interrupt, to defend my home city and its folk. It was hard to bear the accusation that my father and his fellow council men would be swayed in their decision by money. Yet what other reasons they might have I didn't know. And I did know it was not my place to speak.

His anger fading and his features sharp with weariness, Edward flopped into his chair. The earl pulled up another for himself.

'I have sent word ahead to Tanfield where Francis stayed last night. He will meet us on route and have time to think on what to do next. Don't forget, he knows the city well. He was also there last year, when he persuaded many men to rise against Tudor. Their executions will be fresh in the minds of the council and may also be behind their answer.'

Little detail of Lord Francis's attempted rebellion in York had reached me. (How I missed letters from my family there!) But hearing of such reprisals made the council's fear of aiding us more understandable. Yet I knew fighting men from my city would be a valuable addition to our army.

'Matthew!' The earl's imperious voice brought me back to the present. 'Go fetch the servants. Tell them Edward and I will break our fast here as soon as we may.'

As I hurried to do his bidding, I set my mind to what, if anything, I could do to help. My father was a member of the council, after all.

The army was on the move earlier that day, crossing the gentle country Edward and I had ridden through the afternoon before. Lord Francis and his party – Giles and Robert among them, of course – met us at a small village on a crossing of the river. They emerged from a magnificent gateway of many-coloured stone, accompanied by a score or so of armoured men. Upon the steps of the fine old manor house beyond, a small group bade him farewell, an older lady at their head. She turned away, head bowed, as Lord Francis greeted Edward and the earl and rejoined our company.

We halted at midday within sight of the town of Ripon. Its church towers jutted up into an almost cloudless sky. Their lordships held a council with Sir Thomas and Captain Schwartz while taking their dinner in a hastily erected tent.

My letter-writing skills were not required, so, after eating, I strolled along the nearby riverbank with Giles. Now Alys and Roger were no longer with us, I viewed him as my closest friend on the march. But when I spoke to him of my concerns about my home city, he only shrugged.

'Cities' loyalties change, Matt – turn and turn about. They always have, depending on the way the wind blows. There's nothing you can do.'

But still I wondered. And when we made camp that evening, close to the river crossing at the settlement of Boroughbridge, I begged an audience with Lord Francis. I hoped he would at least listen to me as he had on occasion before.

He ushered me into his tent.

'Well, Matthew?'

'My lord, if I may ask, what has been decided about York?'

He eyed me for a moment, as though weighing me up.

'You have heard that the city has refused us entry?'

'Aye, my lord. I was with Edward when the messenger returned this morning. Both he and Earl John were ... disappointed. But no more than I at the news from my home city.'

'Ah, I had forgot. That it was your home. Well, the army shall not go nearer than this, do not fear. Tomorrow we shall march due south from here. Down the ancient road towards London.'

'But, my lord, Earl John says the army needs all the men it can get. '

'That's true.'

'The men of York are stout-hearted and were ever loyal to ... well, to King Richard. I know how much he did for them.'

A faint spasm contorted his lordship's face, but it was gone in an instant.

'Aye, Richard did all he could for your city, Matt. But that was then. We are in different times now.' He pushed himself up from his seat and began to pace about the confines of the tent. 'We more than half expected they would refuse us. After last year – my attack on Tudor. Too many good men died – fathers, sons, brothers. Because of me. That is how they will see it.'

He halted, swinging round and leaning on the back of his chair.

'Still, it will do no harm for the army to move quickly south before my lord of Northumberland can ready his forces north of here. Or perhaps before Tudor can prepare fully against our advance.'

The name of Northumberland was like a stab to me. The man who had treacherously held back at King Richard's final battle – and who, even before then, had been little liked in my home city.

I thrust him from my mind, as I said, 'My father is a member of the city council. It may be that he—'

'What can one man do, Matthew?'

'Perhaps if I go to see him, talk to him. Tell him,' I cast my thoughts back to all my friends and I had heard while in Ireland, 'tell him that Edward is who he says he is. That he is the true son of old King Edward.'

I paused, half expecting his lordship to dismiss my words. But he was watching me, his eyes narrowed, so I went on.

'I know your worry – and Edward's – is that people will not believe he is King Edward's son, and therefore rightful king. That Tudor's proclamations have said he claims to be the little Earl of Warwick, his cousin, instead. Even though Tudor has him imprisoned in the Tower in London.'

'Aye,' said Lord Francis, carefully. 'That may be why some will not join us.'

'Not only is my father known in the city,' I persisted, 'some council members may remember me too. They may also remember I served King Richard. My father even told me the mayor spoke of me when …'

I hesitated, my cheeks of a sudden burning as I recalled the reason. When my shame on leaving York had been turned to a minor triumph at King Richard's hand.

'Well, it may be that they will listen to him.'

I stumbled to a halt, my face aflame. Had King Richard ever told Lord Francis the story of my expulsion from York? Perhaps on that very first day when I had mistaken one friend for the other. But would his lordship even remember if he had?

A smile ghosted across his face. His eyes were distant though, focused elsewhere. Then they snapped back to me.

'Very well, Matt,' he said, his voice betraying no emotion. 'You may try your best. So long as Edward agrees, you may accompany Giles.'

'Giles? He's going to York?'

'He will be setting off this evening.' His half-smile returned. 'You did not think we had given up on the city, did you? The letter to the council was only ever one part of our plan.'

Not for the first time I felt small and foolish in

Lord Francis's presence.

I bowed my way out and went to seek Edward. He was in his tent, reclining on his campbed, one hand draped across his face. He didn't bother to look up as I entered. I was sorry neither Alys nor Roger – nor even the hounds – were around to bring him some cheer.

'Do as you wish, Matt.' He barely lifted his head when I made my request. 'I shall retire early tonight, so will not need you or your harp. I do not care to think of York any more today.'

'There are many men there loyal to your father,' I reminded him, 'as well as to your uncle.'

'Yes, of course, my uncle.' Tired and listless he might be, but tetchiness scratched in his voice. 'I always hear how much he did for York after my father sent him there. He and his Neville wife certainly gained the city's favour.' He rested his head back again and closed his eyes. 'Well, you may try, Matt – see if any will join our cause.'

As I stepped out of Edward's tent, Giles collared me.

'Lord Francis tells me I'm to have the pleasure of your company tonight, little man. We'll leave in two hours, once it's fully dark. Catch a bit of supper and some sleep while you can. We have to be off in good time and we won't be stopping on the way.'

Of a sudden, worry bubbled up in me.

'You won't leave without me, will you?'

'Why would I? Lord Francis has told me to take you. He tells me it's your home town.' Then Giles's lips twitched. 'Although between you and me, I think he sees it as a good chance to be rid of you – I mean, for you to be left in a safe place.'

'But I'm not going to stay there!' A different fear struck me, forcing itself into my voice.

Giles's mirth dropped away. He thrust out a hand to grasp my shoulder and said, his tone deadly serious,

'If I were you, I'd take your chance while you have it. No one would think the less of you – Lord Francis and me least of all. We both know you're not cut out for this. And so do you, don't you, Matt?'

It stung me to hear that yet others doubted me, not just Edward.

Yet the trust that King Richard had placed in me – the belief he had shown on that far-off morning before the battle – came back to me. He at least had had faith in me.

'But I've sworn to Edward that I'll stay with him. And – and I promised King Richard I would …'

That I would do what exactly? What had I promised?

Yet the details mattered not to Giles. His fingers gripped my arm again.

'King Richard, eh? Have no fear. I would have no man break an oath, nor would Lord Francis. I won't leave you there if you choose to return.'

And so, after supper and the briefest of rests, Giles and I set off on the dark road towards York.

16

Homecoming

'Hurry, Matt. We must be off the streets before the townsfolk are abroad. Word will have got around about the army's approach, and they will be wary of strangers.'

Giles's hiss in the darkness was accompanied by a shove and, exhausted as I was, I stumbled through the gateway. The pitted wooden door was held open by a figure hidden in the shadows. A soft chortle came from it now, but also a helping hand, which caught me before I fell headlong. In its other hand was a shuttered lantern, revealed only by the escape of tiny threads of light.

'Come, lad,' said the quiet voice belonging to the chuckle. 'He's right that you must make haste. It'll do me no good if it's discovered I've let you in.'

We had tethered the horses in an area of coppiced woodland outside the city and crossed the last half-mile or so to the walls on foot. This postern gate, set in a half-ruined tower, was one of several down by the river and little used now by the townspeople. Its hinges sighed with a rusty creak as it was pushed closed behind Giles.

'They're expecting you at the sign of the Fleece.' The voice from the shadows again. 'Take my lantern and be quickly on your way. I'll send my boy to tend to your horses once it gets light. They'll be ready for a swift getaway if need be.'

Iron scraped on leather as the lantern was passed from one gloved hand to the other, and another push propelled me up the narrow path away from the postern. After a few paces, with a quiet snap Giles opened one shutter of the lamp. In the slender stream of light, I could at last see where to place my feet, though my lack of sleep meant I hardly had strength to place one in front of the other. The alley widened before long, joining a cobbled way, and the light from the half-moon and sprinkling of stars trickled down to us. Giles fully shuttered the lamp again as we turned on to a grand paved street, of the sort of which my city was so proud.

Here and there a lantern burned above a shop or a light showed in a window, but all was still quiet. Few people other than bakers and brewers would be astir at this early hour. How I longed to be abed too! But we prowled through the silent streets like wakeful tom cats on the hunt. From time to time, real cats' eyes caught the moonlight or a tail twitched in the shadows as an animal ran off. But mostly it was just Giles and I to be seen, if anyone had peeped sleepily from their homes.

Soon we entered a street I knew well, and my heart leapt inside me. I tugged on Giles's sleeve to halt him.

'Giles, we're on Stonegate. Here is my home.'

I pointed to the tall, familiar house. Its jutting upper storeys of black timbers and white moonlit plaster threw the street-level storefront into deepest shadow.

'I doubt your family will happily welcome you this early, Matt,' he whispered back. 'Not without warning. No matter how much they may have missed you. Come with me to the inn. Eat, wash, and sleep. Then return to them in a more civilized fashion.'

He was right, of course. It would not be kind to rouse my family so long before dawn. But my disappointment weighed heavy alongside my tiredness as we passed that long-yearned-for house and those sleeping, unaware, within.

My sadness was soon driven away by the welcome we received at the Fleece inn – after Giles's tentative tap on the door, when the bolts were shot back, and we were urged into the cosy, fire-warmed chamber within. Cups of good ale, new-baked crusty bread and salty lumps of local white cheese were thrust into our hands. Then, at the landlord's summons, two yawning, half-dressed men stumbled down the stairs into the room.

As Giles stepped forward to embrace them, I wished I had a hand free of food and drink to rub the befuddlement of fatigue from my eyes. For, not only did both the newcomers resemble Giles in height, looks and broadness of smile, but – but they were the same man.

Was my lack of sleep making me see double?

At my sharp intake of breath, a crumb of cheese caught in my throat and I choked. Giles swung round to slap one hand on my back to dislodge it, then waved the other hand at the two men – or was it one?

'Matt, these are my older brothers – William and John. Come up from Northamptonshire to join us.'

Then he spied my face, agog as it still was, though the coughing had ceased.

'And, yes, they are twins. Both born of my mother on the very same day.'

I closed my mouth in embarrassment, then opened it again.

'I have heard tell of such people but have never seen them.'

As I spoke, I wished I had not. Yet again I sounded like a half-wit. Of course I had known twins, but not …

'Never seen twins?' said Giles, eyes wide with surprise. 'Why, surely they are everywhere – even here in this backwater of York. Lord Francis himself is such a one. Though to be fair, you might not be able to tell if ever you met his sister.'

'As he and Mistress Joan are not identical twins, like us,' said John with a grin. Or was it William?

'On account of her being a woman,' finished William, laughing. Or was it John?

Flames blazed in my cheeks and I gulped a little of the sour ale to quench them. But I need not have been concerned. Giles and these latest brothers had no more interest in me and had moved on.

'And how are our parents?' asked Giles. 'And Geoffrey?' Was there yet another brother? 'Has Margery had her baby yet? I forget when it was due …'

Their talk about people unknown to me, and the warmth, and my full belly, lulled me soon to sleep. How much later did the chink of empty cups being cleared away and the stirring of the fire puncture the grey swirling fog of my dreams? I knew not, but I opened my eyes to a golden, sun-filled but otherwise empty chamber, save for the bustling tavern keeper, now rearranging the chairs about me.

'Morning, master,' he said on seeing me stretching. 'I trust you've slept well? Your friends retired to their room to sleep, but asked that you be left undisturbed.'

I thanked him with a small coin from my pouch and he eased back the bolts on the door to let me out into the street. From the place of the sun in the sky and the throng of people, pack animals and carts hastening every which way on the paved thoroughfare, I reckoned it was a fit time to spring my surprise visit on my family. I stepped lightly into the tangled lanes of my home district, and the bells of first one, then another and another of the many nearby churches tolled for prime. Then, ahead and above them all, resounded the great bells of the Minster.

I was home again, after more than four long, turbulent years.

In just a few minutes the black-and-white frontage of the house on Stonegate loomed above me. I paused with my thumb on the doorlatch. I had so looked forward to my return after such a length of time, yet had given no thought to the manner of my arrival or my reception. I was no longer the boy I had been. My family too might be very different. I had received no letters from them since before I left London to travel to King Richard on the eve of his final battle, and I had no idea whether any of those I had sent from time to time in after years had ever reached them. For safety's sake – both theirs and mine – I had never enclosed a return address.

I drew in a breath and pressed down on the latch.

The tiny bell on the door top tinkled to announce me as I stepped down on to the well-worn stone flags. As always, the interior of the shop was at first in shadow until my eyes adjusted. The familiar smell of lanolin, leather and ink wafted into my nostrils, and I was transported back to my childhood. To the many hours I had spent helping – and sometimes hindering – my father as he conducted his business here.

A figure emerged from behind bales of colourful cloth and stacks of books in the corner. A tall figure. Taller than I remembered.

'Yes, master? Can I help you?'

A deep voice, yet not so deep. A courteous, bland smile on the face – younger, thinner. Then the eyes widening.

'Holy mother of God! Is it – Matthew? Is it you?'

Not my father. A brother.

'Fred?'

He lunged forward, caught me up in his embrace, buried his head in my hair. His breath tickled my ear as he spoke again.

'Matt! You're safe. I thought— we thought—'

'Yes, I'm alive. I'm safe.'

We broke apart. He held me at arm's length, looked me up and down. His smile returned, broader now.

'You've grown. I never thought—'

'Fred, I'm seventeen. You've not seen me for four years. Of course I've grown.'

If not so very much. And so had he grown – far more than I ever would.

'Has it been so long? Well, we should have known you'd turn up soon.'

'Really? Why? Oh, the army, I suppose.'

'No, it's …' He paused, eyes narrowing in surprise. 'The army? Is that why you're here?'

'Of course. I've been travelling with King Edward all this time.' For a fleeting moment, I wondered why else he imagined I had come home, but my mind hopped back to another thought. 'Did you receive none of my letters then? After I left London?''

'Two or three.' He was more sober now, after the first excitement of meeting. 'And not for more than a year now. But they never really said anything. Beyond that you were still living.'

'I couldn't say much in them. And had to be careful of what I did say. I could never be sure if they would reach here, or whose hands they might fall into.'

'Well, now we know you're alive, and here. And with this army that threatens us and King Henry. No wonder you worried about who would read them.'

'Not threatens, Fred,' I insisted. 'Not York anyway. The council wouldn't let us in, so the army's marching on south away from here today. But it is the army of the rightful king. King Edward the Fifth – son of old King Edward.'

Fred's brow wrinkled again.

'Son of King Edward? But they say he's an imposter – a ten-year-old boy, pretending to be the Earl of Warwick, son of the old Duke of Clarence.'

My heart sank. So Tudor's lies had spread this far and were believed, even here in York.

'No, he truly is Edward, son of King Edward the Fourth. I know. I—'

And so I told my brother the story of all that had happened over the past four years – from the day I had last left York, to my meeting with Edward when he was newly king in his Uncle Rivers's care, through my time in London, then on to the days after King Richard's death and the almost two years since.

I spoke as briefly as I could. As Fred listened, myriad emotions fleeted across his rapt face. Once or twice, his hand crept out to squeeze my arm to comfort me. Once only did he interrupt me.

'Were you at the battle when King Richard died?'

I shook my head, silenced by my memories of all I had witnessed that day. Then, nudged by a remembrance of something I had not seen – the banners of the men of York, including my archer brother – I asked, 'Were you?'

'No.' Anger sparked in his usually mild brown eyes. 'My lord of Northumberland didn't muster us. The council sent a message to ask for advice, but it was too late. Only afterwards did we learn of Northumberland's treachery. Many in the city have sworn to make him pay for it one day.' From his fervour, I did not doubt he was one of them.

After his outburst, he settled again to hear the rest of my tale. As I reached the end, he said,

'So it is true. You know for sure this Edward is old King Edward's son. Father said there were some on the council who argued it was, and that the city should declare for the rebels. But others preferred to believe Tudor's version. They debated long into the night after the letter came, but the cautious men prevailed.'

If only I had been there to add my voice – for what good it might have done. But at least Fred no longer spoke of 'King Henry'.

'Where is Father now?' I asked.

'Another council meeting was called early this morning to discuss things further. Do you know the Earl of Northumberland is on his way with troops? He warned us of your arrival before the council received your letter. I don't know how he found out so quickly, if you only landed on Monday.'

I sighed.

'Men such as he and Tudor have spies everywhere. I learned that to my cost before, in London.'

'Well, he will be here later today. And Lord Clifford arrived with four hundred men last evening. There is quite a force building against your king. And it will be to his rear as he moves south.'

And to the south waited Tudor himself. Maybe now, with Tudor's forces all around, it would be impossible to persuade the council to support Edward.

Disappointment yawned like a pit in my stomach.

'Oh, that reminds me.' Fred cut into my thoughts. 'Just before Lord Clifford arrived, so too did our visitor.'

It was my turn to frown.

'Visitor?'

'The young lady who claims to be our cousin. The reason we should have known you would turn up before long.'

'What young lady?' Then an idea struck me with the force of cannon fire. 'Oh no! Not Alys!'

'Alys?' Fred's forehead crinkled. 'That's not the name she gave. But then she called herself Mistress Wansford, from the city of Northampton, and we know of no such cousins from the south.'

He pulled me to my feet.

'Come on. She may be awake now. She was so adamant she was a Wansford and knew you that Mother insisted we put her up overnight at least. So she slept in Agnes's old room. Peter bunked in with me, and Sarah and little Richard back in with our parents.'

'Agnes's old room?'

'She's married. Remember?'

Of course I did, now I thought of it. She'd been preparing for her wedding last time I was at home.

'And she has a little one of her own on the way now.'

So much had changed.

'And Richard?' I said. 'I've never yet seen him. He must be …'

I searched my memory for when my little half-brother had been born. Surely it was only months after my father told me his new wife had been praying a long time for a baby of her own.

'He's almost three,' supplied Fred. 'A bonny lad. And Mother has had another child since.'

'Another?'

'A girl. They named her Anne. Because of everything Queen Anne did for you and for this city. Mother was devastated when she died, and that she was never able to pay us that visit she promised. Talking of visitors, come on. You have a mystery to solve.'

He grasped my arm and hauled me from the shop, shoving me up the narrow staircase towards the first-floor parlour.

My feet dragged upon the steps. Never before had I been reluctant to meet Alys. Not, at least, since our difficult first encounters at Middleham Castle. But now, after our parting at Jervaulx just two mornings ago, I dreaded seeing her. She had made a solemn promise to remain there, safe, far away from the army. What possible reason could she have for breaking faith with Lord Francis?

17

The Distant Cousin

I mounted the final step with a heavy tread and turned into the large airy room. An unexpected tableau startled me to a standstill.

Our young stepmother was pacing to and fro, humming a wordless tune to a swaddled bundle cradled in her arms. And beyond her – perched on a windowseat, a small boy clinging to her skirts and a baby-sized linen garment on her lap beneath a poised needle – was, not Alys, but

'Elen!'

The name echoed around the quiet chamber.

Mother spun round in alarm, pressing the tiny baby to her bodice. The little boy whimpered and clutched great fists of Elen's crimson skirts, stuffing them against his face as though trying to hide. Elen soothed him gently with a stroke of his brown hair as she laid down her needlework and rose to her feet. Though her back was to the light streaming in through the window, the rosy glow on my friend's dark cheeks was vivid to my eyes.

My own cheeks flared in turn. To conceal them, I stepped quickly forward, bending over her upraised hand to kiss it in greeting.

'Matthew,' she said softly. I sensed the faintest of pressure on my hand before she released it.

'Matthew?' My stepmother was hovering nearby, her shock giving way to disbelief. 'Is it really you? After all this time?'

'Yes, Mother, it's really me,' I said, embracing her and taking care not to squash the bundle she held. The baby's eyes were tight shut and its breathing quiet, oblivious to the scene playing out around it.

'He appeared in the shop not half an hour ago,

Mother,' Fred told her. 'He gave me the surprise of my life too. I thought it best to bring him up to meet our mysterious visitor as soon as possible.'

'Is this the young lady you used to write about so often in your letters, Matthew?'

Mother's surprise might have vanished from her face, but her words made the heat rise again in mine. I was glad Elen cast her eyes down demurely at her needlework rather than look at me, as she settled herself again on to the windowseat. She no doubt knew, as well as I, that it was my tales of Alys my stepmother recalled from my letters.

'Mother, this is my friend Elen,' I said, sidestepping the question.

'But not Elen Wansford?' inquired Fred, a teasing smile lurking about his lips. 'Are you not a distant cousin, mistress?'

Our stepmother's quick eyes must have spied Elen's discomfort as she fidgeted on her cushions. With her free hand, she took hold of Fred's arm.

'Come, Fred,' she said. 'I have need of your help in the kitchen once I've put the baby down in her cradle. We should let Matt speak to his friend in peace. We can catch up with all his news later.'

Fred allowed himself to be drawn downstairs, although he threw me a knowing glance as he called to little Richard to follow.

I stood for a few moments, listening to their footfalls fade. Then, as Elen cleared away the litter of tiny clothes from the windowseat, I lowered myself on to the long padded bench beside her. She picked up her sewing again, deftly plying her needle in the scrap of white fabric. Silence lingered between us for a little longer.

'Are you well, Elen?' I asked at last, to break the uneasy quiet.

'Yes, I thank you, Matthew. Are you?'

Her soft tone was the same as ever. Her face beneath her white netted coif had also returned to its usual calm, her long lashes hiding her eyes as she focused on making minute stitches in the linen.

'Aye,' I said. 'But somewhat perplexed to find you here this morning, helping my mother with her sewing. I thought you were still at my Lady Tyrell's house at Gipping, or perhaps in London.'

A sigh trickled from her lips. Then, threading her needle into the tiny garment, she folded the fabric and put it to one side, before raising her midnight eyes to mine at last.

'I have letters, Matthew, that needed to be brought here. Or rather, those with whom I travelled have them. They are staying at an inn not far from here.'

'What letters?' I could not conceal my surprise at her words.

'From Lord Lovell's wife, and to the Earl of Lincoln from his lady mother. Oh, and also for King Edward from his brother.'

'From Richard? Where is he now?'

She shook her head.

'I don't know. Nor does Lady Tyrell. But somewhere safe, we trust. The letter looks like it passed through many hands to get to us.'

'But why have you come? You say there are others with the letters.'

She glanced down at her now empty fingers.

'I have so missed Alys, Matthew. This is the longest we have ever been apart since we were small children. I knew that somehow she would be with King Edward's army. Though it is no place for a lady.'

I smiled. 'You know her so well. But, still, why – I mean, how—?'

Elen hesitated, toying with a plain gold ring upon one slender finger. She appeared to be sifting her words to select the right ones.

'We knew the army must be landing soon, and that it would make for York. And we heard Tudor was mustering to march north. When Lady Tyrell decided to send messengers, I persuaded her to let me go with them.'

'But why would her ladyship do that? Surely she knew it would be dangerous.'

She lifted her head again. Was there a touch of defiance in the jut of her chin, the black flash of her eye?

'In such times as these,' she replied, 'a lady visiting cousins in York, with two gentlemen to protect her, may perhaps travel more safely than two men alone. If stopped, she may be less likely to be suspected than they – and less likely to be interrogated for any spoken message. We were useful to each other.'

Not for the first time, I admired her courage. It might be quieter than Alys's, but it was as keen.

'So you used the name of someone you knew to be living in York? You presented my family with quite a mystery.'

A blush stained her cheek once more.

'They have been most hospitable – though they had no notion they had any such cousin as me. I have been helping your mother with the little ones and with her mending as some recompense since I arrived.'

She took up her sewing again, and for a while I watched her dark fingers work the needle through the pale linen. What had my father and mother thought when this 'cousin' knocked at their door? Though they were used to encountering foreign merchants from every land known to trade – from the exotic east or the west, from the cold northern realms or the distant south – such men usually did not claim their kinship.

But now I had to turn my mind to more immediate matters.

'Elen, Alys is no longer with the army.'

Her needle stopped its darting.

'Not with you?'

'She disguised herself as a boy to travel with us.'

The shadow of a smile tremored across her lips before it was banished.

'But when Lord Francis discovered her, he insisted she and Roger were left behind at Jervaulx Abbey.

That is thirty miles or more from here.'

Her eyes sought mine again.

'Then what must I do, Matthew? I hear the army will not now come to York. Lord Francis will not welcome another lady on the march. And the messengers, the letters…'

I had no answers for her.

'Let me think about it. And I'll ask Giles. He travelled here with me. He's Lord Francis's man, but he helped Alys and me before.'

The regular thuds of feet running up the wooden stairs struck our ears. They paused at the top, even as our words paused. Then a small face peeked into the room, breathing fast. A wide-eyed, eager face. But one that vanished again, reddening as I caught its eye.

'Come in, Peter,' Elen said, gently. 'It's only Matthew. He will not hurt you.'

The tousled head poked once more around the door jamb.

'Aye, mistress, I know.' My younger brother sidled into the room as though to gain a closer look. 'I recognized him, though it has been so very long since he visited. My mother told me he was here. She says you must now come to the kitchen to break your fast.'

Still sheepish, he backed up his words by beckoning to us. Then he edged from the room again.

Elen and I exchanged a smile, then followed him downstairs, and for a time my worries were forgotten in the warmth and joy of a family reunion.

Father himself did not arrive back from his meeting until more than an hour had passed. When he saw me, he enveloped me in a wordless hug. Then, after having the main details of my story from Peter, Fred, my mother, then Peter again, he ushered me into another chamber for a private talk. He clicked the door shut behind us, then turned to face me.

'You've grown,' he said in his usual gruff manner.

I nodded, without a word.

'It's been a long time since I saw you last. In London.'

'Almost four years, Father.'

'A great deal has happened in that time.'

'Aye.'

More silence. It hung heavily between us like a curtain of smoke.

'We have been discussing your king and his army again in council.'

'Will they change their minds, Father?'

'With Lord Clifford already here and Northumberland on his way? Don't be a fool, boy.'

I flinched at his harsh words, his curtness. But I knew he was right, and I said nothing.

'Had your king but come a year ago,' he carried on, 'our answer would have been different. The appetite for rebellion against the usurper was still strong then.'

'But, Father, he couldn't have. He was recovering from his wounds. It was even thought he might die.'

I cursed myself inside as I said it. I had been part responsible for those wounds, with my delays and failures after the battle. But my father knew none of that. He only knew what was before him now.

'There are many in the city and on the council who support your new king, who have long been faithful to the Yorkists and believe he is who he says he is. But there are others who prefer to believe the lies Tudor puts out – that he claims to be young Warwick. They may know in their hearts he is the true king. But they think few men are rallying to him, and see the wind blowing for Tudor.'

'But our army is many thousand strong.'

'We hear it is mainly Germans and Irish.'

'They are stalwart soldiers, Father,' I protested. 'And there are many true Englishmen with us too. Good Yorkists who came to join us in Dublin, and many who have arrived since. Edward is their king, and York's too. If York declared its support for Edward, surely the wind would turn and blow for him, and other men would rally to us.'

He held me in his gaze for a long moment, then a sigh hissed between his teeth.

'The council must be practical, Matt, and look to the good of all its citizens. We have our livelihoods to think of. We cannot afford to be punished by Tudor as other cities were last year. He has already made his threats clear.'

Silence descended again. It was as though his words were a portcullis that had clanged down between us.

I swallowed, trying to force down a lump that had sprung into my throat.

'Then you condemn your king, Father.'

My father did not speak.

'And – and you condemn me.'

I dragged open the door and stalked away down the passage, past the kitchen from which happy family noises spilled out. My father's voice, raised, followed me.

'You need not go with him, Matthew. Stay here with us. None shall know. You will be safe.'

I stopped. Turned.

He stood in the open doorway, his hand lifted towards me, beseeching. All sound from the kitchen had ceased, and Peter was peering round the door jamb at me.

The sick feeling welled up in me again.

'I have given him my promise, Father. Would you have me betray that?'

18

Farewell to York

I stood outside the shop, gulping in lungfuls of fresh air. Around me the street was abustle with people going about their business, and the cries of street hawkers mingled with the squawking of chickens carried in crates and the rumbling of passing carts. Above it all pealed the bells from the nearby Minster – whether for terce or sext I had no idea.

As I hesitated, uncertain what to do or where to go, the shop bell jangled as the door swung open again. A glance over my shoulder revealed Elen in the doorway, with Fred at her side. Then my name was hollered from among the crowds out in the street.

'Matthew! So this is where you've been hiding yourself.'

Giles and his two brothers were winding their way towards me through the throng.

The last thing I wanted at that moment was to speak to any of them, let alone introduce them each to the others. I shut my eyes tight until lights danced within the lids, as though in hopes I could hide away inside myself. Then I hauled in another deep breath and tried to force a smile on to my face.

It wasn't needed. John and Will were already bowing low to Elen and kissing her hand, before turning to Fred to clasp his in a hearty shake. And John – or was it Will? – was gesturing at Giles.

'This is our unruly youngest brother, Giles. And Giles, this is the brave young lady we told you about. Mistress Elen. And … and her distant cousin, Master Frederick. Young Matt's brother, we believe.'

'Though we are not so certain of that relation,' joked his twin.

So it was all explained. John and Will were the messengers sent by Lady Tyrell, accompanied in their deceit by Elen.

Not for the first time this day, Elen's cheeks were tinged with a deep pink as Giles bent to kiss her hand with a gallant flourish. He then shook Fred's hand before addressing me.

'Matt, we've had news that must change our plans. Is there somewhere private here where we can talk?'

Fred took charge.

'You are welcome to our parlour, gentlemen. It is unoccupied at the moment.' He looked pointedly at me. 'Our father will be going out again soon, once he has taken some ale, or I'm sure he would greet you himself.'

I was reluctant to re-enter. But Fred ushered everyone, myself included, inside, through the shop and back upstairs. The chamber was indeed empty. Our mother was no doubt attending to Father down in the kitchen, with Peter and the younger children still about her.

Once we were all seated in the parlour, with Elen taking up her needlework once more, Giles said,

'We've heard not only that Lord Clifford has brought troops into the city, but the Earl of Northumberland is expected to arrive any moment with several thousand men. Also Lord Scales is advancing with considerable cavalry from the south.'

I sensed Fred's eyes upon me, but I could say nothing. After what had passed between Father and me, I was too bruised to think of what this all meant. In a moment, Giles continued.

'My brothers and I will return to the army. There is little more of use that we can do here, apart from sow a few seeds.' Small smirks brushed the faces of both Will and John, but they did not speak. 'We shall take the letters with us. And, Mistress Elen, we need your message from Lady Tyrell to deliver to his lordship.'

'Should I not take it myself?' Her soft voice trembled with uncertainty.

'It wouldn't be safe for you to travel any further with us,' said one of the twins. 'But we shall encounter no hostile forces between here and the army. The message is no doubt promises of men and support from the southern districts?'

'Yes, but ...' Elen hesitated. 'But Lady Tyrell was unsure of many of them – of whether the promised troops would be ready in time. No one expected King Edward's advance to be so swift.'

'All will be well so long as Tudor and his men are caught out too,' said Giles. He laughed, but the sound was hollow.

'Maybe some, but not others,' warned his brother. 'And it may be that those troops we can raise in such a short time will be outmatched in numbers by those he can.'

'It was always a gamble by his lordship to advance so far so fast without being sure of his support.' His other brother was equally serious.

'If I may have paper and pen,' said Elen, 'I will record all that Lady Tyrell entrusted to me.'

Fred shot up to collect what she needed, placing our mother's sewing table before her to write upon.

'And what of the lady herself?' he asked as he turned again to the three Mallarys. 'She can remain here if she wishes. I'm sure our father will not object.

Elen paused in her writing, her pen poised, her eyes seeking me.

'I would prefer to travel to Jervaulx Abbey, if that is possible.'

'Jervaulx?' said Fred, his eyebrows raised in inquiry. 'Why so? That is quite some way north of here.'

'Her friend ... our friend is there,' I said. 'Alys Langdown.' I explained as quickly as I could.

Fred swung back to Elen and bowed.

'Then I would gladly accompany you there, good cousin. I have several days free.'

'Free?' I echoed. 'But your master never gives you extra holidays.' I remembered well the irascible old bookbinder to whom Fred was apprenticed. Or, at least, to whom he had been apprenticed last time I was home.

Fred's eyes flicked towards me. His face was unreadable.

'I had been due to play the part of Isaac in the Corpus Christi pageant next week,' he said. 'But now, thanks to King Edward's approach, the plays have been cancelled. I can easily escort Mistress Elen to Jervaulx and return before work begins again.'

My heart went out to him, both in gratitude and because he had always longed to have a role in the mystery plays. All the years he'd spent hammering and sawing and slapping paint on the scenery carried by the stage-wagons, and now this chance had been snatched from him.

'Then that is settled,' declared Will – or John – unaware of his sacrifice. 'Our thanks, Fred. We can travel to join the army without concern for my lady's welfare.'

'And Matt?' asked Giles. 'What is your decision?'

'I will travel with you, of course,' I said without an instant's thought. 'When do we ride?'

So it was that, soon after nightfall, having heard trumpets and marching feet in the city through much of the afternoon, Giles, Will, John and I were sneaking out through the river postern to retrace our early morning steps to the woodland where our horses awaited. I had enjoyed a few hours' sleep, followed by a family supper with our 'distant cousin' and our new Northamptonshire friends. I did not speak with my father again in private. But despite our earlier disagreement, as I embraced him in farewell he repeated his oft-spoken words to me on departure: 'There will always be a home here for you, Matthew.' And then he added, 'Keep yourself safe, if you can.'

A clear night with a moon almost half full helped us on our way, as we travelled through the gently rolling country surrounding my home city towards the army's planned encampment at Bramham Moor. Once I twisted in my saddle to gaze back at the twin towers of our mighty Minster, just visible as dark patches against the star-strewn sky. How long would it be before I set eyes on it – and my family – again?

Our journey that night was shorter than the night before and I looked forward to stealing more hours of sleep before the army moved off again in the morning. But not long after we left York, that wish seemed likely to be thwarted.

The first herald of a problem came in the sound of hooves pounding along the lane ahead. We had not seen or heard a soul since the boy who had guarded our horses, let alone anyone travelling at speed through the deserted countryside. Yet here was the growing clamour of a galloping horse.

The three brothers exchanged glances, then Giles thrust out a hand to grasp my rein.

'Off the road, Matt,' he hissed, and kicked his horse's flanks to lead us all into a nearby copse.

We had to duck beneath the lowest branches but soon were deep enough among the trees to hope to remain unobserved. Yet our view of the lane, dappled with moonlight and shadows, allowed us a clear sight of the approaching rider. Crouched low over his mount's neck, he swept past us in a swirling second of thundering hooves, glinting armour and choking dust, and then was gone, the hammering on the hard earth dying again into the distance.

'Clifford's livery?' A Mallary voice from the shadows.

'I think so,' came another. 'Though it was difficult to tell at such speed.'

'I wonder at the need for it. Clifford's men only rode out from the city this afternoon. What message can require such urgency already?'

'Aye.' This from Giles, still with his hand on my rein. 'I think we must take extra care as we ride on.'

Our pace was slower as we set off again. None spoke, each of us straining to listen beyond the dull thudding of our own horses' feet. And such caution proved its value before long. We had just skirted a small hamlet, when another wave of noise rolled towards us. More hoofbeats, and with them the far-off flare of lights across the fields.

A whispered curse in the darkness, then, 'Back to the village. We must find cover.'

A tumbledown barn was a welcome sight as we dashed back along the lane. We slipped down from our saddles and the twins wrenched open the doors, barely clinging to their hinges. We led our horses inside. A stark ribcage of rafters offered little protection from the midnight sky above, but what remained of the walls would shield us from the eyes of anyone passing.

The loud drumming of many hooves drew closer. I peered round the ramshackle door out into the darkness. At first little was visible bar those spangles of flame some way off. Then around a bend in the lane charged a horde of galloping horsemen.

As it thundered towards us, hands grabbed me from behind. I was dragged back and shoved against the wall. In the dim light I could just make out Giles, his finger to his lips. One of his brothers was hoisting himself to the top of a broken-down wall. He crouched there, a dark shadow amid the rafters.

The tumult passed in seconds. In the ensuing hush, a harsh whisper dropped down from above.

'Two dozen or more, some men two upon a horse. Clifford's men, from their livery. They carried a tattered standard. I would say a rout.'

'Are there more?'

'Perhaps. Certainly on foot. There are torches scattered across the fields heading this way.'

'As ever with no thought to the crops.' Giles almost spat the words, quiet though they were. 'That won't make it easy for us to get through.'

'Best to stay put then,' breathed his other brother from the darkness behind us. 'If Will's right and our boys have driven off an attack from that fool Clifford, the army won't be off early in the morning. We can find and follow them at our leisure.'

The three brothers agreed. My opinion wasn't sought. I was simply told to rest while they took turns to watch from atop the half-ruined wall.

A pile of hay in a corner of the barn offered a soft mattress, as well as supper for our horses. But sleep stayed far from me that night.

Instead I lay there, wakeful in the dark, listening to the normal night noises. The soft hooting of an owl overhead, the rustlings and scurryings of rats in the hay, the shifting from hoof to hoof of our slumbering mounts, the deep breathing of two sleeping Mallarys. And, from time to time, different sounds. The clip-clop of lone horses upon the track, the faint jingle of harness, the heavy tramping of dozens of marching feet. Calls from one man to another, curses and complaints too. Then, later, fewer, leaden footfalls, and shuffling, uncertain steps. Muffled scraping of weights being dragged, the moans and pitiful whimpers of wounded men. Sometimes the darkness was disturbed by the flicker of torches or the sliding shadows cast by moving lamps. All – noises and lights – passed, on one side of the barn or another, moving towards the village.

Except in one terrifying moment.

Scuffling footsteps on hardened dirt. Hesitation. Creeping closer. A scratch of rough skin on wood, the creak of a hinge.

Heavy breathing in the darkness.

Mine?

My body tensed, ready for flight.

The scrape of a blade being drawn. Thud of feet landing from a height.

A muffled cry cut off. A gurgling, choking, dying away.

Silent darkness.

A sickly sweet scent I had smelled before, seeping towards me.

Then the scuff of something heavy pulled away, a thump as it was dropped.

Leather boots, fingernails, grazing a stone wall. A shadow looming against rafters and star-spangled sky.

Silence again.

I lay awake until the stars dwindled, the sky faded to grey, the first chirruping of the birds. Giles nudged to rouse me. As we resaddled our horses and crept from the barn, I took care to look nowhere but in front of me and out into the new-awakening day.

19

'The Bloodiest Battle'

We caught up with our army not long after it broke camp close to the small town of Tadcaster. Lord Francis welcomed Will and John as old friends, their brother Robert grunted his greeting, and Giles gave our report to their lordships while riding alongside.

The mood of the royal party was buoyant despite our indifferent news. After Edward and their lordships received their various letters and Giles told of what happened overnight – save the fate of one lone straggler – we learned the Mallarys' guess was correct. Lord Clifford's troops had indeed mounted an attack, on a company sent to seek provisions in the town. But after a violent skirmish, they been put to flight once soldiers from the main army had arrived. Several men had been killed, but all on Clifford's side.

'So what you saw was their retreat back to York,' said Lord Francis.

'With their tails firmly between their legs,' Sir Thomas added, grinning.

'And let us hope that is a good omen,' finished the earl. A cheer rose from the men riding about us.

Lord Francis's good humour was dulled somewhat as he read Elen's letter. I knew what it contained, of course – or believed I did – about likely additions of troops as we journeyed south. So, after his early frown, I was surprised to see a smile ghost across his lips. He plucked from within the folded paper a smaller note, handing it to Giles.

'Please give that to Matthew,' he said. 'It seems he has a correspondent too.'

Giles's arched eyebrow and teasing air as he passed it to me sparked more flames in my face. I caught sight of 'For Matthew Wansford', penned in Elen's neat handwriting, before I thrust the paper deep in my pouch. As so often, I cursed my weakness in blushing. I had no wish for Giles or anyone else to suspect an intrigue between Elen and me.

We had not been riding very long with the army when the royal party broke away, turning on to a lane running down towards a wide, slow-flowing beck. Not far from its banks, among rough pastureland, stood a stone chapel. Its walls were solidly constructed, while its windows gaped, glassless, and above, only rafters outlined its roof.

I shivered despite the warmth of the day, remembering a similar skeleton stark against a darker sky. This building, though, appeared half-built, not half-ruined, its timbers new wood, not shattered by age.

Their lordships swung down from their horses, the gentlemen following suit. Edward remained in his saddle. As I lowered myself to the ground, Lord Francis walked towards us.

'Come, Edward,' he said in his quiet tones, resting his hand upon Storm's neck. 'Here is the place we told you of. The chapel to commemorate your father's great victory here and the soldiers who died that day.'

'But it is unfinished.'

'Sadly, yes. It was only begun once your uncle Richard became king.'

'But he didn't fight here, did he?' Edward's brow puckered in puzzlement. 'Surely he was only a boy when my father won his crown.'

'Aye,' agreed Lord Francis. 'But he knew it was important to honour those who fought here, as well as celebrate your father's achievement. He had many of their bodies moved here for reburial. Perhaps you will decide to pay for its completion. But now, will you come to pay your respects?'

'Between this and my promise to the abbot of Jervaulx, my treasury will be half gone as soon as I reclaim it.'

His face expressionless, his movements reluctant, Edward dismounted. Throwing Storm's rein to me to hold, he followed their lordships.

Lord Scrope's chaplain and the clerics who had accompanied us from Dublin led the gentlemen into the roofless building, carrying aloft a processional crucifix. The morning sun glinted off its rich gilt and jewels, and I was transported back, unbidden, to another chapel, also open to the sky. That day on the headland in Ireland. The mist, the babbling crone. Edward's mesmerized state. Her warning.

I held back, did not follow them inside. Sent up my prayers for the dead and the forgotten here, outside the holy building. Stood watching the rooks wheeling, circling, about their nests in the nearby trees, cawing to one another in their lazy voices. Tried to rid my mind of those evil memories. Here in this place of the dead.

Giles sauntered over, leaving his brothers chatting quietly with other gentlemen who remained outside. He halted beside me, his arms folded, as his gaze also wandered about the surrounding fields.

'Twenty thousand men died that day.' His words splintered my reverie. 'The bloodiest battle ever fought on English soil, they say. Old King Edward's crown was costly won. Let's hope his son does not have to pay so dear.'

I swallowed. 'We have only seven or eight thousand in our army.'

'Give or take.' He did not look at me, but reached out a hand to grip my shoulder. Had he detected a tremor in my voice? 'Though it appears we have one man less since last night.'

'One less? A deserter? But one will make no difference either way.'

'It might to you, lad. Robert tells me your friend Hugh Soulsby could not be found when the army regrouped this morning.'

'Hugh?' I had done my best to avoid him on our

journey, indeed had tried not even to think of him since my mishap on the Sands. 'But where's he gone?'

He shrugged. 'Who knows? Who cares? He was part of the troop sent to aid the foraging party last night, and then he disappeared.'

'But his men? Or, rather, his uncle's men?'

'Still with the army – to a man. Robert said their captain was happy to see the back of Hugh. Good riddance I say too.'

He patted me on the shoulder again, then returned to his brothers, leaving me to think over this revelation. Yet I had little time to digest it before the congregation emerged from the chapel, returning to their horses. Edward's face was sombre as he joined me. He seemed in no hurry to remount and, beyond him, both Lord Francis and Earl John were still standing too, tearing open the letters the Mallary twins had brought.

Edward was staring out across the countryside as I had earlier. But he was looking back more than weeks – indeed, rather more than twenty-five years, to a time long before his birth.

'So this is where my father fought his first great battle. And by his victory claimed the throne.'

He fell silent, into memories that were not his own. Some minutes passed before he spoke again.

'He was only eighteen, little more than a year older than I am now. I wonder if I—?'

Silence once more.

With a jolt I recalled another king telling me of a first battle when he was just eighteen. As I stood beside him, like this, one morning, awaiting a different clash of armies.

I shook away the memory.

'He was a great man, my father,' Edward went on, oblivious. 'A great warrior. He often told me of his battles. He even acted them out with my brother and me, any time I was with my family in London. He had servants playing the battle formations of old mad King Harry, or Queen

Margaret or his cousin Warwick. And he would laugh and say England would not see battles like that again, not while he was king. How I wish he still lived!'

The yearning in his voice – yearning for a time long lost, never to be regained – tugged at my heart. How many others here – and far from here – would also wish for that time to return?

'Sometimes I think he is the only person who didn't betray me.' His voice was plaintive, as when first I met him, all those years ago, at the time of which he now spoke. 'My mother fled to sanctuary when he died rather than stand by my side. My uncle Rivers and brother Grey, with their schemes and ambushes, seeking to grab power. My uncle Gloucester, stealing my throne. The royal council, my uncle Buckingham – conspiring with him. Even my sister Elizabeth. Marrying the usurper and giving him an heir.'

I said nothing in their defence. Long and painful experience had taught me there was no point when he was in this mood. I could only listen and wait.

'And then I remember he did not marry my mother. Not properly. Not even when his first wife was dead. He could have chosen to then. In secret again, if he wished. Known only to God and the priest. Why didn't he? Then my brother and I would not have been—'

He choked at the word, could not utter it.

This was not a matter I could speak on. So I stayed silent, and let his thoughts turn, as turn they did.

'My brother. Dickon. Perhaps he alone has not betrayed me.' A tight smile, and he glanced at me for the first time. 'And you, Matt, and Alys and Roger. And your loyal hounds. You have all stuck by me, and I thank you for that.'

'And Lord Francis and your cousin the earl,' I reminded him. 'Sir Thomas and Lord Kildare. Duchess Margaret too. They are loyal to you. Their presence here – this whole campaign – proves that.'

'Aye.' His blue eyes were pensive as they gazed

again at the fields and the trees and the still-circling rooks. 'To me, perhaps. Or maybe only to my name, our family. I suppose, when you are king, it can be difficult to separate the two. If I should fail—'

'Edward!' I cried, but he waved my protest aside.

'If our attempt should fail, and I with it, will the same attempt be made for Dickon instead? I am just the present heir to the Plantagenets, to our crown. Will they be just as loyal to the next, and do as much for him?'

Those words were unanswerable too. But they nudged me to say, 'Your letter from your brother. Have you read it?'

A smile of genuine pleasure flitted on to his face.

'I have. In the chapel. When the service began to bore me. He writes of all the wonders he has seen and the fun he is having. Though he is careful not to say where he is – or with whom. Although I suspect our cousin George may be with him, from some of the scrapes he hints at. Perhaps we should have had a code – like yours and Alys's. Then he could have told me everything.'

That notion prompted a recollection for him too.

'And have you read your letter, Matt? The one Francis gave you.'

There was no edge to his question, only curiosity. But my cheeks flushed once more.

To hide my embarrassment, I rummaged in my pouch for the note. As I unfolded it, a scrap of paper slipped from within and fluttered to the ground. I picked it up, telling him as evenly as I could, 'It's from Elen. Though what she has to write to me about when I met her only yesterday, I don't know.'

I glanced down at the flattened-out note, with its trails of elegant writing, then at the smaller fragment held lightly between my fingertips. This letter within a letter – if such it was – had no marks of any sort upon the outside, save a small flat seal of whitish wax.

Elen's brief note began:

Fgct Ocvvjgy
Vgnn Gfyctf, yjgp zqw jcxg vjg ejcpeg, vjcv jku ukuvgt
Gnkbcdgvj jcu ytkvvgp vq og. Ujg ucau ujg nqxgu jko...

'It's just half a dozen lines, all in code,' I said to Edward. 'She must have written it while we were still making plans. Though I didn't see her consulting a cipher.'

Edward gestured to where the rest of the company were still unmounted. Lord Francis, Earl John and the Mallarys were deep in discussion with Lord Scrope and his brother, Thomas.

'It looks like you'll have time to decode it, if you wish.'

I fished out my cipher and set to. Elen had not dated her message, but I knew, of course, that yesterday had been Sunday – the last before Corpus Christi. In a few minutes I translated the whole missive. To my surprise – and Edward's when I shared it with him – it read:

Tell Edward, when you have the chance, that his sister Elizabeth has written to me. She says she loves him and longs to see him again, and that their father would have been proud of him. She prays that he will stay safe, whatever comes. And she asks that you give him this note if you should be able.

Her only other words were,

You take care and stay safe, too, Matthew.
Your good friend always,
Elen

Edward's smile returned. He accepted the scrap of paper I offered and his deft fingers snapped the seal. As he opened the note, he said,

'So, my sister is still faithful too. There are more

numbered in that party than I calculated. Do not heed my bitter words earlier, Matt. You know me well by now – how I am blown this way and that by the wind. I know I have much to be thankful for and to look forward to. I hope it will not be long before I meet with my family again – or you with yours.'

His eyes flicked down to the paper he held. They ran along the lines written there, once, perhaps twice. Then he drew a hand across his face, as though weary, before crumpling the note up and tucking it in his pouch.

He did not look at me again. Without another word, he took Storm's rein from my hand and swung himself into the fine-tooled saddle. All about us other gentlemen were doing likewise. The Lords Scrope embraced Lord Francis, then made their way over to Edward. Doffing their caps, they bowed to him, each swarthy face beaming.

'Farewell, Your Grace. We ride to reap the crop sown by our young Northamptonshire friends. We will join you again when we can. God speed.'

Their words were a mystery to me. If Edward knew more, he did not show it, only returning their farewell with a silent bow of his head. In moments the royal company was trotting on to rejoin the army, its tail end visible not far ahead as we regained the great highway. My Lords Scrope and their retinues turned away to canter north, back towards my home city.

Soon my curiosity about their plans and about Edward's note was banished. My thoughts now were all about what lay ahead for us.

We were travelling due south again. Towards – who knew what?

20

Storm Clouds Gather

A strange hush settled over everything. Only the piercing song of a wren in the trees behind punctured the silence. Then a tumbling of sweet notes drew my eyes upwards to the cloudless sky. A lark was soaring high above, a dark speck against the blue, uncaring of anything happening below. All other sound and movement around me had ceased now, though from time to time a horse shifted on its hooves or tossed its head, scraping the dry earth or jingling a harness.

All appeared ready at last. All were waiting, all were watching.

Down the sweeping slope before us, beyond the far-off road, I could see movement still. The dawn breeze had veered to the south and now wafted muted noises towards our position. The faint tramp, tramp of marching feet, the tinny blare of trumpets. The masses of men and horses were advancing towards the road like the gathering of black clouds at the approach of a storm, darkening the bright fields of midsummer crops. Most came from the west, but some also from the east, cutting us off from the tall spires of Newark, a few miles distant.

I swallowed. The gulp was deafening to me, but none around me heard. All their ears and eyes were on the tempest massing below. Countless men, and beasts, and wagons, and cannons. Never before had I seen so many.

Save once. Another early morning like this, when I had stood atop a church tower and watched two immense armies assemble. Facing one another across a place called Redemore Plain. Yet then I had myself been far away, a spectator only.

Now I sat upon Caesar, heavy with unaccustomed armour, a sword sheathed at my side. Close to my king and his courageous knights.

Once I had dreamed of this. Once, when I was so very young. Now it was no dream. It resembled more a nightmare.

Eager to escape my fear, I cast my gaze one way, then another.

At the forefront of our company was Edward, erect aboard Storm. He was staring straight ahead, stony-faced. Sunlight gleamed on his finely worked Flemish armour and on his golden circlet, worn again upon his helmet. His deep red and blue surcoat dazzled with the leopards courant and fleurs-de-lys of the royal arms alongside a sparkling sun in splendour. A gilded belt was looped about his waist, from which his father's sword hung in its jewelled sheath. At his other hip was a cruel-edged battle axe.

To either side of him were Lord Francis and Earl John, equally finely attired, their warhorses also encased in bright-burnished armour overhung with trappings of murrey and blue. Lord Francis's mailed fists were tight about his reins, and the deep-etched lines upon his face were visible even in the shadow of his raised visor. Earl John's eyes were roving, hawk-like, about the scene unfolding before us, one gauntleted hand resting upon his sword hilt.

Behind all three, their huge multi-coloured standards streamed proudly in the stiff breeze. The oaken staffs were clamped in the sturdy grip of the standard bearers, each astride his mighty stallion. And about this heart of the army clustered the remainder of the royal party – lords, gentlemen, squires, the Mallary brothers and me.

And I felt myself an imposter of the worst kind. As I sat there, atop an aged, borrowed warhorse. Clad in polished plate mail lent me by a duchess's assistant armourer from among his stores, refashioned to fit my small frame by a pirate-blacksmith at a makeshift forge in the half-ruined castle of Dublin. A disgraced choir boy, dismissed page, never-made-squire, failed messenger (several times over now, for more than one master), afraid of battle and unfit to be a soldier. What right had I to be there amidst the valiant knights of an anointed king?

A rider on a compact bay horse cantered towards us, tearing into my musing. He halted in front of Edward, lifting his visor and bowing.

'Your Grace.' Captain Schwartz's guttural voice was unmistakable in the quiet. 'Your army is arrayed. We await your signal.'

Beyond him, stretching the full length of the ridge before the royal party, overlooking the road and the gathering storm clouds, were ranged a multitude of men. Edward's loyal troops. Mounted or on foot, bristling with pikestaffs, halberds, handguns and longbows. Bunched together round the scattered standards of their lords and masters. Patiently awaiting their commands.

These were the soldiers we'd travelled with across the sea from Flanders and from Dublin. Who had joined us at Piel, Swarth Moor, Cartmel and a score of places since. Who had trudged across the Sands, and marched through Garsdale and Wensleydale, and down the Great North Road. Who, last evening, had forded the wide and shallow River Trent, and camped upon its banks and in the fields about the nearby village, knowing what awaited them this morning. Who, in Irish, Flemish, French, German, English, had pledged to serve their masters loyally. As had I.

Their numbers had been swelled again over recent days, as we rode south from the battlefield chapel at Towton, making slower but steady progress along the great highway. Everywhere we were joined by more men, on foot or on horse, heavily armoured or only lightly equipped, clutching longbow or crossbow, pike or battle axe, sword or mace.

Our spirits rose with every new arrival. Edward's moroseness at the chapel melted away and he did not speak to me again of betrayal or disappointments. I rode beside him each day, witnessing his pride in the army that flocked to him. Then, late in the evenings, after all work was done, he listened contentedly to whatever tunes I could muster on my harp. Perhaps he had been thinking less of Alys, or perhaps more of when he would meet her again once this journey was done. But he did not speak of her. And so neither did I. Though she – and Roger, Elen and Fred – were often in my thoughts.

After the victorious skirmish at Tadcaster, those days also brought small triumphs. When our scouts came across a company of knights under Lord Scales, far in advance of Tudor's slowly mustering army, and our own advance cavalry had driven them off. And then, when the company had regrouped, our men put them once more to flight. When news came that the two Lords Scrope had joined with many local men – sown seeds bearing fruit – to assail one of York's great gateways, forcing the Earl of Northumberland – then on our tail with four thousand men – to return to defend the city. When my home city declared its support for King Edward, and Northumberland had wisely retreated to his manors far to the north, rather than continue south to join Tudor and risk leaving the city in his rear. And when Lord Scales and his knights were beaten once again and fled still further south. Each messenger who brought such news was welcomed with joy and a reward of coin.

Then scouts returned with news of Tudor's forces gathering around Nottingham and Newark, and further west and further east. But also then messengers arrived from Edward's supporters in the south. Their way was now blocked, they said. They couldn't get through the Tudor lines. They could not harry him from the rear as they were so few. They would join us when they could, once we broke through. Lord Francis's lips would tighten, but Earl John's smile didn't fade, and his buoyancy carried Edward with him.

Finally, after our crossing of the river, as we camped close to the squat grey-stone church of the small village of Stoke, a last messenger arrived. I had been summoned to attend Edward in the royal tent where their lordships were holding a council of war. The news from deserters and scouts alike had made clear the enemy was close – so close a meeting of the two armies must be inevitable. Giles had said, over supper, 'Tomorrow – unless Tudor turns tail and runs at the speed of our advance, like Lord Scales.' But his jest rang hollow.

On my way to the tent, I was overtaken by men-at-arms, escorting an unarmed but armoured gentleman. Upon his surcoat the red Tudor dragon breathed fire on a green field, and his mailed fist clutched a letter. As I ducked inside the tent flaps after him, he had already removed his helm.

Edward was seated in his great carved chair, beneath the royal standard, draped from the tent's rafters. His jewelled coronet encircled his fair hair. As ever, Earl John and Lord Francis stood one to either hand, sentinels both. The foremost lords and captains of the army were grouped about them, hands resting lightly on the pommels of their swords, observing, silent, like crows waiting as the ploughman slices the soil.

The new arrival bowed to Earl John.

'My lord of Lincoln, His Grace King Henry has sent me with a letter for you.' He stepped forward and proffered the square of parchment. Its shiny red seal glinted in the light of brands dotted about the tent.

Earl John did not stretch out a hand to take it.

'I believe, sir, your message is for my beloved cousin, His Grace King Edward the Fifth, King of England and France, and Lord of Ireland.' With an elegant wave, he indicated Edward.

Tudor's messenger cast a glance towards the seated figure, before turning back to the earl.

'Indeed not, my lord. My liege recognizes no one of that name. My message is only for John, Earl of Lincoln.' He thrust the letter towards him once more. 'My lord, my master King Henry urges you to surrender yourself to his mercy, and assures you he will be lenient.'

Edward and Earl John both drew themselves up at his words. For perhaps the first time, I was struck by the close resemblance of these cousins – both tall in stature, fair of hair, eyes reflecting the torchlight with an ice-blue glitter, square chins jutting with pride. But now, elder deferred to younger – earl to king.

My lord of Lincoln made way for his cousin, gracefully bending his head to him. Edward rose to his feet, then waited a moment in silence, eyes steady upon the visitor. The man shuffled the letter from one hand to another, fidgeting upon his feet. Finally Edward spoke, his words measured.

'I bear you no ill will for your master's disrespect, sir. Hand your message to our squire there.' To my surprise, he pointed at me, lurking in the shadows near the entrance. 'My men will find you food and drink, if you will await our response.'

The messenger hesitated, before bowing first to Earl John, then, after a heartbeat, to Edward. His eyes sought me out, then he pushed the parchment into my waiting hands and retreated through the tent flap.

When he had gone, Earl John seized the letter from me and broke it open. He read briefly, before tossing it on the table in front of Edward. Lord Francis stepped forward to pick it up.

'The usurper offers me a pardon if I throw myself on his mercy,' said the earl, his voice cool.

'And he does not speak of Edward?' asked Lord Francis, eyes scanning the parchment.

'Nor of you.' Earl John shook his head. 'He seeks to divide us at the last. Perhaps our suspicions are correct. That we have come upon him so fast he is not ready to meet us. He gambles on my accepting him, and our forces splitting and melting away before he has to engage with us.'

'If that is so – and the deserters suggest it is – then this is our best time to strike.' Edward's words were more like a question.

Lord Francis, as ever, was cautious.

'Perhaps. But our scouts believe his forces already outnumber our own by some way – even if they are not fully assembled and prepared. If we do strike tomorrow, we will be taking an immense risk.'

'Maybe,' returned Earl John. 'But will there be another opportunity?'

The other gentlemen, who had remained silent until this moment, all began to speak at once, clustering around Edward. As always, Sir Thomas Fitzgerald's powerful brogue rose above all others, although Lord Scrope's robust tones almost matched him as he threw his pennyworth across the hubbub.

After some moments of chaos, Lord Francis had raised both his hands and his own voice.

'Gentlemen, gentlemen, pray hold your peace. I believe it is for our young king to decide on our course of action.'

Edward waited while the commotion subsided. Then, clearing his throat, he spoke to the one man in the room who had not joined in.

'Captain Schwartz, what is your view of our position?'

The German had been ready with his answer.

'We have many very good troops among our army, Your Grace. Others are less so. And we have fewer of both than I would wish. But kingdoms have been won by men with fewer. By Henry Tudor himself, I believe.' Earl John inclined his head to him in assent. 'And he did not have my Germans about him with their trusty pikes and handguns, or these gallant gentlemen here.'

Bows were made all round.

'I have walked the terrain hereabouts,' Captain Schwartz continued, 'and we will command a strong position on the ridge. It overlooks the old roadway where Tudor's forces must assemble. The sun will not be against us until late in the morning, the wind perhaps for us. It is not an unfavourable situation. Those who have read

Madame de Pizan may agree.'

My perusal in Mechelen of that celebrated lady's book on battle strategy led me to nod without thinking. The warmth of a blush crept up on me at the idea any of the gentlemen might see the gesture, but I was back in the shadows, so surely was safe.

Edward had also inclined his head. His own face flickered pale in the light of the guttering torches, but his voice was firm as he said, 'Then we shall tell Tudor that we reject his offer. Matthew? You must write our refusal.'

Startled, I had clutched at my pen and ink bottle, and hurried over to the table where parchment awaited me. Captain Schwartz and the other gentlemen moved away to discuss plans while Edward dictated to me. As he finished the letter, brief but full of defiance, and took hold of my quill to sign it, Lord Francis spoke quietly.

'Edward, are you sure? It is not too late to change your mind. None will call you coward if you choose not to fight.'

Edward completed his signature with a flourish, handing the pen back to me, then reached for the length of wax to seal the reply. As he held it to the candle flame, he said,

'I am a crowned and anointed king, Francis. I will not flee. I will not be king of nowhere.'

The memory of those words uttered long before, on the headland overlooking Dublin, stabbed at me and I dropped my quill and bottle of ink at the shock. The bottle's stopper broke as it struck the tabletop and ink oozed darkly on to the wood before I could stem its flow. I mopped it up as best I could with my kerchief. The black stain seeped into the clean white linen like blood soaking through a bandage.

Edward hardly noticed my confusion. He was gazing up at Lord Francis.

'And you, Francis? Are you sure? Tudor has not offered you a pardon like John.'

'Not this time, no. I had my chance two years ago,

after your uncle died at his hand. The usurper sent messages to me in sanctuary. He would have had me deny my oath of loyalty, then bow to him and kiss his hand.'

'You spurned him? Then made an attempt on his life in York? No wonder he does not look upon you kindly now.'

'And nor should he. I'm here to finish what I started then. I mean to avenge Richard.'

His words circled now in my head as I sat atop Caesar, surveying the massing armies. My mailed hand crept to my chest. A faint ringing arose as the metal gauntlet brushed against the badge pinned to my surcoat. I glanced down, my movement stiff in my weighty gear. The silver boar gleamed against the blue fabric, like the brightest star on the velvet of an early evening sky. Did it tell the story of why I too was here?

Down the long slope in front of us, beyond the road, all movement had now ceased among the enemy troops strung out in either direction. Our companies were also standing to attention as their commanders strode among them or rode before them, encouraging them, urging them to strive to their utmost on this day. Edward had visited the camps at daybreak and walked among the men as they assembled, speaking with individual soldiers, laughing with them, taking a little of their bread and ale, to show himself to them. I knew he would have eaten little, that he dared not attempt a rousing speech now before them all, in case his voice should falter – that, as before his coronation, his insides and mind will have been churning all this morning. As were mine. His face was calm now as he sat upon Storm, but I suspected it was a mask only, a shield for the turmoil within.

'Have the spotters spied Tudor?'

Lord Francis's question rang out in the quiet.

'Nay,' Sir Thomas replied, a grin lighting up his helmet-shadowed face. 'He'll be leaving the real fighting to my lord of Oxford there in the vanguard. No doubt the usurper is sheltering behind his mother's skirts or watching from a church tower somewhere.'

Laughter rose from all the troops within earshot.

'Perhaps he's learnt from his past mistake,' declared Earl John. 'When King Richard came so close to killing him, although he cowered behind his bodyguard to the rear of his army. Gentlemen, what say you? Does a true king hide himself away like that? Or does he show himself upon the field of battle?'

The response was deafening. Soldiers all around shouted, 'King Edward, King Edward!' and 'A York, a York!', or hollered wordlessly and clashed their weapons and stamped their feet. And from the German troops, stationed to both sides of us, rolled the hammering of drums and the high-pitched piping of their fifes. The clamour and thunder unfurled along our battle lines until our whole world shook.

Then, and only then, did movement below catch my eye. Far down the slope, the first lines of the enemy were stealing forward. They crept towards, then across, the ancient roadway. What had appeared little more than grey banks of cloud now could be seen as row upon row of men, sunlight sparking pinpoints of silver off armour and pikes, bright colours reflecting from huge flowing standards. Trumpet blasts whipped towards us on the breeze, accompanied by the tramping of hundreds, maybe many thousands, of booted feet.

My chest tightened, my breathing almost ceased. I saw Edward raise his hand, shining steel against the glowing blue of the summer sky.

21

The Advance

A moment of stillness.

Above us, the uncaring lark still soared, its sweet song spiralling down from the heights. A breath of breeze feathered my cheek, carrying with it scents of meadows in flower. Caesar's black-tipped ears twitched, one way, then another, prickled by the tension in the air.

Then Edward brought his arm down with a sharp chop, as though it were an axe or the brutal downswing of a sword, and all stillness was banished.

Our own trumpets blared. To our rear, the colossal cracks of cannon obliterated the birdsong, followed instantly by heart-stopping blasts that struck deep within my chest. Then all about us hundreds of bowstrings sang, the arrows soaring across the sky towards the distant army. Men in those far-off shadowy lines fell, scythed down, but still the grey mass stole forwards, and our cannons' crashing and archers' shooting were echoed and answered. Red flames spat far beyond the enemy lines, and across and up the slope sped a black hail of lead balls and goosefeathers. All fell far short of where I stood, but many must have hit their mark. From the foremost ranks of our men tore screams and cries the like of which I had never before heard and pray never to hear again.

Cannon boomed once more, and the sharp retorts of the Germans' handguns ripped the air. I heard the creaking of crossbows cranked back and shot, warlike, blood-curdling shouts and shrieks swirling all around. The acrid stench of gunpowder drifted to my nostrils, lay grittily on my tongue.

Down the slope, not so far now, the dark storm clouds rolled on, on, edging forward, wreathed now in smoke from their own guns. Flashes as of lightning flared, thunder roared, and their rain of shot and arrows rushed up towards us, even as ours poured down upon them.

As the tempest crept nearer, nearer, the men at its heart were revealed more clearly, the companies of armoured riders on its flanks, the jewelled banners flying aloft. Upon one reared a huge boar, not the pure shining white of my master King Richard, but a tawdry blue. I had seen it before, once carried into battle, then in peeling paint on a tavern sign. I knew it was the symbol of the Earl of Oxford – he who had led the army for Tudor on that fateful day two summers before. And beyond it now marched, through the fog spewed by the guns, more waves of soldiers, of cavalry, of standards – sprawling off into the grey, mist-shrouded distance.

How many thousands were mustered against us? They seemed beyond numbering, like sand grains upon a beach or ants within their colony, scrambling over one another to get to us. And every one bristled with weapons.

A wave of horror and nausea rushed over me, as though I were peering over the parapet of a lofty building. More cracks from our cannons thudded against my chest, and I clutched at Caesar's mane and rein to stop myself toppling. Giles manouevred his horse beside me and stretched out a hand to grasp my steel-clad arm.

'Steady, lad.' I saw him mouth the words, inaudible above the racket. A smile too.

I tried to return it but managed no more than a grimace. Had Giles witnessed this before? He had never spoken of it in my hearing. Yet he appeared calm. As did his brothers alongside him. All three were seated steady on their mounts, watchful, waiting for orders, never flinching at the cannons' blasts. And all the lords and gentlemen too. Messengers would scurry or canter up from all directions, bow, doff their sallets or touch their caps, bellow their reports. Their lordships conferred, agreed, responded, signalled to and dismissed the men to their commanders, conferred again, eyes ever alert to all that was about them. Once Sir Thomas guffawed, swigged long from his leather water bottle as though quaffing fine wine at a feast, then kicked his horse to follow the messenger, being swallowed up by the rows of troops in an instant. Lords Francis and John exchanged a glance across Edward – who stared still straight ahead, his open helmet revealing his stone-still face.

The cacophony continued, with the enemy stealing ever closer. No matter what torrents of arrows, bolts, shot we sent their way, they seemed unstoppable. What was it I had heard from the grizzled old soldier viewing the battle with me two years before? The sky is black with arrows. Men, comrades, fall alongside you, in front. Still you have to move on, clamber over bodies, slipping in blood and broken flesh. Was that how it was for the enemy soldiers I could see, still advancing over their comrades who had fallen? And how about the men in our own front lines? Standing waiting, watching, maybe struck by the rain of arrows, the hail of cannon balls. Seeing, hearing their companions falling, perhaps even dying beside them.

How did they bear it?

A lull in our firing. We had few cannons, I knew, hauled with us all the way from Piel, and little shot. Tudor's cannons continued their distant rumble, and our handguns cracked and bows twanged in response, among the shouted orders and cries of the troops. But in the relative quiet, Sir Thomas returned to the royal party, with Captain Schwartz cantering at his side. They reined their horses to a halt in front of Edward and their lordships. Neither doffed his helm this time, or even bowed.

'Your Grace, your lordships.' Sir Thomas's voice rang clear above the battle noise. 'We cannot be waiting any longer. We must advance the army to meet them.'

Edward looked towards Sir Thomas's companion. 'Do you agree, Captain Schwartz? Is it the right time?'

The captain bowed his head. 'Aye, Your Grace, it is.'

Earl John urged his horse a pace forward, towards the two men.

'But we must not advance too soon, gentlemen. We have the high ground still. It is not ideal to move—'

'Not ideal, no,' Captain Schwartz interrupted, neglecting his usual politeness. 'But little here is ideal – we know that. And it is not ideal that my men – and yours – are being injured, dying, without any defence. My Germans cannot use their pikes, their halberds, from a hundred, two hundred paces distant. No matter whether we have the high ground or not. We must engage.'

'We're giving Oxford's archers and cannon too good a target here,' agreed Sir Thomas. 'We soon will have no army left to hold the high ground if we do not engage.'

Earl John swung his horse around to face Edward and Lord Francis. Beneath the raised visor of his burnished helm, I could see his iron-strong profile, the blue eyes of his family frost-touched and hard. So different to the gallant, elegant aristocrat I had come to know before this morning.

'We shall keep the heavy cavalry in reserve. But with your permission, Edward …' He left the words hanging.

Edward glanced once at Lord Francis, who nodded without speaking.

'Then, Captain Schwartz, Sir Thomas, ready your men for the advance.'

Cheers rose from those troops close enough to hear his command.

Sir Thomas, with his usual broad grin, set his spurs to his horse and disappeared among the close-packed groups of men. Captain Schwartz drew his sword and saluted Edward with a flourish before cantering off in the other direction. Other lords and gentlemen from the royal party – the doughty old knights Sir Henry Bodrugan and Sir Thomas Broughton and both Lords Scrope among them – also made their bows and rode off to join their men, standard bearers trotting in their wake.

Messengers carried on scurrying here and there

between the companies of soldiers. The whole body of men in front of us and so far to either side became a seething mass of movement, like a huge beast slowly awakening and stretching. Arrows and shot still flew, both from our army and into it, and sharp retorts and spurts of smoke rose from the handgunners. But now the pipers piped and the drummers drummed all the harder, the tall gleaming spikes of halberds and pikes stabbed upwards among the foremost ranks, and more and more banners lifted, proud, above the soldiers. Yellow, blue, sea green, blood red – all rippled against the azure sky as they caught the breeze.

Earl John, eyes running across the frantic activity, must at last have spied the signs he awaited. He leant to speak to Edward, who once again raised his arm aloft.

No stillness this time. No birdsong soaring above the never-ceasing thunder of Tudor's cannon or our own gunners. As Edward's gauntlet flashed earthwards, trumpets blasted all around, shouts arose from many hundreds of mouths, fifes shrilled, drums pounded, the thumping march of thousands of booted feet began.

The beast was on the move.

22

'Arise Sir Matthew Wansford'

My breath caught in my throat. The sights and sounds stirred me, but terrified me too. That these many thousands of men were marching down the slope of the field towards the wave upon wave of soldiers marching up, and in minutes only, they would crash together, intending to kill, knowing they could be killed.

And all for the whims and desires of two men – one barely more than a boy, younger even than I.

I watched fascinated, unable to tear my eyes away. The cheers and fanfares and bobbing forwards of the glistening steel of the foremost pikes and flags told me the front lines were already on the march, yet it was an age before the soldiers towards the rear took their first steps. Only then did I see with my own eyes those men with whom I had sailed and ridden, laughed and joked, broken bread and drunk ale, sung and prayed over the weeks, hitching their gear upon their backs, hefting their weapons – whether axe or sword, javelin or pikestaff – and marching towards … what? Their destiny? Ours? Certainly many were marching to their deaths.

Enclosed within their metal gauntlets, my fingers gripped Caesar's reins, even while I fought to hide my emotions. No one must see my fear, my dread. The relentless beat of the guns, the drums and the marching feet hammered in my head and at my chest, echoing, driving the beat of my heart. Terror clutched at me from all sides.

What would happen next? How would the coming minutes, hours play out? What would be my fate – and that of my companions here on the ridge?

None of their lordships spoke now. Earl John had wheeled his horse about, taking his place beside Edward again, he and Lord Francis like protective standing stones, one either side of their king. Sitting upright upon Storm, his own fists tight upon the fluttering murrey and blue trappings of the reins, Edward's face was wan, but set, obstinacy carved deeply on it as so often. All eyes marked the advance of our army under the continuing onslaught of the enemy's shot and arrows.

As the troops moved onwards, like the ocean tide rolling back down a beach, dark scraps, as of driftwood or jetsam, were left behind on the churned-up grass. Only as scores of figures flooded on to the field from behind us and both sides did I realize what those scraps were. Bodies – of dead and wounded men – together with their gear, left high and dry as the rest of the army passed over them. The hurrying figures were campfollowers, many women, some children, who had also travelled with us over the days and weeks. They now searched among the debris littering the ground. Where they found life, they clustered together and carried the man from the field. Where there was death, they moved on to the next – perhaps with a bag, a weapon, food, coin, a keepsake, whatever they could gather.

My stomach roiled again and I tore my eyes away. All around us, companies of heavily armed and armoured horsemen had remained behind as the footsoldiers moved on. They regrouped now about the royal party, several hundred men and horses in all, waiting and watching what was happening further down the slope.

Slowly, so slowly, as though time were shuddering to a stop, the waves of soldiers were drawing closer to one another. Our cannon had now fallen silent, but Tudor's were still firing, though many balls whistled over the heads of our army. They smashed into the ground beyond, scattering the scurrying campfollowers. His archers altered their sights more easily and more bodies were left stranded as our army moved on.

Then, as I watched, either time speeded up again or our men did. Were the soldiers in the front ranks breaking into a run? Could they now see the faces of the men further down the hill? Was there fear in those English eyes at what approached them from above? The arrow-sharp tips of pikes wielded by the fearless Germans – on staffs twice the height of a man? The razor-honed heads of the mighty halberds? The steel-tipped javelins of the Irish – thrown at and deep within your chest before you even saw them coming? Did the fearsome war cries and wordless roaring of this onrushing tide strike terror into their very hearts?

Like the turbulence where two fast-flowing rivers meet, the two armies finally burst together. Though hundreds of paces distant, the mighty clash of weapons and bellowing of our men was ear-splitting. Only in my mind's eye could I see the brutal downhill charge of our iron-clad wall of warriors, their wicked blades raised ready to spear and spit all who stood in their way. But the shrill screams and shrieks told all.

Our vantage point on the ridge, I knew, gave the best view of the battle – better by far than any to be had by Tudor's generals far down the slope behind the action. Yet to my eyes all was chaos. Just a shifting, plunging jumble of men, dark against the green-brown fields. Here and there, sparks of sunlight flew from polished helm or upraised axe, midnight blue or sunshine yellow silk revealed a standard held aloft, and riders of horses the colour of beaten copper or palest grey slashed their bloody way through companies of earth-bound footsoldiers. But mostly it resembled the nameless, faceless fury of a storm-racked ocean. Grey, turbulent, eddying seas. Thunderous, tumultuous, black-as-pitch clouds. A violent, chaotic tempest, tossing our stomachs, fears and emotions this way and that, with no light breaking upon the horizon and no apparent end in sight.

Messengers and spotters still scuttled to and fro. Campfollowers still darted about the debris-strewn landscape. Rank upon rank of shadowy troops still moved up towards the ancient roadway to bolster the force fighting under the rippling blue boar banner. And still my insides churned at the slaughter playing out in front of us. Every glint upon a falling blade was a brutal blow or stab, every scream a man or horse injured or worse. Each surge or eddy within the heaving crush of men was a small victory for some lord or gentleman, his men clustering, breathless but fierce, triumphant about his standard. Yet, in seconds, all could change, as other lords or gentlemen charged, and that small victory turned to a defeat, a rout, carnage.

But who could tell? Not I – sitting astride Caesar, aghast at all that unfolded before me. I had no clue how one side or the other was faring in this immense struggle. Other, more experienced eyes must tell. And yet ... and yet, even I could see the relentless, never-ending march of reinforcements to our enemy.

A flurry of horse and rider galloping up the slope from the rear of the battle lines. Skittering to a stop before Edward. The rider bowing, his surcoat torn, bloody, muddied. Raising his visor. Revealed – Robert Mallary, his breath coming fast.

I had not even seen him leave. Giles, beside me still, was leaning forward to hear his report. His brothers Will, John, beyond, did likewise.

'Your Grace, Captain Schwartz reports our charge almost broke through Oxford's lines. But his men are now sorely pressed. The Irish have fought bravely, but they are ill-equipped for such fighting as it now is. Sir Henry Bodrugan has fallen, and no news is to be had of my lord of Kildare. Captain Schwartz begs your further orders.'

Earl John rattled off questions. Lord Francis interjected one or two. But between them, still seated upon Storm, Edward remained quiet. I suspected my face mirrored what I could see of his – ashen, hollow-eyed. That bluff Sir Henry was no more, and that laughing, good-humoured Sir Thomas might also be dead ... these were thoughts I did not wish to dwell upon.

'With Lord Scales's cavalry on their right flank,' Earl John was saying as I shoved my attention back, 'we would perhaps be wise to focus our attack there. At worst, it will compel Oxford to wheel his troops about to face us and take the pressure off our main force. At best—'

'At best,' put in Lord Francis, 'Scales will recall how you and your men beat him back all through Yorkshire. He may be put to flight again, right into Oxford's men.'

Cheers and jeers greeted his words, though his own face was serious.

'We can but hope,' said Earl John with a grim smile. 'If Tudor's main force is made up of the poor troops our scouts suggest, any retreat by Scales and Oxford might well put them to flight too. Beyond them, Lord Stanley's men form the rear guard. Who knows what his response would be to such a rout?'

'Ever waiting to see which way the wind of battle blows,' said Lord Francis, a bitter tinge to his voice.

'He might then throw in his lot with Edward,' returned Earl John, 'and we could crush Tudor's force between us. It is a gamble for us to ride into the attack, of course, but we did not hear from Soulsby that he and Stanley would not join us. And Soulsby's northern troops are still within our ranks.'

'Aye,' said Lord Francis. 'And have acquitted themselves well fighting in our vanguard, Robert says.'

Their words took me back to that night on Swarth Moor, when Hugh had brought his uncle's message, and to the troop of his men who had joined us at Cartmel. Was it possible that he – and Lord Stanley – would prove loyal to Edward and turn traitor to Tudor after all?

'And if we cannot turn the flank,' said Earl John, 'at least the way to Newark would be open to us. It might offer a chance to retreat and regroup.'

'For what purpose?' Edward's voice broke into their urgent discussion. Clear and strong though it was, did I sense a tremor beneath? 'What use is it to retreat?'

Their lordships both turned to face him. Lord Francis raised his hand, but did not reach out.

'Edward, do not make the same mistake as your uncle. It is possible to withdraw and fight another day, as he could have two years ago.'

I winced at the mention of King Richard, knowing all too well Edward's customary response to his name. But he did not look at Lord Francis. His gaze was fixed on the fray before us.

'My uncle, Lord Lovell? Usually you implore me not to repeat my father's mistakes. But this time – my uncle?'

'Your father made a wise decision to withdraw from Doncaster,' replied Lord Francis. 'He returned with an army that won at Barnet and Tewkesbury.'

'Indeed, my lord. But if we do not prevail here, who now will come to our aid?' Edward's face and voice were bleak. 'This surely is our last chance … my last chance. I will not have others die on my behalf and not fight and take the risk alongside them.'

Their lordships were struck silent. Far down the slope, the battle raged on.

Was it my imagination, or was the great tangle of men and horses closer now? Were our troops being driven back a little? Here and there, odd straggling figures were running from the rear, fleeing towards the village, or away from it. As I watched, horsemen broke from the melee too and, pursuing the lone runners, hacked them to the ground.

I pulled my eyes from the sight as Robert's gruff voice rose above the tumult again.

'Begging your lordships' pardons, but whatever your decision, it would be best to make it soon – or the chance may pass.'

Lord Francis glanced at him, then back at Edward and Earl John. Neither spoke, but the earl nodded.

'Then so be it,' said Lord Francis. 'We roll the dice. Your father would be proud of you, Edward – as I am proud to ride with you.'

In his eyes shone a fierce light I had never seen before. He and Earl John turned their mounts about, spurring them towards the company of riders at our backs. All was a-bustle again, with squires and messengers scurrying about, horses being led forward, lances and war helms handed up to riders, and above it all the voices of their lordships raised in command as they addressed the gathered knights.

Edward himself did not stir, staring still at what awaited us.

I urged Caesar forward a few paces to stand beside him. He did not turn to me, but, stretching out, slapped Storm on the neck.

'This is a very good horse, Matt,' he said, gazing ever ahead. 'He has carried me well so far. Please thank your friend Elen for acquiring him for me.'

His remembering her service at a time like this amazed me – as did the gentleness of his tone.

'You can thank her yourself when you meet her at court,' I replied, uncertain what else to say.

Edward looked at me then, his familiar taut smile upon his lips. Then he drew his sword. The curlicue inscription on the blade stood out, dark against the sunlit steel, like fine-inked script on the costliest parchment.

'When all this is over,' he said, 'I think I shall knight you, Matt. For all your good service to me. And you shall arise Sir Matthew Wansford.'

Somewhat awkwardly, he leaned towards me and tapped his sword tip, first on one shoulder, then the other, then again on the first. The metallic tap, tap, tap on the armour beneath my surcoat sounded oddly dull in my ears.

'Then you will be a fit companion for me. And for my ladies Alys and Elen.'

Was he serious? There was no time to wonder. Squires were hurrying up with lances and he had sheathed his sword and flipped down his visor before I had a chance to study his expression. He reached down to accept a lance, hefting it with the ease of long practice in the tiltyard. I had viewed his successes often during our stay in Mechelen.

I shook my head to refuse the lance offered me, drawing my sword instead. For all Edward's promise of impending knighthood, I had never been made even squire before, so had never handled any weapon other than a sword and a bow.

My mouth was suddenly dry as I tried to swallow. Ranks of full-armoured horsemen were lining up in front of us, and Lord Francis and Earl John took their places again to either side of Edward. As I pulled Caesar back into position to their rear, Giles Mallary kicked his horse alongside. He thrust an open leather bottle into my awkward fist.

'Drink. It may be some time before you have the chance again.'

I tipped the bottle up, its mouth hard between my lips. Cool clear water trickled into my tight, parched throat. But I felt little relief, as I handed the bottle back. Giles stoppered it, stowing it in a saddlebag. Then he smiled, though it was only a grim shadow of his usual expression.

'Stick with us on the charge, lad.'

His twin brothers loomed beyond him, saluting me with their lances and identical grins.

'We'll see you through if we can,' said Will. Or perhaps John.

All three snapped their visors closed, hiding their reassurances.

I followed their lead. In an instant, everything was even less familiar. The slit in the visor narrowed my world, darkened it, smothered it.

A shouted command, muffled by the metal encasing my head. Then another.

A moment of stillness once all were gathered.

Edward raised his hand and let it fall once more. Then, with a last blast of the trumpets, we were on the move.

Slowly, slowly at first, then quickening our pace as the riders in front began to pull away down the long slope. From all sides the Plantagenet battle cry rang out, as it had for Edward's father, uncle, grandfather before him – 'A York, a York!'

Caesar tossed his head as he ran. I hung on tight to the reins, fighting to keep control, scared he would break into a full gallop and outpace the Mallarys, speeding alongside me, or even cannon into Storm. The grey stallion was racing ahead of me now, his sleek haunches gleaming golden-white in the bright sunlight as he carried his rider towards the fray. Edward blazed in his red and blue surcoat and shining-silver armour, his lance clenched in his gauntleted fist, levelled straight at what lay ahead.

How I clung on to Caesar with one hand and my knees only, and stayed upright, my sword thrust out before me, I knew not. But somehow, somehow, as this great body of horsemen thundered down towards its enemy, I was carried with it. Dirt kicked up by other horses dinned as it struck my helm, the wind of our speed buffeted me, the pounding of a thousand hooves assaulted my ears. But somehow, somehow, I stayed on.

The boiling whirlpool of the two mingled armies was coming nearer, growing immense as we sped towards it. The ringing of weapons, the blare of trumpets, the roars and screams of men, the squeals of their mounts, became deafening. Directly ahead was a vast tangle of horses, their riders struggling to haul them round to face us, standards flapping, mangled bodies upon the ground. A great groan arose as if from one throat, then our foremost knights were among them – with an uproar of clashes, clanging, thuds, a chaos of hacking, slashing, slicing, shrieking.

Caesar's speed – a gallop now – careered me into this terrifying, baffling morass in a second. A rider clad in green and yellow, surprise scrawled across his face, loomed before me and I flailed at him with my sword. Did I hit him? I knew not – so confused did all become. But I forged on through the muddle of men and horses, striking out with my sword where I could, ducking to avoid others' blows, unheeding when my sword arm jarred as it met with metal, leather, flesh, bone.

Nothing in my training at Middleham had prepared me for this – no footwork, no feints, no chivalric salutes. Nothing perhaps save the animal terror, the fear of pain, the horror when facing an opponent much larger, more brutal, with intent to kill, to maim, in his eyes.

But the training – or was it instinct? – of my horse helped. He seemed to sense when a threat was close, and would twist and turn with little prompting from me, presenting the smallest target possible to an opponent, but allowing me to strike – before carrying me on, picking his way across bodies and past other horses and men, fighting mounted or on foot upon the ground.

In this way, somehow, we survived and kept going. Until, somehow, the heaving, surging mass of men and horses was behind us.

I dragged Caesar about, gasping to catch breath, my aching arm with its red-stained sword hanging loose at my side. We were on the edge of the fighting now, and perhaps, again, could see a little of what was happening.

I had long ago lost sight of Edward and Giles. Will and John too, and their lordships. Were they even still alive in there?

Scanning the melee, shielding my eyes with my gauntlet, I caught a flash of sun's rays upon a distant standard. Edward's was still raised, at least. Other banners were aloft too, but I could not identify them. I had no time. Of a sudden, the turmoil was about me again. Mostly it was men upon the ground, unhorsed or footsoldiers. Many were fighting, but some were running – away up the slope or to the east. There the squat tower of the village church rose above trees – much closer now than I had thought. Had the battle shifted so much since our charge? That way lay the Newark road. If the fight had been pushed in that direction, our attack had not forced its way through, but had been ... repelled. Had the tide of the battle turned once more?

Men soon surrounded me again – of which army I

could not tell. I could no longer spy the telltale signs, the colours, the liveries – all mired in blood and filth. None took notice of me. Some were fighting still, but now many more were running. The horsemen closest to me engaged with one another no more, but were pursuing those on foot – the easier target. Several runners were hacked down, their cries shrill in my ears despite my sound-muffling helmet.

An icy chill sluiced through me but, reminding myself of my duty, I swung Caesar's head back towards the fray. Yet now it was like swimming against a river's current. I could not force my way back, was swept off in the flow of teeming, screaming humanity. And my mount's size was no help. Soldiers blindly struck out at all around them with axe or dagger, trying to shove a way through, uncaring of hooves kicking out or a bloodied sword raining blows down at them.

Fighting to avoid them, Caesar twisted about and about, whinnying frantically, no matter how I fought to regain control. Then, with one final exhausted effort, I wrenched his head around. But there behind us a giant warhorse was rearing up. I had not observed its approach in the tumult. I caught a glimpse of blue and white upon the rider's surcoat as I thrust my sword wildly up towards him. A shudder ran the length of my arm. Had I struck home?

The huge horse reared again, lashing out with its hooves. I saw sunlight glancing off a raised mace as it scythed towards me, felt a colossal clout upon the side of my helm.

Then I was slipping from the saddle.

And falling.

Falling.

All the breath whooshed from my body as I hit the ground.

I lay there, face in the dirt, waves of nausea, pain, blackness rising to smother me.

Caesar, panicked, was cantering off, swerving

round knots of men slicing and slashing still.

Then a tremendous jangle shattered in my ears, a crushing weight crashed upon me, and, sinking into the swirling darkness in my head, I knew nothing more …

23

Playing Dead?

… until … until … a nudge, a whimper. A moist warm touch on my cheek.

I tried to brush it away. Found I could not raise my hand. Whirls of black and grey spinning in my head, a muffling rush of noise. Swimming upwards from the dark comforting depths of oblivion. Breaking the surface. Ambushed by searing pain.

My head heavy with pain. Heavy with cold hardness pressing against my scalp.

Warm salt blood trickling across my lips.

My eyes flickered open, reluctant. Inches away a glistening nose poked towards me. A shaggy brown face. Whiskers. Grinning mouth with pink lolling tongue. A single bright-black eye, puckered scarred skin where the other should have been.

Another whimper.

The dog or me?

Red, blue, white spangles rippling across my sight and nausea rising. But I forced my eyes to stay open.

Where was I? What was happening?

The dog nuzzled my face again, then disappeared. Claws rang on metal, scraped on leather. Pawing. At my waist.

My pouch. Home to the tidbits I always carried. Once for Murrey, then for Shadow, Belle.

I tried to fish one out now for this dog. But still my hand wouldn't move. Numb. Trapped beneath me. As I lay face down.

My legs too. Heavy, metal-laden. Wouldn't budge.

Why? Why couldn't I move?

Armour. It struck me now. I was wearing armour. A helm upon my head. Sharp edges of metal close to my eyes. Hand immobile in its steel gauntlet. Legs weighed down.

Yet once I could move in armour. Couldn't I? As I walked, mounted, rode. But now …

Something else.

Weight pinning down my whole body. My other arm also useless. Up behind my head. I could feel it, but could not even wiggle a finger.

But now the numbness was ebbing. Now, as I struggled to move, soreness seeped in – to fingers, to arms, to legs, to torso. Stinging, smarting, aching. Throbbing beneath my bruised skin. Bone-deep pain. Sharp skewering pain. Battered, immovable, my body shrieked.

But I must not panic, must not shriek aloud.

I breathed in slowly. My chest was cramped in its iron casing. I let the air trickle out, breathed in again.

Straining my neck muscles, I craned my head up. Half an inch, then an inch off the ground. Pains stabbed, brilliant lights shot through my eyes, forced me back down. But I had looked. And I saw.

Saw, lying across me, a huge armoured figure. Scarlet soaking his blue and white surcoat. Pooling, darkening, beneath us on the dry earth.

Everything flashed back. The battle, the screams, the blood. The loss perhaps of Edward, Giles, their lordships. My terror in those last moments. The man I had killed.

I closed my eyes against it all. Against the fear, the horror, the death. But the pictures and screams swirled still in my head. I could not hide in darkness.

Yet I tried. I had no strength, could barely move, could not push the dead weight from me. If I lay still, perhaps I could be sucked back down. Into the seething, eddying depths. Into unconsciousness. Perhaps escape the pain, the horror.

I lay motionless. Eyelids tight shut. Dazed mind drifting. Sounds oozing in.

From above, the cawing of crows circling. The

breeze sighing in tree tops recalling the restless waves of the Celtic Sea. The shouts and calls of men, some distant, then some closer. The clatter of horses' hooves. The creak and rumble of wagons. A blood-freezing screech cut short.

And I knew what I would see if I could raise my head. Soldiers, campfollowers, scavengers. Roaming the battlefield. Searching for the living, stripping the dead of valuables.

What would happen when I was found? Alive, but unable to move. Clad in armour most men could not afford with a year's wages, maybe even a whole lifetime's.

Would I be able to bargain my way out alive?

Another scream. Closer this time.

I tried to swallow. But the inside of my mouth was dry, scratchy. Like ancient leather. The tip of my tongue rasped as it ran across my lips. Then I felt slobber on my cheek, my nose. The dog licking me once more.

As I screwed up my face at the touch, the clip-clop of horses approached from beyond my head. Several voices talking.

I froze. Not that I could move much. But even the wrinkling of my nose could give me away.

I remembered the old soldier I had met. Who played dead when lying wounded on the battlefield at Barnet and had survived to witness King Richard's final battle years later. Would the same work for me? Or should I call out and place my trust in God that these people would be friends?

I opened my eyes a crack. I could see little beyond the long brown nose and shining watchful eye of the dog, now staring down at me. Just the rising expanse of grass, littered here and there with far-off dark figures, some lying, some moving about slowly. The blow to my head must have forced my visor partway up. The shape of the window opened allowed me to see only what lay straight ahead. It would perhaps be best for the moment to wait, and hope the newcomers did not slide a blade into my body before checking I was alive.

The clopping of hooves came nearer. Three or four horses at least. They halted just a few feet from me, though I could see nothing of them. But their riders' voices I now heard clearly. The first, a dry, nasal voice. A hint of French accent tingeing its words.

'They must be found. I must know they are dead.'

The second voice, deeper, older. Bringing with it a memory of the north.

'They will be, Your Grace. All the troops have orders not to strip the corpses until Lincoln and the others have been found.'

I flinched at the name. Then prayed this tiny movement would not betray me.

I need not have worried. The first man just laughed, though it was a grim enough sound.

'I doubt these men's discipline will be that good.'

'The order is upon pain of death, Your Grace.' The second voice again. 'Now the battle is won, the men understand we don't need them any longer and will not hesitate to punish them.'

Just in time I stifled a groan, as if at a fierce blow.

The battle had been won. But not by our side if these men were seeking Earl John. Was he indeed lying dead, somewhere on the battlefield, waiting to be found? And what of the others?

Yet, even in my anguish, a further thought struggled in my head. Who was this man who was so eager to find them, this man who must be addressed with such respect? 'Your Grace'? Had there been a duke among Tudor's army? I racked my sore, fuzzy brain, but could recall none being mentioned. Lords there were a plenty, an earl or two. But none of these would be called 'Your Grace'.

But the speakers allowed no time for more thinking. The next name uttered by the thin voice of the unknown lord threw all into further confusion.

'And is this the boy you told me of, Soulsby?'

'Aye, Your Grace. My nephew here brought him

down from Jervaulx as you ordered.'

Soulsby? Despite the warmth of the sun on my face, inside me ran rivers of ice. This gruff northern voice belonged to none other than Lord Soulsby? And he spoke of his nephew. Did that mean Hugh was also here?

My eyelids squeezed shut before I could stop them. Waves of cold terror welled up within me until I feared I would choke. Were it not for the dead man weighing me down, surely the convulsion would have given me away. Then another thought leapt. What boy? Yet the full horror of my predicament dawned with the first speaker's next words, like light piercing through fog.

'Bring him here. If he's as alike as you say, Soulsby, you shall receive a fine reward. You will have served your king well.'

His king? Could this unseen man really be . . . Henry Tudor?

'Your Grace, Your Grace!'

Shouts from away beyond my feet.

'What is it?' Soulsby's voice, raised.

Many, hurrying feet. Grating of metal, heavy dragging sounds.

'Sire, we have them!'

'At last!' The first voice, triumphant.

My eyes fluttered open as the shuffling, scuffling noises drew close.

The dog had turned, fur bristling, towards the sounds. Though its ragged form obscured half my eyeline, just yards beyond I could see several soldiers in grey and green livery. They were half-shoving, half-dragging two men. One could barely set one foot before another. He fell to his knees, slumped forward, head down, as the group halted. The other walked, stiffly, stumbling, but upright. One gauntleted hand held his other arm, which hung awkwardly by his side as though broken. Both wore surcoats soaked with blood. Yet through the deep red blotches and the haziness of my view, the familiar symbols stood out.

'Remove their helmets,' commanded Lord Soulsy.

The soldiers grappled for some moments with buckles and straps, though neither captive resisted. Moans escaped from both before first one helm, then the next, was set aside to reveal –

'So – my lord of Lincoln. And—'

The nasal voice was interrupted by Soulsby.

'And Lambert Simnel, Your Grace.'

'Ah, yes. So it is. Of course. That was the name we chose, wasn't it, Soulsby? Master Simnel. Like the grain, or the cake.' A dark, hollow laugh. 'I see your resemblance to your father. A miller of Oxford, is he not? Or was it a carpenter?'

Though my vision blurred and shifted, I saw Edward's white but bloodied face held high, his eyes flashing his defiance.

'My father was true King of England. As am I.'

That laugh again.

'So you seem to believe, boy – or you would not have dared wear the royal arms or fly the royal standard.' The voice sharpened. 'But there is only one king here, and we would have you kneel to him. As I see my lord of Lincoln already has.'

The soldiers obediently took their cue from this. They guffawed loudly at the lame joke, those with hands on Edward trying to force him to his knees too.

But Edward's strength still held. He wrenched himself from their grasp and took a step forward to stand beside Earl John, placing his good hand on his cousin's armoured shoulder. The effort sent a spasm of pain across his face. Yet he stood firm as the earl tentatively reached up to grasp his hand, pulling upon it to heave himself with difficulty to his feet. Soon both Earl John's boots were planted upon the ground, albeit very unsteadily. More bright blood gushed beneath the arm he raised to Edward's shoulder, as his cousin turned back to face the hidden riders.

'Neither the Earl of Lincoln nor I, Edward

Plantagenet, shall kneel to a usurper.'

No one who had known the late King Edward could have mistaken these two young men as anything but his kin. They were so alike. Tall and fair, blue of eye, open of face, royal of bearing – for all they were battered and bruised and broken of head and limb. All the blood and mud and filth upon them could not hide their royal blood. And the soldiers about them knew it and stood back silent now.

The horses beyond my sight shifted upon their hooves. A muttered curse and the twitch of a whip sounded as though one of the riders was impatient with his mount. Then the first voice – was it truly Henry Tudor? – snapped, 'Where is that traitor, Francis Lovell? I know he was behind all this.'

A shadow flickered across Edward's hollowed eyes.

'Viscount Lovell is dead. I saw him fall. In the thickest press of the fighting. He was a brave man, and no traitor. He was loyal to his king.'

'Unto death this time, it seems.' Once again, the mirthless laugh. 'He did not flee the battlefield this day, unlike before.'

Earl John's mailed fist tightened on Edward's shoulder and a grimace passed across his begrimed face.

'Francis was loyal to us, as he was to our uncle.' His words were slow and slurred. But did I detect anger beneath them – echoing that rising within my own heart? 'He fought alongside Richard until there was no hope. To stay on the field thereafter would have been suicide, with your murderous thugs slaughtering all who remained alive. As I see they are doing here today.'

'And suicide is a mortal sin, punishable by all the torments of Hell.' A sneer touched the man's voice. 'Hah! I would have found torments aplenty in this life for him if he had lived. He was a thorn in my side too long. But no more. A pity though. As you say, he was a brave man and true. I would have valued his service once. He had his chance to serve me, yet spurned my pardon. I had hoped then he would swear his oath to a true king. As you did yourself then, John, when I first claimed my crown.'

Following the words was not easy through the pain and nausea throbbing and rushing in my head. But the speaker's tone had changed. A little warmer, perhaps. Almost a plea within it?

But Earl John's response was wintry.

'My uncle Richard was the true king. Parliament decreed it.'

'Ah, but not God, I think,' came the reply. 'Or he would not have willed my victory.'

The earl's eyes shifted to one side, as though looking at someone else.

'Perhaps not. But I always believed that victory was due more to treachery than to any plan of God's. Today has been no different.'

Gathering himself, he spat towards the unseen horsemen. The effort racked him with coughing and doubled him over in pain. He sank again to his knees, a burst of fresh blood flowering upon his surcoat. Edward knelt beside him, cradling his upper body.

Lord Soulsby's voice growled out above the anguished sounds.

'It will be a mercy to dispose of him here, Your Grace. He'll not survive to be interrogated off the field. We'll get nothing out of him – no matter what methods we might use.'

'Did his thrust hit too close to home, Soulsby? For you and Stanley both perhaps.' Tudor's words were waspish. Then, once Earl John's spasm subsided, he continued, 'But yes, we must move on. We have a great victory to celebrate. Yet not before we tell these two what we have planned. Where is the boy?'

The noise of a horse urged forward, then the thuds of two sets of boots hitting the ground. A muttered 'Go on!' and into my dazed line of sight moved two figures. One, the larger, held back a little, while propelling the other, far smaller, forward. The first was Hugh Soulsby, but the second sparked my astonishment. It was the young servant boy from Jervaulx Abbey. John Broom.

He stood in front of Hugh, trembling. Pasty-faced and eyes wide in bewilderment, he was staring at the two lords kneeling upon the dirt before him. He appeared younger even than before, in this stark sunlight rather than the soft glow of church candles, but his strong resemblance to Edward struck me again.

'Yes.' The word was breathed out in satisfaction. 'He is very like. You have done well, Soulsby.'

'Thank you, sire. It was my nephew who spotted him.'

Hugh stepped smartly forward and bowed. Even through the swirling of my vision, I could see his broad face flushed with pleasure at the praise.

'The boy has no family.' Lord Soulsby again. 'He will not be missed. The friars will no doubt think he has simply run away.'

'Good. Now turn and face me, boy.'

When the lad didn't move, Hugh grabbed him by the shoulders and shoved him towards the riders. John stumbled and fell headlong upon the ground towards where I lay. The sudden movement spooked the dog, still lurking beside me. It crouched and snarled defensively against the imagined threat. In one smooth motion, Hugh stooped, scooped up a stone and threw it at the dog. It yelped once as the missile struck home, then limped off out of my sight.

Hugh dragged the boy back to his feet, facing the horsemen.

'What was that?'

'Just a mangy cur, Your Grace,' he said, bowing again. 'It's run off now. Nothing to worry about.'

My breathing had stopped dead at the flurry of movement. Now I had to fight not to haul a deep, shuddering breath back into my lungs, to counter the nausea that surged through me. For a split second I had believed that all was lost. That Hugh would see me lying there, eyes open. That even the faintest of movements would give me away. But the dog's protective action had saved me, even as it had been injured itself. Hugh paid no more heed to me than he now did to the dog that had fled.

'Has his lordship told you of your fate, boy?'

John was gazing up at the speaker, his mouth agape, shivering again in his terror.

'My f-f-fate, my lord?' he said at last, at a nudge from Hugh.

'What shall happen to you. Where you shall be going.' Tudor's voice was impatient.

'N-n-no, my lord.'

'Be not so afraid. It is nothing bad. Unless you yourself are bad, and do not do as you are told. Pay attention to what I say and to Lord Soulsby here, and you shall not be harmed.'

'Y-y-yes, my lord.' The boy didn't sound convinced, but Tudor carried on, raising his voice a little so all those gathered about could hear.

'Your name is Lambert Simnel, boy. You are the son of a carpenter from Oxford. But these wicked men here told you you were Edward, Earl of Warwick. They placed a crown upon your head, then forced you to lead an army against me, your rightful king.'

The boy was staring up at him still, his eyes stretched wide.

'But, but, my lord, my name is John, not L – Lam—'

'Silence!' roared Lord Soulsby. The boy tottered backwards into High's waiting grip, buffeted by the force of the word. Tudor continued as if there had been no interruption.

'From now on your name is Lambert. I have forgiven you your sins. And I shall be generous in my forgiveness. You shall return to London with us. There, all will see just who you are and how you are sorry for what these men forced you to do. I shall reward you with a job, perhaps in my royal kitchens. And if you do well and as you are told, maybe you will rise far in my service.'

John was struck dumb at all he was being told. But beyond him, Edward raised his head from tending to Earl John.

'Lambert Simnel?' he said. 'But—'

'But what?' Tudor's voice was sharp again. 'You thought you were Lambert Simnel perhaps? Oh no, that moment has passed. You are no one. Nor will ever be. None here will even remember you existed – on pain of death.'

The soldiers who had dragged Edward and Earl John to this place snapped to attention, exchanging glances amongst themselves.

'We shall allow a kindness to your cousin of Lincoln. For his past service to us. We shall say he died of his wounds, having fought bravely for the imposter – perhaps aiming ultimately to seize the crown for himself. It will be a comfort – and a warning – to his father and his family. But you—'

Edward struggled to rise to his feet to protest, but the soldiers, having lost their earlier sense of awe, forced him back down. Earl John's head now lolled, eyes half closed, against his bloodied chest.

'But you – you have no name, and no family. None shall miss you or mourn you or say masses for you. And young Lambert here—' John Broom had turned at the scuffle and was gazing now at Edward, their blue eyes almost on a level, 'young Lambert will see what happens to you and never forget it, lest it happen also to him.'

Edward tried to wrench himself from the men's grasp to lunge towards the riders, but he was held fast. His face was livid white as his eyes flared up at Tudor.

'And what will you tell your wife – my sister Elizabeth?'

'Never fear. She will never know it was you. She will only know this boy – the imposter put up so Lincoln could claim the throne for himself.'

'There is still my brother.'

'Your brother Richard? He is but a boy.' The scorn burnt like acid through the maelstrom in my head. 'We shall find him and deal with him. He will have no support after this. He will not trouble my kingdom.'

Though on his knees at this man's mercy, and no longer struggling to be free, Edward held his head up straight. My vision was still wavering, yet I could see that he did not. His chin lifted, his mouth was set firm, and his eyes blazed in defiance.

'So I see that, at the end, you do kneel to your rightful king,' sneered Tudor. 'Soulsby, finish it. Then strip them and bury them on the battlefield, a last insult to them.'

A click of the tongue and a jingle of harness, and Tudor must have twitched his horse around to trot away.

Before me swirled John's face, white with shock, and Hugh's, pale too as he jostled the boy to one side. The dark shadow and scuffle of a great horse urged forward, a burly knight upon its back.

A curt command – 'Bare their necks.'

Soldiers' arms wresting the cousins apart.

The earl slumping, Edward pushed forward.

The upward flash of steel.

My gorge rose and my head swam and my eyes closed themselves tight as I lost my senses once more. But I knew the horror of what I saw and heard in that final instant would stay with me through all the rest of my life.

24

Aftermath

The hum was like the buzzing of a fly on a hot summer's day. Insistent, urgent. Blundering through the muffled roaring in my head.

'Matt? Matt?'

A cool touch upon my cheek.

A gentle whimpering. Me? Or that dog again? But speaking? And my name?

I eased my eyes open a crack. A shadow loomed above me, cutting out half the brightness of the blue sky. I blinked to clear my sight, heard a cry of happiness.

'It is Matt! And he's alive! Oh, Alys!'

A second shadow loomed.

'Well done. But – alive he may be, but is he all there? Does he know us?'

I tried to speak, but barely a croak emerged. My head pounded again and my eyes closed against the pain.

'I don't know. He needs water.'

'We must move this body off him if we're to help. And find out if he's wounded. Fetch Roger and Fred. And get that dog out of the way.'

A shoo. A soft warning growl.

'Oh, just leave it, Elen. It's not hurting him. Get the others.'

A few moments passed, then came the scuffling of feet, confused words, a scraping of metal on metal, a rolling and a thump. And the great heaviness that had been pinning me to the ground was gone. Cool air forced its way into my lungs at last. I choked at the rush, gagged, felt pain shoot through me again.

'Turn him gently and take his helmet off.' A deeper voice. 'Where's the water?'

Hands upon me, moving me on to my back.

Fingers fumbling at my neck, sliding beneath my head. The vicious metal eased from me, smarting, stinging where it left its touch. Then my head laid gently back, propped on softness. Something hard thrust against my lips, my teeth. Cool liquid slopped upon my tongue.

I opened my mouth wider, gulped eagerly.

'Easy, Matt.' The man's voice again. Familiar? 'Just sip it at first. Till we know where your wounds are.'

'Head,' I mumbled. 'Shoulder, I think. Where am I?'

'On the battlefield, of course.' Alys's voice.

I knew that.

'No, I mean …' What did I mean? 'Battlefield?'

As I rasped out the word, all the horrors of the day flooded back.

The waiting, the cannon roars, the death screams, the advance.

Sir Henry, Sir Thomas.

The desperate charge. My bloodied sword.

Edward, Earl John. Lord Francis.

My head twisted to the side and I vomited with a violence I had never known before.

The sour taste dragged me back to the present. More water was put to my lips and I gulped it again to wash the foulness away. Then I opened my eyes.

Immediately above me, Elen's face, dark against the bright sky. My head was pillowed on her lap. My brother Fred offering the water bottle, eyes full of concern. The tip of his longbow jutted above his shoulder, where it was slung across his back. Standing, Alys, her hands upon her hips, staring down. At her side, Roger.

'How long …?' My words less of a croak.

'Have you been here?' finished Fred. 'Not so very long. We arrived after the battle turned into a rout. We've been searching for you since it's been safe to do so.'

Elen's face twisted. 'We hardly hoped to find you. In all this—'

Her words choked to a halt.

Alys knelt down beside me, pushing something to one side. A whine of protest. The dog again. And for all her impatience, Alys abandoned her attempt to be rid of it and was absently stroking its bristly head as she said,

'What happened, Matt? Can you tell us?'

So I did tell them, as briefly as I could, the words catching in my mouth at both dryness and fearful memory. I sipped more water. Saw the horror grow on their faces. Then I reached the last, when I had first come to, lying pinned down on the battlefield. My voice broke, once, twice, then again, as I told them how it ended.

Sobs dropped down from Elen. Alys's hands flew to her mouth. Roger lurched off to one side and sounds of retching assailed our ears.

Fred's face turned sickly white.

'He had them executed?' he said quietly.

I nodded, and pain shot through my temples. Elen dabbed again with the damp cloth she had been holding against my head, even as a tear fell from her eye.

'I can't believe it.' Alys's anguished voice broke through as the pain settled. 'Surely even Tudor is not such a monster.'

Roger hove back into view. He was wiping his white-rimmed mouth with a kerchief.

'There's a fresh mound of earth over there.' He gestured back the way he had come. 'Just the one. He didn't even have the decency to give them separate graves. Just threw them in one atop the other.'

A gasp, more sobs.

Alys stood up, averting her eyes from where Roger pointed.

'We must get moving. We cannot stay here. They're scouring the field for survivors. Killing most as far as we can see.'

Fred started running his hands over me, inspecting what he could between the plates of my armour. I winced from time to time, while he said, 'We've been lucky to find you while their efforts are focused elsewhere. Lucky too that you're well away from where most of the troops fled and have been butchered. We may be able to move you away without attracting too much attention. Just another group of campfollowers or scavengers.'

He finished examining me and stood up, brushing his hands upon his jerkin.

'No major wounds that I can find, other than the nasty gash on your head. And the bleeding from that seems to have stopped. Can you get up?'

Though the pain still drummed in my head, that in my shoulder had receded to a dull ache and he didn't appear concerned as I struggled to right myself.

'I think so.'

'It's not so far to the horses,' he said, as he and Roger hooked their arms beneath mine and hoisted me to my feet.

My whole body was suddenly aflame at the movement. But I gritted my teeth against a cry, clutching at my helpers to stop and wait while the batterings and bruisings ceased their screaming. As my head cleared, a new thought swam into it.

'Horses? But won't they all have been taken by…?'

'Our horses,' said Fred. 'How we got here. We left them in those trees.'

He waved his free hand towards the thick woodland behind the ridge. The ridge where the royal party had lined up before the battle. It seemed so long ago now. The ranks of trees ran along the top of the ridge here, but some way further along, towards the village, they swept out across it, their dense cover almost hiding the church tower. That way, perhaps two or three hundred paces distant, were not just odd knots of people or single men – walking, crouching, staggering away – but many men, horses, milling about, in and around the trees. Some banners still aloft. Far-off shouts. Was that where Fred had said Tudor's men were focusing their attention?

'We had to be careful they weren't stolen by

anyone fleeing the field,' Alys was saying. 'So we left them with—' She broke off, shaking her head. 'Oh, I hope they're both safe. We must hurry.'

'With whom?' I asked, bewildered.

Roger squeezed the arm he was holding.

'We found John Mallary, Matt.' His tone was unusually serious. 'He was hardly wounded, but stunned, like you. I thought it was Giles at first. But when he came round, he told me … John told me … Matt, Giles is dead. And his brother Will. And Robert too, he thinks. But not far from him was Lord Francis.'

'What?' I almost staggered despite their support. 'Giles dead? And his brothers? And … and Lord Francis?'

Edward's words slammed back into my mind. About how Lord Francis had fallen in the thickest press of the fighting.

'Not dead,' said Alys, her eyes shining with unshed tears. 'Not yet. But he's very badly wounded. He's been drifting in and out of consciousness. He may not live. But together we managed to get him on a horse. John's watching him and the dogs, keeping out of sight while we tried to find you. We have to get back there. Come on!'

With Roger and Fred one to either side, I stepped gingerly forwards, my movements stiff and unsteady at first. After half a dozen paces, my boot trod on something. Something that yapped.

I glanced down. There was the small brown one-eyed dog, looking up, holding a paw towards me.

'What is this, Matt?' asked Roger, amusement in his voice. 'It seems to know you. A new friend? Your protector?'

'He's just a mutt that found me on the field. He woke me up. I think he smelt the tidbits in my pouch.'

As I gazed down at the whiskery face and the raised paw, the thrown stone, the yelp, the limping away thrust themselves into my memory.

'And – and, yes, I think he saved my life too. Can you reach into my pouch for a treat for him?'

Alys flung an impatient glare at us but said nothing. Roger did as he was bid and, as I bent down awkwardly to offer the scrap of dried meat to the dog, he said cheerfully,

'He looks half-starved. But he'll be your friend for life now I should think. And mutt? There's his name then. Perfect! Matt and Mutt.'

I couldn't help but smile at his words, and at the greediness with which Mutt wolfed the scrap from my hand. Then, as I went to straighten up again, tensing against the soreness in my back and shoulders, the glint of something on the ground caught my eye.

There, half-hidden in the trampled grass and earth, was a silver badge, almost the length of my thumb, its catch broken and mangled.

I reached for it, ignoring the stabs of pain. Picked it up with my clumsy mailed fingers. Turned it over.

It was a silver boar.

My other hand clutched at the breast of my surcoat. Found there only the torn flap of blue fabric that told where the badge had been ripped away in the dying moments of the battle.

So many memories came flooding back they almost swamped me. The handing of the badge to me, the promise made as it was given, the blue eyes of he who had bound my loyalty with it. The nephew who had scorned him.

As I straightened up, Alys urged again, 'Come on, Matt. We must hurry.'

'I failed him,' I blurted out. 'I failed both of them.'
'What?'
'Edward. And King Richard.'

Her eyes caught sight of what I grasped in my hand, then snapped up to my face.

'Don't be silly, Matt,' she fired back. 'You did what you could. You couldn't have fought alone against the might of Tudor's army.'

'But I could have—'

'Could have what?'

'Maybe ... maybe I could have persuaded him not to.'

'Matt!' Her voice could barely contain her exasperation. 'He was a Plantagenet. You can't persuade Plantagenets. And both he and King Richard would want you and Lord Francis to be safe if possible. Now, come on!'

She elbowed Roger out of the way and, slipping her arm through mine, heaved at me. A smile tugged at the corner of Fred's mouth as he also urged me on. Folding my steel-clad fist about the badge, I set off again, carefully placing one foot before another. Mutt stuck close to my boots, dodging my clumsy steps this time.

The distance to the woodland gradually shrunk and walking became easier as the stiffness left my limbs. I also learnt the movements to avoid to ward off the sharpest pains. Then, as my head cleared, so too did my thoughts of what lay ahead.

'Alys, what will Lord Francis think of your breaking your word?'

'Breaking my word? On what?' She glanced at me as we carried on walking.

'On not leaving Jervaulx. Or coming here.'

'Oh, that.' Her words were abrupt, but was there a touch of guilt in her tone? 'Well, he only made me promise not to be near the battle. We heard there had been one at Tadcaster. Elen and Fred told us when they arrived at the abbey. How were we to know he didn't mean that one?'

'We tried to stop her,' said Elen. 'But she's no more persuadable than a Plantagenet.'

'And then, of course, we had to come with her,' said Fred.

'Anyway, if we hadn't come,' insisted Alys, 'you and Lord Francis would still be lying there on the battlefield. It doesn't bear thinking about. That surely makes up for any promise that might have been broken.'

She hesitated, then added, 'Not that one was.'

Her smile at me was more a grimace. For all her bravado, her green eyes had the sheen of tears again. And for the first time I registered what she was wearing. Her kern's cap again, though her pale red hair was no longer pinned securely up beneath it but poked out at all angles. And the rough jerkin, hose and boots she had worn on the voyage from Dublin and after. All were dust- and dirt-covered now after her latest journey.

'So you kept hold of your boy's clothes. Even at Jervaulx.'

'What? Yes, of course. It's always easier to travel as a boy. Even though I couldn't persuade Elen that it was safer.'

Elen was indeed walking alongside Fred in the same deep red travelling gown she had worn in York, though now also mud-speckled.

'But you didn't plan to break your promise and come after the army?' I persisted, directing my question to Alys.

'No, of course not. But you have to be prepared for anything and everything in times of war. You know that.'

'That's true,' agreed Roger. 'I thought it might be safer if I dressed up as a girl too. But I don't think anyone would ever mistake me for a soldier and kill me for it, do you?'

He threw wide his arms as he walked, revealing he had jettisoned the livery that proclaimed him as Earl John's squire in favour of a simple dull-coloured doublet.

Fred half-laughed at his jesting, but then said darkly, 'No one is safe on a battlefield, man or maid. The sooner we are away from it the better for all of us – no matter what we're wearing.'

By now we had reached the first of the trees and had to take care winding our way between the closely spaced trunks so as not to snag my stumbling feet on stray roots or fallen branches. Not far within the shadows I soon spied two ghostly hounds and a cluster of horses in a small clearing. On only one of the horses was a rider – no, two riders. One was sitting upright in the saddle, clasping the other to his chest with one mailed fist. The second man's head, helmetless, lolled forward.

'At last!' a voice hissed through the trees. 'I can hear them coming closer. We must be away or else we shall lose our chance.'

The rider was John Mallary. His visor was raised, revealing his blood-encrusted face. One eye was blackened, half-closed with the bruising.

'Hurry. His lordship is barely clinging on to life. We must get him somewhere safe if we can.'

The drooping head rolled a little to one side, then lifted with a great effort and a groan. Lord Francis was barely recognizable, so gory and battered was his face. Blood was still oozing from a deep wound in his side, below John's protective arm.

'I will not flee another battlefield.' His words hardly crept to my ears, so weak was his voice.

'My lord, you have no choice,' declared John. 'Otherwise you will die here and be tossed into a common grave with the others.'

Lord Francis, his head now resting back on John's shoulder, shook it minutely.

'I will not have men call me a coward – again.'

I stepped forward, closer to him. Though it was hard to see him in this state.

'None will call you coward, my lord. Edward and Earl John called you a brave man and loyal – to them and King Richard.' The memories were agonizing. But I drew a breath, before continuing. 'I even heard Henry Tudor—'

At those words, Alys nudged me out of the way. She took hold of his hand, till then dangling loose by his side.

'Think of your lady wife, Lord Francis,' she beseeched him. 'Think of Anne. She will be praying for you to come home safe to her.'

His gaze, hardly focusing, alighted on her. The pain within it was distressing to see. He struggled to swallow as though his mouth was parched.

'Anne? She is better off without me. She'll no longer be under suspicion. Perhaps she will marry again, have the children she always longed for.'

'Let us allow her to make that choice if we can, my lord,' Alys said firmly.

His head sagged forward again, exhausted. John's arm tightened around his chest.

'We must be on the move if we too are to live.'

'We have just three horses between the rest of us,' Fred said, taking charge again. 'Matt, are you fit to ride alone? I'm not sure any of these horses will be able to carry more weight than you and your armour. Roger and I can take the ladies behind us on the other two horses.'

I nodded. Stars spun in my eyes as I did so and a muffled roar surged in my head, but I said, 'I think so. Or shall I get rid of my armour? It might be safer. And it's of little use to me now.'

'There's no time,' said John. 'Fred, help him to mount. Then we must make our way down through these trees and out towards the river. We can decide where to head next once we've put some miles between us and the battlefield. It's our best hope, I think.'

In a few minutes, once I had managed to scramble aboard one long-suffering horse, we were on the move. Seven riders on four horses, with three dogs in our wake. After an initial skirmish, with much snapping and yelping, the royal hounds had called an uneasy truce with Mutt. Each dog now trotted at the heels of its human's horse.

We made slow going through the trees. They clung to the edge of a rocky escarpment that I only vaguely recalled climbing up the day before. The horses, with their heavy burdens, found the going hard, picking their way with difficulty through trunks and undergrowth and down the steep slope. But before too long we came to the foot of the hill and the last of the trees, and the water meadows stretched out before us to the distant willow-hemmed banks of the river.

But even as I gazed with relief at the scene, disaster loomed once more.

25

A Matter of Life or Death

Marching along the woodland's edge from the direction of the village was a small troop of heavily armed men. All were on foot, except one man to the rear astride a bay horse, leading another horse laden with a large bundle.

'Should we go back into the trees?' hissed Fred. 'Or try to make a dash for the river?'

'Do you think the horses can make it?' I asked, conscious of the weight of my armour. The horse I rode wasn't the sturdy warhorse Caesar had been.

'I'm not sure Lord Francis would,' replied John. 'Besides, they've seen us now.' A shout had gone up from the soldiers and they were running towards us, the lone rider cantering among them. 'We'll have to make a stand. Ladies, you must dismount.'

Alys and Elen slipped to the ground without a word and the four of us still ahorse urged our mounts into a defensive line in front of them. Fred unslung his bow and nocked an arrow to the string, while Roger unsheathed his sword.

I put my hand to my waist and only then discovered my sheath was empty. My sword had been knocked from my hand as I was knocked senseless from my horse.

John must have seen me clutch at air, or perhaps caught the expression of horror that swept across my face.

'Here, take mine,' he said. 'I cannot wield it and keep hold of Lord Francis. Only use it if you must. They may parley with us. Encourage them to. Offer anything you can think of to get us out of here.'

He handed me his sword, then pulled his horse round behind the other three, still clutching his lordship to his chest. Alys, Elen and the hounds clustered about him.

I could almost taste the fear in the air as, flanked by Roger and Fred, I raised this unfamiliar sword before me to face the approaching soldiers. And what I saw then struck me with terror yet again.

For the rider who now hauled his horse to a halt only yards ahead of us was –

'Hugh!'

Roger's exclamation was as full of surprise as of horror.

'What?' Alys shouldered her way between our horses before we could stop her, Shadow clinging to her heels. 'Hugh Soulsby? What are you doing here?'

'God's teeth!' Hugh swore, a mixture of astonishment and disbelief on his face, visible under his open visor. He alone among the troop of men was in full plate mail, overlain with the grey and green surcoat of his uncle's livery. The midnight bird taking flight upon his chest brought uncomfortably to mind the carrion-seekers still circling the battlefield. 'The brats from the castle. All together again. I thought you'd been split up for good.'

One of the footsoldiers came up beside him. His crossbow was cranked and primed ready to fire.

'You know these people, sir?'

'Aye, I do,' said Hugh. 'Though I had hoped never to set eyes on them again. Save one, perhaps.'

The glance he directed at Alys held something unpleasant. I did not stop to consider what.

'Well, here we are together, wanted or not,' I cried. My voice was firmer than my heart, which quailed within me. 'And we mean to leave together too.'

Hugh looked back at me, the leer growing across his face.

'You mean to, do you? And what makes you think I'll let you?'

I racked my brain. I had to keep him talking, stop him giving any order to his men. I snatched at something, anything. At what had been lurking in the bleary corners of my mind.

'I know a secret,' I said quickly.

'A secret? What secret could you possibly know? And why should it be of interest to me?'

'It's a secret your master Henry Tudor and your uncle would not want these men to know. A secret only they and you and a handful of others know.' As I gabbled, the smirk faded from his face. Was I on to something? 'Concerning a certain Master Simnel. Also called John.'

'What?' Hugh's eyes narrowed. 'How do you—'

'I was there as the truth came out. You thought me dead, didn't know it was me. But I heard. And I saw what you did – what they said and did.'

He shifted in his saddle, glancing again at his men. They were milling about the horses, uncertain what was happening. I jabbered on, conscious of Roger's eyes upon me, of Alys's hand upon my stirrup.

'I see you didn't fight again today, Hugh. Your armour is too clean. Just like before. When your uncle pledged to fight for King Richard but never entered the fray. Unless the bundle there upon that horse is your soiled armour. Are you so rich you had a spare suit to change into when you hastened to fawn upon the usurper?'

Hugh scowled, his eyes flicking back to the packhorse even as the men cast their eyes up at him, muttering. None could spy a speck of dirt or blood upon him or his surcoat. But could I spy a tiny chink of light?

'But you're not ashamed, are you? You were busy doing your job, setting up things for ...'

I hesitated. Suddenly the chink became a yawning crack, as I remembered words he had spoken to me more than a week ago.

'You were setting up things for your uncle. For your uncle's plan. So he has a hold over – over someone I shall not name. Is this all part of your uncle's games?'

The muttering among the soldiers became louder. I noticed now not one of the dozen or so there also wore the grey, green and raven surcoat. Rather they sported a mix of different liveries – different loyalties. Had I found the right track by babbling and good luck?

Hugh's face was purpling. 'They're not games, they're—'

I prattled on. 'What, if not games? A matter of life – or of brutal death? A means to keep a foot in different camps? You once told me it may not always suit your uncle to be Lord Stanley's man – or Stanley to be Tu—'

'Be quiet!' Hugh's anger exploded. 'Not a word more! Or I shall kill you where you stand.'

I fell silent at last, aware of the primed crossbow. But the man who held the weapon had other concerns.

'Master,' he addressed Hugh. 'Lord Soulsby ordered us to kill all who are not German. But these ladies, and the gentleman in the armour ... and if you know them...?'

Hugh stared down at him as if unseeing, his chest heaving as he drew in quick breaths. What was going through his head? What had his uncle told him? And how vital was it that none knew the truth about Edward, and John Broom, and about the Lambert Simnel deceit? Was that why only the Germans were to be spared – because they would not speak of it like the English would? If word got around the army, among the lords, what would Tudor do?

Hugh, perhaps, had no more idea than I. He dragged his horse's head around to face his troop.

'Let them go,' he snapped.

''But, sir—' protested the crossbowman.

'I said, let them go!'

'But, sir, shouldn't we take them prisoner, take them for questioning? They may be of interest to ...'

'No! I'll answer to my uncle for it. One's dead, or nearly dead. What harm can a couple of girls and some scrawny boys do?'

'But, master – their armour, their livery ...'

Hugh rolled his eyes in exasperation, then pointed at me.

'That one.'

All their eyes turned and skewered me, stopping my heart as surely as would spears.

'If you take his armour,' he spat, 'and divide it between you, will that satisfy you?'

The soldiers conferred a moment, then the crossbowman nodded.

My heart beat once more. Without a word, I slid down from my horse, stripped off my gauntlets and began to unbuckle my armour. Two of the soldiers rushed towards me and I tensed again, half expecting one to slip a dagger between my ribs. But they only came to help with the straps and laying the beaten steel pieces to one side. Before long, I stood up in just hose, undershirt and leather jerkin, and the soldiers had collected and carried off every scrap of metal. I shivered though the day was still warm.

Hugh stared down from atop his bay colt, then leant towards me, his broad face unreadable.

'There,' he hissed. 'You told me once you should have killed me and didn't. Now we're even.' He flung a glance at Alys, who was hovering beside me. 'And just pray we never meet again. Things might turn out very different.'

He straightened up and in a louder tone so all could hear, ordered, 'Now be on your way.'

Without the encumbrance of my armour, I had less difficulty remounting my horse, though my bruises and cuts still howled their objections. Then, taking care not to provoke them further, I put out a hand to pull Alys up behind me, while Fred did the same for Elen.

Roger spurred his horse beside mine and together we faced Hugh.

'Well, Hugh,' said Roger, his tone lighter than I would have thought possible. 'I have known you for many years, and may I say, if we never meet again, it will be far, far too soon for me.'

Hugh scowled again. Without another word, he raked his spurs across his horse's flanks and cantered past us, on along the edge of the trees, the packhorse trailing behind. The soldiers exchanged glances, then followed in his wake, each lumbered with some piece of my armour.

We were left staring after them as they retreated into the distance.

Alys curled her arms around my waist.

'All that you said, Matt – what did you mean?'

I shrugged, then regretted it as pain spiked my shoulder.

'I'm not sure, really. It's just things he said to me at Swarth Moor. And what happened this morning. It's all tangled up together in my head. I took a wild stab and it seemed to hit home.'

'You certainly rattled him, talking about his uncle,' said Roger.

'But why did he let us go? So easily too?'

'I have no idea,' I admitted. 'But maybe Hugh doesn't know what's going on either, not really. And to be honest, I think he was as shocked as I was by what they did to Edward and Earl John.'

'Well, whatever just happened,' said Fred, 'we have to get away from here before he changes his mind.'

'Agreed,' said John. 'His lordship can't hold out much longer. We must get him to a physician. Or find a priest to shrive him at least.'

He kicked his horse into a slow canter, heading across the water meadows towards the river. Fred turned his mount to follow, glancing back at us past Elen, who now clung on to his waist.

'Come on, you three. We have a long road ahead of us – wherever it leads.' And he urged his horse after John.

Alys, Roger and I were left alone, watching them ride away. A huge hollow emptiness yawned inside me and I was glad when Alys broke the silence.

'What will you two do – once we know how Lord Francis fares?'

It was Roger's turn to shrug.

'I don't know. Go back to my parents to begin

with, I suppose – now Earl John is dead. See what my father wishes me to do next. And you?'

'I think I'll return to Duchess Margaret. If I can. I'm sure she will offer me a home.'

I twisted round to Alys as she spoke. Her eyes were bleak as she watched Fred and John ride across the flat meadow.

'Go all the way back to Burgundy?' Roger was aghast.

'I dare not stay in England now that Tudor is my guardian. And that look of Hugh's, what he said to Matt ... What on earth did that mean?'

I had not yet told her all that Hugh had said to me at Swarth Moor. About becoming his uncle's heir in place of his cousin Ralph – and the hint about Alys and marriage. And I didn't have the heart to now. So I said nothing.

'Who knows?' said Roger innocently in reply. 'They were both talking in riddles, after all. And what about you, Matt? What will you do? Your brother was telling us about his plans to open a printing house in York one day. Will you join him in that venture?'

Until that moment I had given my future no thought at all. Though the pain in my head had lessened, my brain was still swirling in confusion. But now, at Roger's words, a sharp prick stuck my thumb and I cast my eyes down to where I had been absent-mindedly fingering the broken-pinned boar badge. It shone still, though I had not yet brushed away all the dirt.

'There's still Richard,' I said.

'Richard?'

'Wherever he is. I'll find him and serve him. If he wants me.'

'No, Matt!' cried Alys. She was peering over my shoulder at what lay in my hand. 'Whatever you promised King Richard, it wasn't that. You've done enough. Everything he could have asked of you – and more. You're your own man now.'

'Am I?'

Her arms gripped tighter around my waist.

'Yes. This ends today, surely, this fighting. Now Edward … now Edward is dead.'

I craned back to her as she said this. But nothing showed in her face beyond the shock and sorrow we all felt. She shook her head as she carried on speaking.

'Not now Tudor has secured himself on the throne, for better or for worse. No one will rally to support Richard in any attempt to claim it. Not after what happened today. Even if Tudor doesn't get to him first. And people will prefer to believe all Tudor's lies. It's safer for them. Easier too, not to challenge them.'

In the silence that followed, I thought back to what my father and Fred had said, about the men of York wanting to believe Tudor's story rather than the truth. And I recalled all the lies that had been told about King Richard – both before and since his death. That he had been a tyrant, a usurper. That he had threatened Parliament to force it to make him king. That he had wished to marry his niece. That he had murdered his own nephews. Would people continue to believe the lies about both him and Edward? For how long? Months? Years? Longer?

Roger broke the quiet with a laugh. A false-sounding laugh, aimed, I knew, at distracting us from Alys's words.

'Well, I suppose it all means that the old Order is finished anyway.'

'Does it?' shot back Alys. 'I thought we swore a lifelong oath.'

'I certainly did,' I said.

Roger looked sheepish. 'I guess so.'

'And we still have the code,' said Alys. 'We can use it to keep in touch wherever we are – and whenever we might need each other. Although, frankly, Roger, I'm not sure why I should ever have need of you.'

Her words were sharp in tone but accompanied by an arch of her brow, as though teasing.

Roger smiled, if a little uncertainly, then gathered his reins in his hands.

'I suppose we should catch up with the others.'

I could see Fred and John, with their precious burdens, now almost halfway to the willows fringing the riverbank. No one else was in sight. I sent up a prayer of thanks for that small mercy.

Alys whistled to the dogs. All three of them pricked their ears, white or brown, and gazed up expectantly.

'Come on, then, Roger,' she cried. 'Race you!'

And she kicked her heels against the flanks of our horse.

I was not ready for the sudden movement as the horse shot off and the silver boar badge was almost jerked from my hand. My fingers closed over it just in time to stop it falling as my other hand grabbed tight on to the reins and my knees gripped the horse's sides.

Somehow, as we thundered into a canter – with Roger's horse sprinting alongside and the dogs at full pelt behind – I managed to manoeuvre the badge safely through the mouth of my pouch and into its depths. I pictured it lying there, nestled among my other precious things. A leather-bound book, letters, the code. A gold coin depicting the head of an unrecognizable king.

Then, leaning over my horse's neck and clutching at reins and mane, I focused all my efforts just on trying to cling on.

Post Script

The Year of Our Lord 1497

You lay the letter down on the table. The candle flickers and shadows dance on the walls of the room, the oak panelling looming closer in the gloom.

It is an excellent letter, you know that – like the ones you used to compose. Written also in a well-formed hand. Just the signature stands out in your brother's scrawl, familiar to you from your childhood. Did Dickon have a good secretary to scribe his letters as you yourself once had?

Matthew. That was his name, of course. Matthew Wansford. Though it is so many years since you have seen him, you will not forget him. Or his loyal friends. Or all that they did for you.

Does Matthew still live? You lost sight of him almost at once as you charged together into the fray on that fateful day ten years ago. When the chaos of battle was of a sudden all around you, and your only concern was to kill or be killed. Your cousin Lincoln was struck from his horse, then Lord Francis too. Good men, both of them, as you said later to—

You shake your head at your own thoughts.

No, you will not say that name. Not even in your head, in the privacy of your own room. You must no longer let yourself think of that man, of what he has done. Of what he continues to do.

Yet what else can you do except think? You can do nothing now. Nothing to change what happened that day ... or since ... or now. Too much has changed. Too many people have sworn you to this life you now live. Your sister, your half-brother, your mother – while she was yet alive. Lord Soulsby. And surely you can do nothing for your brother Dickon – not now.

You sweep the letter aside with an angry hand. Anger you have not let yourself show for many years.

Your trusty hound raises her head from her paws, blinking sleep away from shadowed eyes. You reach down to stroke her old grey head. The action soothes the hound, but not your thoughts. As she lowers her head to sleep again, you remember …

Remember those long minutes after the battle. When soldiers in grey-green livery hauled you and your cousin John to face the victor. When you would not kneel to him and John defied him. When young John Broom was brought forward, to the usurper's delight. When the order to kill you was given.

You remember Tudor twitching his horse to ride away. Hugh Soulsby dragging the wide-eyed boy to one side. Lord Soulsby urging his mount about to face you. The curt 'Bare their necks.'

Remember rough hands shoving you down. Remember fighting against them. Twisting, struggling, despite the pain in your arm, your jaw. Forcing your head up, round, to see soldiers drawing their swords. Their blades flashed in the morning sun. Seeing Soulsby raise his gauntleted fist, glance once behind him …

Then –

'Wait! Hold your hands.'

Soulsby's words. Hissed to the soldiers wrestling you to stay down, holding John still, weak as he was. Tearing aside your tunic collar and fine white linen undershirt. Lifting their swords to strike the deadly blows.

'Let the boy watch his cousin die first.'

Soulsby again.

Grim laughter from the men. Fingers clenching in your hair, wrenching your head up further, towards John. John – bloodied and hanging from two soldiers' arms. A third soldier's hand clasped upon his collar, his sword upraised, waiting for the order.

Grim laughter, but nervousness in their eyes, their faces. To kill an earl. Even here on a battlefield. In cold blood. And then –

Then to kill a king …

Soulsby's eyes glinted, watching you like a cat watches a mouse trapped beneath its velvet paw.

But you would not watch John die. They could not force you to.

You closed your eyes, tight, your head tense against the restraining hands.

'End it!'

You heard the blow fall, the stab through flesh, against bone. Felt a judder beside you, the hot touch of spattered blood upon your cheek. Heard, felt, the scuffle of hands grasping a slumping weight.

Soulsby's voice again.

'Take him, strip his armour, and bury him here on the battlefield as His Grace commanded. His family can claim his body at their pleasure – if they wish.'

Another snicker of laughter, uneasy once more. Then the sounds of dragging, the scrape of metal across churned-up grass and mud. A boyish moan, the noise of retching.

'Take the boy too. Remind him what will happen to him if he ever speaks of this.'

A squeal of alarm, a gruff reproach.

You opened your eyes a crack. Watched the young servant boy from the abbey hustled away by soldiers, wiping his mouth with his hand, goggle-eyed in terror as he glanced back. You glimpsed beyond him other soldiers hauling their burden like no more than a block of wood or sack of turnips. You tried to smile to reassure the boy. The jab of pain in your battered jaw made you wince, and you tasted salty blood upon your tongue.

Then you saw again Soulsby staring down at you, his nephew hovering nearby, alone now, save the soldiers still clutching your arms, your hair, your collar. The soldier standing behind you, waiting to strike.

'Now you.'

You tensed, squeezed your eyes shut. Waited for

the blow that must surely come.

You would not struggle now, would not give them the satisfaction of a fight this time. Soon the stab, the hack, would come. The searing pain.

The darkness and oblivion.

The never-more-knowing.

A burning rose within you, then ice cascaded down to your very fingertips.

But all that came was a thump upon the ground. The pacing of boots towards you. Hot breath in your face.

'Open your eyes, boy.'

You were stubborn, screwed your lids tighter still.

'Get it over with.' Your words a croak. 'What are you waiting for?'

'For you to face me, boy. For you to listen.'

A hand firm upon your chin. You gasped as pain shot through your jaw. The fingers slackened their grip a little but thrust your head upwards.

'Look at me.'

You obeyed.

Soulsby stood before you, leaning down, bending, so his eyes were only inches from yours, his mouth just inches from your ear. His voice rasped your ear, his breath rasped your face.

'I'm going to let you live, boy.' His words were scarce above a whisper. 'Despite all you've done here today, I'm going to let you live.'

Deep within you, a scream welled.

'No! Kill me now. As you did my cousin.'

'Oh no, boy. You shall live.'

You stared at him, your eyes wide now in confusion. Stammered, 'I … live? Why? How?'

'Why? Because your sister, your mother, your brother Dorset – all pleaded for your life. Begged me to spare you this day – if I should be able. And how? Here I am.' He glanced about, behind him again. 'My lord and master departed in distaste at what needs to be done. Unwilling to watch, coward that he is. Here I am. With only my own men about me. Able to grant your family's request.'

The shriek bubbled inside you.

'But Tudor? He—?'

'He will never know. Not if you do as you are told. You will give up your claim to his throne. You will retire to a place that has been chosen. You will never speak of who you are, what you have done.'

'But I cannot.'

'You must. It may be hard for you – you who should have been king. And you have played your part well this day, I cannot deny. But now you must think of your sister who will be queen. Of your mother. Did she not write you about it?'

'But – all those men died for me. My cousin John too. Francis Lovell. I could not desert on the eve of battle.'

'They would also want you to live.'

'No!' The shout escaped you. The horror. The shame.

Soulsby clapped his hand over your mouth, ignoring your shudder this time. He cast a look over his shoulder again.

'You have no choice now. You must do as I say. It is for your own good. And think always of what Tudor will do if he discovers you – and what your family have done behind his back.'

You bit at his gloved hand, teeth closing on thick leather, then wrested your arms from the soldiers' grip and lunged for Soulsby's dagger. It slid easily from its sheath into your uninjured hand and he flinched away.

'Stupid!' he spat. 'Very stupid.'

But he held himself back from the dagger's point and gestured to his men to be still.

'I will not play your games, Soulsby,' you whispered. 'You betrayed my uncle in battle, toyed with my cousin Lincoln's good faith. And now you would have me believe you will be true to my sister's wishes, my mother's?'

'They have given me money and pledges to secure my loyalty. Promised me favours.' No emotion now touched his face or voice. Both were flat, blank. 'And I was ever loyal to your father. Why would I not be true?'

'Because some time it will not suit you. Some time you will offer us all up to Tudor if it serves your purposes.'

The silence lengthened as he watched you. When you did not move, did not speak again, he broke it, his tone now brutal.

'Then what do you plan? You cannot escape. There are five of us to one of you.'

The silence stretched out once more.

Then, slow, deliberate, you turned the dagger until its point pricked your throat.

'Ah, I see.' His eyes became slits. 'You will kill yourself rather than suffer this humiliation.'

'Not humiliated.' You stumbled now on the words. 'Ashamed.'

Soulsby growled a laugh.

'Ashamed? Is the fear of that worth all the torments of Hell? For that is where you'll end, boy, if you cut your own throat. And what good will that bring to your family?'

You stared at one another for long moments. Cruelty shone now in his eyes, then triumph dawned as your fingers loosened, as the dagger slipped to the ground.

He stepped forward, drew back his fist, and …

Stunned by his punch, you knew no more until you awoke again, much later, stifled and blinded within a filthy sack, tumbled upon the back of a horse, swaying its way far from the battlefield.

Hugh Soulsby brought you here. Once you were awake and safely distant from Tudor and his men, he released you. Let you ride, silent, sullen, for several days' journeying. Into the secret south-west of the country. Past downland and moor, across a wide-horizoned plain, along ancient, hollowed roads. To this secluded manor house where you have remained these ten years past, hemmed in by your grief, your guilt, your shame.

Ten long years you have lived here. When you came you were a boy of sixteen, whose life had been turned on its head by the death of your father and what happened after. Now you are a man of twenty-six and you live quietly in retirement after the horrors you witnessed … the horrors you caused.

The ice in your insides remains. Not now fear for yourself, for your soul, but shame for what you did. For the deaths of all those who fought for you, stood by you. For your betrayal of them, of all your friends, of your brother. Even of your father who died so long ago. If only he—

You shake your head again to dispel your thoughts. No more. You must think no more.

Not of your father, your family, of what might have been. If you had made different choices – in Flanders, in Dublin, on the battlefield … with Alys.

Where was Alys now?

You remember your last sight of her. Standing, forlorn, in the abbey courtyard.

You should not have given in and left her there. Should have run away with her when you had the chance. Not faced the shame that awaited you on the battlefield.

She'd have gone with you – surely. For all that she had rebuffed your declaration the evening before. She would have come round.

Wouldn't she?

Your sister never sends news of her, though they had once been such friends.

You have never married. Never will marry now. You cannot trust anyone with your secret. Cannot risk harming anyone else. You remain alone with your memories and self-loathing.

No. No more thinking. It will change nothing. And you will play others' games no more.

You grasp the pen, a fresh sheet of parchment.

Fumble with the tiny scroll again. Spread it out upon the table, weigh it down with cup and ink bottle. Begin to write slowly in the code you have used in the handful of letters smuggled to your loved ones. The simple code your sister sent you all those years ago.

In a few minutes you will summon the messenger – the young Cornishman who, among so many others, flocked to Dickon's invading army when it landed in the far south-west. But first, in your fine well-formed handwriting – taught you by the best tutors in your youth – you scribe:

To my beloved brother Dickon
I send you greetings, but also crave your pardon. I cannot join you at this time.
Do not think ill of me. I swore upon the lives of our sister and our mother – when she still lived – to give up forever my claim to the throne. But may God be with you in your quest for it. And may we one day be reunited – in Heaven if not before.
I remain your loving brother
Edward Plantagenet

You lay down your pen. Fold and seal the parchment and push it away across the table. Pick up your brother's letter and offer it to the candle's flame.

It twists, and burns, and blackens into ash. The beautiful writing vanishes into nothingness.

Edward Plantagenet.

Once he was king of England. Now you are king of nowhere.

Here ends SONS OF YORK, the fourth book in the sequence called THE ORDER OF THE WHITE BOAR, ending the story of the Dublin King begun in KING IN WAITING.

Author's note

This is a work of fiction. I don't know who the Dublin King was. I don't know whether Edward Plantagenet, the eldest son of King Edward IV, was alive in 1487 and crowned King Edward V in the Irish capital. I don't know who Henry Tudor really thought the Dublin King was. But one thing I do know is that the 'official' story that has come down to us over the past five hundred years – that the rebellion was in favour of a ten-year-old boy called Lambert Simnel, who claimed to be the Earl of Warwick but was not – only evolved over some months and is contradicted by many items in records during that time and after.

This book presents the 'facts' that we do know, that are agreed upon by several sources. For example, someone was crowned in Dublin by two archbishops; an army landed probably at Piel island, including two thousand German troops commanded by Captain Martin Schwartz, funded by Margaret of York and led by John, Earl of Lincoln and Francis Lovell. The march across the spine of England, the approach towards York, the skirmish in Tadcaster, the battle near a village called East Stoke ... All these things occurred.

Do I think it likely that a young boy called John Broom was taken from Jervaulx Abbey because of his resemblance to Edward and substituted for him after the battle? Not really. And do I think what is written in my 'Post Script' happened? I'm not sure. But I do think it possible that some young boy called John was substituted for whoever the Dublin King was. This could explain the report of a herald which named a 'John' found on the battlefield as the boy king, and perhaps the later story that none of the Irish lords who had been at the coronation recognized him a few months later when Henry Tudor paraded 'Lambert Simnel' before them. And who knows what happened to the young man he replaced?

The plain truth is that all we can say about the fate of Edward and Richard, the young sons of Edward IV, is that they were not *officially* seen *in public* after the summer of 1483. 'Officially' because the official version of events in government proclamations and records was controlled by the Tudors. Anything else – including suggestions the boys may have been murdered on the orders of their uncle, Richard III – is just speculation. Maybe one day we will know. Perhaps future discoveries by the Missing Princes Project, under the direction of Philippa Langley (who, as part of the Looking for Richard Project, was behind the rediscovery of King Richard III's grave in 2012), may show my own speculations in the *Order of the White Boar* sequence to be far wide of the mark. I await such developments with interest!

In the meantime, I hope you have enjoyed reading the adventures of Matthew Wansford and his friends as they seek to bring their version of the story, and their memories of the real King Richard III, to modern readers. After all, the main purpose of much historical fiction – my own included – is to entertain readers. If, as an author, I can also encourage my readers to think in greater depth about the history itself on which it is based, so much the better.

The four books of the *Order of the White Boar* sequence have taken me a little over nine years to write and publish – since the day of the press conference that announced, in February 2013, that King Richard's grave had been identified, 'beyond reasonable doubt', thanks to the efforts of Philippa and her colleagues in the Looking for Richard Project. I'm indebted to Philippa, the late Dr John Ashdown-Hill (including for the term 'the Dublin King'), Annette Carson, and Dr David and Wendy Johnson for everything they have done to find the King's grave and to encourage people to re-assess his reputation. I have also been helped by many other people along the way, too many to thank individually without risk of omitting names. So instead I would like to thank all Ricardians who have fought for King Richard's reputation in any way, great or small, over the years and everyone who has helped me bring a little more of the story of his life and legacy to a wider audience.

Loyalty binds us.

About the author

A Ricardian since a teenager, and following stints as an archaeologist and in publishing, Alex now lives and works in King Richard III's own country, not far from his beloved York and Middleham.

The discovery of Richard's grave in 2012 prompted Alex to write *The Order of the White Boar* and its sequel, *The King's Man*, to bring the story of the real man to younger readers. *King in Waiting* and its sequel, *Sons of York*, explore his legacy in the following years.

Alex has also edited two anthologies of short stories by authors inspired by King Richard III: *Grant Me the Carving of My Name* and *Right Trusty and Well Beloved...*, both sold to raise money for Scoliosis Association UK (SAUK), which supports people with the same condition as the king.

A standalone book, *Time out of Time*, following the timeslip adventures of Allie Turner who discovers a doorway into the history of Priory Farm, an ancient English house, was published in 2021. Alex is currently working on another novel based around an archaeological dig in Scotland, and has not yet ruled out continuing the story of the 'sons of York' beyond 1487…

Alex enjoys visiting schools to talk to students about the books and the history. If you would like to arrange a school or library visit, please email AlexMarchant84@gmail.com.

If you have enjoyed *Sons of York*, please consider leaving a review on Amazon and/or GoodReads and follow Alex on social media at:

Website: alexmarchantblog.wordpress.com
Amazon: www.amazon.co.uk/Alex-Marchant/
e/B075JJKX8W/
Facebook: www.facebook.com/AlexMarchantAuthor/
Twitter: twitter.com/AlexMarchant84
GoodReads: www.goodreads.com/author/show/
17175168.Alex_Marchant
Instagram: www.instagram.com/alexmarchantauthor/

Elen's note to Matthew

The full text of Elen's note to Matthew from York found in the chapter 'The Bloodiest Battle' reads as follows. If you wish to decipher it for yourself, the code of the Order of the White Boar can be found at the beginning of the book, after 'Cast of Characters'.

Fqct Ocvvjgy

Vgnn Gfyctf, yjgp zqw jcxg vjg ejcpeg, vjcv jku ukuvgt Gnkbcdgvj jcu ytkvvgp vq og. Ujg ucau ujg nqxgu jko cpf nqpiu vq ugg jko ciockp, cpf vjcv vjgkt hcvjgt yqwnf jcxg dggp rtqwf qh jko. Ujg rtcau vjcv jg yknn uvca uchg, yjcvgxvt eqogu. Cpf ujg cumu vjcv aqw ikxg jko vjku pqvg kh aqw ujqwnf dg cdng.

        Aqw vcmg ectg cpf uvca uchg vqq, Ocvvjgy

        Aqwt iqqf htkgf cnycau

        Gngp

The mysterious letter for Edward enclosed by Elen in her note to Matthew (later encoded using the Order's cipher) reads:

Xyulymn mih

C vya sio, acpy oj siol zoncfy unnygjn un nby nblihy. Zil nby muey iz siol mcmnyl, siol fcnnfy hyjbyq uhx gy. Filx Miofmvs bum jligcmyx sio u muzy bupyh cz sio qcff von acpy siolmyfz oj nib cg. By mqyulm Mcl Qcffcug qcff ufmi jlipy nloy ni om. Myye nbyg vyzily uhs vunnfy iwwolm. Nlomn nbyg ni eyyj sio mywlyn uhx muzy.

        Ohncf C myy sio uauch, C ug

        Siol fipha ginbyl,

        Yfctuvynb L.

Also by Alex Marchant

Time out of Time

Welcome to the golden summer of 1976. Year of the Heatwave, year of the Drought.

Normally sun-starved and grey, England is plagued by endless blue skies – no rain for months, the country scorched and parched, standpipes in the street.

But 12-year-old Allie has other worries. When her family moves to ancient, ramshackle Priory Farm – far away from her friends and everything she has ever known…

Then she discovers a doorway into history – and her adventures begin. What secrets will Priory Farm reveal?

An exciting timeslip adventure by the author of *The Order of the White Boar* sequence, *Time out of Time* whisks the reader off to explore one small part of England through the ages – with some explosive moments in time…

For readers of 10 and above

'A wonderful timeslip adventure.'
Pam C. Golden, author of *A Tree in Time*

'An absorbing and thought-provoking read. I absolutely loved this book!'
Wendy Johnson, Looking for Richard Project

Available from Amazon, all good bookshops or direct from Alex: AlexMarchant84@gmail.com

Grant Me the Carving of My Name
With a Foreword by Philippa Gregory

&

Right Trusty and Well Beloved...
With a Foreword by Philippa Langley

Two anthologies of short fiction by authors inspired by King Richard III, sold in support of Scoliosis Association UK (SAUK)

'I want you to tell my real story... Use any talent you have to show me in my true light, not painted black with Tudor propaganda. My new army must be wordsmiths, not soldiers; artists, not knights; musicians, not warriors. We will lay siege to the towers of Tudor lies and bring them crashing down...'

Who, for you, is the real Richard III?

Is it the boy, exiled in fear to the Continent aged seven? The loyal warrior, brother to Edward IV? The young man struck by tragedy? The just and rightful king? Or Thomas More's and Shakespeare's infamous villain?

You can meet them all within these pages ... or can you?

'An inspired idea.'

'A mixture of the serious and the light-hearted, this anthology of Ricardian short stories is a must read.'

Available from Amazon, all good bookshops or direct from Alex: AlexMarchant84@gmail.com

Printed in Great Britain
by Amazon